BLACK DRAGON

An Adam Drake novel

SCOTT MATTHEWS

Copyright © 2022 by Scott Matthews

Published by Vinci Books 2024

All rights reserved.

No part of this book may be reproduced in any form or by any electronic or mechanical means, including information storage and retrieval systems, without written permission from the author, except for the use of brief quotations in a book review.

All characters in this work are fictitious. Any resemblance to actual persons, living or dead, is purely coincidental.

Chapter One

ADAM DRAKE WATCHED his new bride dive down in the turquoise waters of Catseye Bay to get a closer look at a brown spotted Wobbegong Shark. Resting motionless on the rocky bottom next to an outcropping of coral, the shark's camouflaged coloring made it look like a shaggy carpet.

If they hadn't been floating side by side watching a school of yellow and black butterfly fish swimming around the outcropping, they wouldn't have noticed it when the little shark lifted its head and swallowed a small neon blue tang fish.

Drake was also keeping an eye on a large Hammerhead shark shadowing his wife at a distance. Hammerheads are apex predators that feed on smaller sharks, like the Wobbegong. He knew they rarely attack humans, but he was ready if this time proved to be an exception.

He took a deep breath and dove to position himself between Liz and the shark, slowly circling fifty feet away. When he stopped beside her, he tapped her shoulder with his left hand and pointed at the hammerhead. His right hand held a dive knife drawn from a sheath strapped to his leg.

Liz turned to look and opened her eyes wide when she saw the hammerhead.

Drake mouthed "slowly", took her hand and started for the surface. On the way up, they watched as the hammerhead whipped its body sideways and made a lightning-fast lunge down to the little shark on the bottom. With its mouth opened wide, displaying rows of long triangular teeth, the hammerhead struck the smaller shark and swam off with it clamped between its jaws.

When they broke the surface, Liz shook her head and shouted, "Wow, that was amazing!"

"I've never seen anything that big move that fast," Drake said.

Liz moved closer and wrapped her arms around him. "Thank you for watching out for me."

Drake smiled. "I didn't think you were in danger. The hammerhead was after the Wobbegong, but you're welcome."

She kissed his cheek and held up her white G-shock dive watch. "We better get the dingy back to the marina before we have to pay for a full day," she said and swam toward the dingy bobbing twenty yards away.

The "dingy" was a twenty-two-foot Zodiac Pro 7, with a two-hundred-fifty horsepower Mercury outboard motor and a sunroof. It was more boat than they needed to explore the coastline of Hamilton Island, Australia, but it was the only boat available at the marina for a half-day rental when they decided to snorkel the reef off Catseye Beach.

The newlyweds were staying at the Qualia Resort and Spa in the Whitsunday Islands, off the coast of Queensland, Australia. Liz had been diving and snorkeling the Great Barrier Reef that was on her bucket list and their honeymoon had been the perfect time for her to cross it off.

After a small private wedding on Drake's vineyard and a long flight from the mainland to their luxurious Windward Pavilion suite, they rested for two days and just enjoyed being alone and married. The panoramic views of the Whitsunday Islands from their covered terrace, the soft tropic breeze at night, and time spent in the infinity-edge plunge pool had worked their magic for both of them.

Re-energized, they'd been to Bait Reef to scuba dive a thirty-meter vertical wall and were mesmerized by the colors of the soft corals, yellow sea fans, and red feather stars. They'd explored the deep fissures in the wall, surrounded by schools of greenish-blue yellowtail fusiliers and saw huge bumpheaded parrot fish. They'd kept their distance, however, from a grey-silver barracuda, black-tip sharks and lines of great manta rays when that swam by.

To see everything the island offered, they bushwalked the trails on the island, hiked to its highest point, Passage Peak, and enjoyed a gourmet picnic lunch at Coral Cove the resort's chef prepared for them.

Tomorrow night, they planned on a sunset cruise around the island following a round of golf at the Hamilton Island Golf Club on nearby Dent Island.

But tonight, Drake had made reservations for the resort's signature food and wine pairing evening to sip champagne and enjoy fresh oysters. Which was the main reason he'd raced off in the dingy as soon as Liz was safely sitting beside him.

With the two hundred fifty horsepower outboard motor running at six thousand RPMs, they were skimming across the flat sea at fifty miles an hour around the northern end of Hamilton Island on their way back to the marina.

At the outer limits of the bareboat holding area north of the marina entrance, Drake reduced the Zodiac's speed to the marina's four knot speed limit to keep its wake from rocking the sailboats waiting to enter the marina.

Liz stood to the left of the center console, waving to a family standing at the railing of their sailboat, when she noticed the tallest of the three children point to the marina's entrance. The bow of a huge white superyacht was coming into view, easing its way out to the Dent Passage.

Drake quickly shifted the motor into reverse to stop the Zodiac's forward motion, staring at the elegant vessel crossing in front of them. His eyes followed the flowing lines of the yacht from the bow along the two decks with dark windows and above to the open sundeck, looking for the superyacht's passengers.

It wasn't until the stern of the yacht came into view that he could see its passengers. The main deck opened onto an open-air platform with orange lounges surrounding a glass-encased infinity pool. The yacht's swim platform was a couple of steps down from the pool.

At the back of the poolside platform, three Asian men in suits and one tanned man wearing an Aussie Outback hat stood holding flutes of champagne. The man with the outback hat raised his flute to them and smiled as the yacht passed by. The other three men stood stiffly and stared into the distance without acknowledging them.

"That's a solemn bunch," Drake said.

"Except for the one who smiled. The others look like pallbearers at a funeral."

"Beautiful boat. I wonder who owns it?"

"Someone in China," Liz said. "It's flying the red ensign of Hong Kong."

Drake shifted the Zodiac's motor out of neutral and moved ahead slowly toward the marina entrance, when Liz said, "There's a man with the binoculars on the breakwater. He was looking at the yacht. Now he's looking at us and waving."

"He's probably waving at you, not me. Someone you know?"

"I don't recognize him."

"You might when we get to the rental dock. He pointed that way and started jogging," Drake said.

Chapter Two

THE MAN with the binoculars was waiting to catch the bow line from Liz when the Zodiac drifted the last ten feet to the dock.

"Good to see you again, mate," the man said to Drake. "What brings you to Hamilton Island?"

"Liz, meet Lucas Barrett," Drake said. "Lucas, this is my wife, Liz. The Great Barrier Reef was on her bucket list, and it's our honeymoon."

"Congratulations to you both, then. Let me buy you a drink. Where are you staying?"

"The Qualia resort," Drake said, and looked at his watch. "We have reservations at seven tonight, but we have time for a quick one. You have a favorite watering hole close by?"

"The Marina Tavern on Front Street," Barrett said. "I'll get a table on the deck while you settle up on the boat."

When they had the Zodiac tied up, Liz asked Drake on their way to the boat rental office how he knew Lucas Barrett.

"I met him on a joint training exercise the Unit did with Australia's Special Air Service Regiment and ran into him twice in Afghanistan. He was a sniper like Mike Casey."

"Is he still with the SASR?" Liz asked.

"I doubt it. He looks like he's physically fit, but not SASR fit. They train hard, like the SAS in the UK."

Barrett was sitting at a table on the deck overlooking the marina and stood when they approached, pulling back a chair for Liz.

"They had a bottle of 2017 Leeuwin Estate Chardonnay. I ordered it for us, since you said you were pinched for time," he said. "It's one of our best wines. I think you'll like it unless you prefer something else."

"That sounds wonderful," Liz said.

Drake sat down across the table from Barrett and asked, "Are you still SASR?"

"I left about the same time I heard you and Mike left Delta. I'm an investigator for the CDPP now, the Commonwealth Director of Public Prosecutions."

"What do you investigate?" Liz asked.

"Transnational criminal activity and terrorism," Barrett said. "Lately, most of my time is devoted to investigating the drug trafficking cartels laundering their profits from fentanyl labs in Mexico through our casinos."

A server came to their table with wine in an ice bucket and Barrett asked Liz to approve it for them. When she inspected the cork and nodded her approval after tasting the wine, Drake waited until the server left before asking, "Is that why you were watching the superyacht flying the Chinese ensign?"

Barrett took his time tasting the wine before asking, "What about you, Drake? What are you doing these days?"

Drake smiled at the deflection and said, "I shouldn't have asked, sorry. I'm the director of special projects and part owner of Puget Sound Security, the company Mike took over after leaving the Unit."

"What kind of special projects?" Barrett asked.

"At the moment, I'm putting together a division of the company that will operate as an intelligence contractor for the government. We exposed a Chinese espionage operation while working for a client of ours. The right people suggested we branch out."

It was Barrett's turn to smile. "Sounds like we're in the same line of work. I'll tell you why I was watching the superyacht. Did you get a good look at the men who were on it?"

"Some of them, probably not all of them. Liz is one you should ask. I was driving the Zodiac."

"I got a good look at the men standing at the rear of the main deck," Liz said.

"Was one of them a man in his forties, five feet ten, slender build, maybe a hundred sixty pounds?"

"There were three Asian men in suits standing together. The man standing next to them had on khaki pants, a maroon polo shirt and an Aussie Outback bucket hat like Adam wears. He would fit the description of the man you described."

"Who is he?" Drake asked.

"My informant and the manager of a casino in Brisbane. He's here with some big-time gamblers that junket operator arranged for the billionaire who owns the superyacht. I was waiting for him to slip away today and meet me. When I saw the yacht leaving, I wanted to know if my man was still on it."

"Is your man involved in money laundering at his casino?" Liz asked.

"They have approached him. Being asked to travel with the billionaire and his friends is meant to be an enticement to get him involved. But that's not what I'm interested in. He heard talk about some plan to cripple America. He's trying to get information on that for me."

"What kind of plan, Lucas?" Drake asked.

"I just heard about this yesterday, before my informant left Brisbane on this yacht. He overheard a conversation that included the words plan to cripple America. That's all I know."

"Who did he overhear?"

"A gambler on this junket with the billionaire."

"Have you identified the gambler?"

"I have a name. It may be false. My informant thinks it is."

"Is there anything I can do to help you with this?" Drake asked.

Barrett shook his head. "No, and please don't repeat anything I've told you. If this involves who I think it does, they have the resources and soldiers to make this very dangerous for anyone who gets in their way. Let me handle this, Drake. It's what I do."

"If this involves a potential threat to America, it's also what we do, Lucas. If you get anything more about this plan to cripple America, will you promise to share it with me?" Drake asked and handed him his Puget Sound Security business card.

Lucas Barrett pushed his chair back and stood to leave. "It was a pleasure to meet you, Liz. I hope you enjoyed the chardonnay."

"Lucas?"

"I'll do what I can, mate. If this turns out to be anything more than some gambler talking big in a casino, I'll let you know."

Chapter Three

THE BENETTI OASIS 40m superyacht entered Cid Harbor and dropped anchor. Visitors to Cid Island harbor regularly report seeing packs of bull sharks swimming there, and the government each year warns divers and snorkelers to avoid the place.

Thrill seeking fools continued to visit to see large bull sharks, considered to be the most dangerous sharks because of their aggressive nature, in their natural habitat.

That was one reason Samuel Xueping, the billionaire owner of the Benetti Oasis 40m, stopped there to have a dinner of shark fin soup to show respect to his Chinese guests. It was an appropriate setting for the evening.

Each man was the highest-ranking members of his organization, and a necessary component of the plan Xueping was honored to be chosen to lead.

The Chinese triad he was the Dragonhead or leader of, was a transnational criminal syndicate that earned twenty billion dollars a year from drug trafficking. It had ten thousand members worldwide and was the most ruthless criminal organization in the world.

His legitimate business enterprise consisted of hotels and

casinos he owned throughout Asia, a regional airline that flew visitors to his widespread holdings, and a fleet of luxury superyachts, like the Benetti Oasis 40m he was on.

He had served his guests dinner in the dining area of the main deck to begin the evening. Ladling shark fin soup from an ornate antique heated tureen into their individual bowls, he'd invited them to sprinkle shredded ham, crisp bean sprouts and red vinegar in their bowls and enjoy the traditional Chinese dinner his chef had prepared for them.

After dinner, he led his guests to the main salon for cigars and whiskey and explained the gaming event for the evening.

"While we enjoyed dinner and got to know each other better, my men have been dealing with the man who stood next to you when we left the marina," Xueping said. "He is the casino manager I wanted to work with in Brisbane. I have learned, however, that he has been talking with an investigator of the CDPP."

"Does he know anything?" asked Ramon Ying, the owner of the largest pharmaceutical company in Mexico. He helped supply the Chinese cartel in Mexico with the precursors it needed to manufacture synthetic fentanyl products as fake opiod prescriptions and move their product to the American market.

"Nothing of consequence," Xueping said. "He overheard an unfortunate conversation by one of my former associates, who mentioned our plan at his casino. I'm convinced all he knows is there might be such a plan."

"Has he mentioned that to the CDPP investigator?" Ying asked.

"Unfortunately, yes."

"How do you intend to deal with this?" Frank Zheng asked. Zheng was the Dragonhead of the syndicate that had split off from Xueping's larger organization. He handled drug trafficking to Canada and America for them from his base in Vancouver, British Columbia.

"The same way I'll deal with this casino manager tonight. I have already dealt with the man who was foolish enough to speak about our plan. I will make sure the CDPP investigation goes no further."

With that, Xueping clapped his hands twice, and two of his men brought the casino manager out to the swim platform below on the lower deck.

The casino manager appeared to be unable to stand by himself and was being held up by two of Xueping's men. His head was bowed, and there were small cuts across his back and lower legs.

"He deserves to die by Lingchi, the 'Death by a Thousand Cuts', but we don't have time for that. So the sharks deal with him. I'm willing to bet ten thousand dollars that it will take no longer than two minutes for the sharks to make him disappear. Does anyone want to bet the over or the under?" Xueping challenged.

When they made their bets and their whiskey glasses were refilled, Xueping nodded and they shoved the casino manager off the swim platform to the cheers of his guests.

Chapter Four

DRAKE WAS STANDING on the deck of their Windward Pavilion suite Saturday morning, looking across the passage toward Whitsunday Island, when Liz walked out and handed him his first cup of coffee for the day.

She slipped her arm around his waist and leaned her head against his shoulder. "I can't think of a more beautiful place to honeymoon. Thank you for finding this place."

"I haven't ever relaxed like this," he said. "I can understand why people come here."

Liz slipped off her white lacy coverup and nudged him toward their private plunge pool to his left. "Coming in with me?"

He smiled lasciviously, admiring her beautiful slender body and the tiny black bikini she had on. "I thought you were going to work on getting rid of those tan lines this morning?"

Liz reached up and pulled the thin bikini top strap aside on her left shoulder. Frowning at the small pale line that remained where the strap had been, she sighed and untied the bikini top. "I guess I could use a little more sun. Now, will you please come get in the pool with me?"

Drake laughed and turned to set his cup down on the glass-topped deck table when he heard his cell phone ring inside their suite. "Let me get the phone and I'll be right there."

He hurried through the suite's living room and picked up his phone next to the coffeemaker on the counter. "Drake," he announced.

"G'day, mate. Hope I'm not interrupting anything."

"What can I do for you, Lucas?"

"I know it's your honeymoon and all, but I need a favor. My informant is missing. I'd like to fly you and your bride to Brisbane tonight for dinner at his casino. If Liz can identify the men she saw on the yacht, I'll have a better chance of finding out what happened to him."

"Are you sure he didn't get off the yacht?"

"They berthed the yacht at the Boat Works marina south of Brisbane. We've checked the marina's security CCTV footage, and he didn't get off the yacht when it tied up."

"You have the CCTV footage. Can't you identify the men from that?"

"They kept their heads down, wore hats and sunglasses, even though it was dark. We don't have enough for facial recognition."

"I'll have to talk with Liz. We're booked on a sunset dinner cruise around the island tonight."

"Tell her I'll reserve a luxurious room at the Treasury Casino and Hotel for you. I'll even use my expense account to cover any shopping she does at any of the top-end casino shops," Barrett said. "I could really use your help on this."

"I'll talk to Liz and call you."

"Thanks mate."

Drake returned to the deck and sat down at the edge of the plunge pool, dangling his legs in the water.

"Who was that?" Liz asked.

"Lucas Barrett. He wants to fly us to Brisbane for dinner tonight to see if you can identify those men on the superyacht."

"Why does he need to identify them?"

"His informant didn't get off the yacht when it docked. He's missing."

"We'll miss the sunset cruise."

"I know. I'll see if we can change the reservations for another night before we leave Wednesday."

"If it will help Lucas, I'm willing to go," Liz said. "How soon will we have to leave?"

"I'll find out."

Drake called Barrett, with his legs still dangling in the water. "How soon will we have to leave?"

"There's a Qantas flight that leaves Hamilton Island at 4:10 this afternoon, arriving in Brisbane at 5:35 pm. I'll make sure your tickets are waiting for you at the Qantas counter."

Drake looked down at Liz, who was standing at the edge of the pool. "You owe me one, Barrett."

"Understood. The Treasury Casino and Hotel doesn't have a dress code, but most patrons dress formally, in case you were wondering."

"Good to know. See you tonight."

Drake set his phone down and jumped in the pool. "Our plane leaves at four o'clock. We might as well enjoy ourselves until then."

QANTAS FLIGHT 729 landed at the Brisbane Airport and Lucas Barrett was waiting with a cab to drive them to the Treasury Casino and Hotel.

Drake asked if there was any news about the informant on the way to the casino.

Barrett turned around from the passenger seat of the cab and said, "His wife hasn't heard from him. His car is still parked at the Boat Works marina where he left it when he boarded the yacht."

"Do you think he knew more about this plan to cripple America than he told you?" Liz asked.

"I don't think so. He's been very cooperative."

"What do you have on him to get him to be one of your informants?" Drake asked.

"He wasn't reporting large tips he receives from the organizers of these gambling junkets."

"But you said he wasn't involved in laundering drug money?"

"All the big casinos bring in as many gamblers as they can who lose millions in their casinos. They comp them luxury suites, extend them credit lines, provide hospitality and other fringe benefits. One of his biggest gamblers lost twenty-three million dollars in one night. Laundering money these gangster gamblers lose, gamblers connected to the Chinese triads, requires someone on the inside to get the money back out. That's what they wanted my informant to help them with."

"The men we saw on the billionaire's yacht are Chinese triad?" Liz asked.

"I believe so," Barrett said. "It's hard to know them all, but we know quite a few of them. The syndicate I think these men are members of have ten thousand men around the world. They don't discriminate and recruit anyone willing to live by their rules. They have members from every race and nationality. That's why they're so hard to identify."

"Do they know who you are?" Drake asked.

"They do, but they aren't foolish enough to move against the CDPP, if that's what you're asking. The men you'll see tonight are well-mannered, clever, and wealthy men. The triads kill each other. They don't go after someone like me."

Chapter Five

THE CASINO and its 5-star hotel were in Brisbane's renovated nineteenth-century sandstone Treasury Building, with architectural features reminiscent of sixteenth-century Italy.

Lucas Barrett ushered them inside the luxurious interior, with its high ceilings and luxurious furnishings that created an atmosphere of old-world charm.

"The hotel has one hundred and twenty-five rooms, the casino has a hundred gaming tables, and there are five restaurants and bars," Barrett explained while they waited at the reception counter to check in.

"I reserved a Casino Parlour King Room for you. I think you will enjoy it. Meet me in a half an hour at the overwater bar, the Will and Flow, for a drink before dinner."

Drake and Liz agreed and followed their porter to the room Barrett reserved for them. After tipping the porter and waiting for the door to close behind him, Liz whistled softly as she gazed up at the eighteen-foot high ceiling and the long gold drapes that hung down to the floor.

"This makes me feel like we're dressing for dinner and a night of gambling across a baccarat table from evil men in some Bond movie," she said.

"Bond meets beautiful women who aren't married to evil villains at baccarat tables," Drake said. "I'm already married to a beautiful woman, and I don't need to waste my time playing baccarat when there are other things I want to do. But I agree, it makes you feel like that."

Thirty minutes later, they were dressed for the evening and walking across the deck of the Will and Flow Bar that extended out over the Brisbane River. Lucas Barrett was sitting at a table, holding up a pint of beer.

"Is your room satisfactory?" Barrett asked when they sat down.

"It will do." Drake smiled.

"It was the only room available when I called," he said, and smiled. "Not that you don't deserve the best for helping the Commonwealth on short notice. What can I get you two to drink?"

"I'm in the mood for a glass of champagne," Liz said.

"Hibiki Harmony whisky, if they have it. I've developed a taste for Japanese whisky staying at the Qualia."

Barrett waved a server over and ordered their drinks before asking, "Are you familiar with the ways criminal syndicates launder their money these days?"

"No," Drake admitted.

"Okay, a little background then," Barrett said. "Junketeering got its start under Mao. He considered gambling to be one of the three evils of society; opium, prostitution, and gambling. With gambling banned on the mainland, junket operators found ways for gamblers to get to Macao to gamble.

"Junket operators today specialize in marketing overseas casinos to Chinese high-stakes gamblers and arrange trips and casino credits for them. They also manage the gamblers' local funds and liaise with the casinos, who pay commissions to the junket operators for the business they bring in.

"The big high-stake gamblers, or whales, can lose millions of dollars in a single hour of gambling. In just a few trips to a casino, as much as a billion dollars can pass through a casino. Once deposited with the casino, that money is then wired, via the casino's accounts, to anywhere in the world."

"How does that launder the money?" Liz asked.

"Because the money the whales lost is then wired back to members of the criminal syndicate to their banks or offshore accounts. In one junket in 2015, they flew several triad bosses to Australia on a private jet and they lost over eight hundred million dollars in high-roller private gambling rooms at the Crown casino in Perth.

"The casino also paid out two hundred and thirty-two thousand dollars in commissions to the junket operator owned by a crime syndicate known as 'The Company'. One junket operator we caught on video depositing thousands of dollars in cash for one of his gamblers said during his prosecution that it was easier to move black money through a casino than through a bank."

"The casino has to be involved for that to work," Drake said. "Aren't your casinos monitored and regulated?"

"They are, and we're doing a better job of it now. But they offer the casino workers huge bonuses for helping the syndicates, sometimes as much as two hundred thousand dollars a year. That's a powerful incentive for lower income employees, like many of the casino workers are."

"Your informant was a casino manager, not a low-income employee," Drake pointed out. "What approach did they use to get him to work for them?"

"His wife is Chinese, and her family still lives in Wuhan, China. They offered to bring all of them to Australia," Barrett said.

"Are you going after the billionaire and his friends?" Liz asked. "Is that why you want our help to identify the men on his boat?"

"Without my informant, that's unlikely at this point. My focus now is finding out what happened to him, and who the gambler was he overheard talking about a plan to cripple America."

When their drinks finally arrived, Barrett ordered another pint of beer and explained his plan for their evening.

"The name of the billionaire is Samuel Xueping from Hong Kong," Barrett said. "His legitimate businesses are real estate, mainly hotels and casinos he owns in Asia, South America, and Mexico. When he visits The Treasury Casino, he always eats at the Black Hide steak house and orders the most expensive Australian Wagyu beef on the menu. He has a reservation for a party of three tonight at seven o'clock. We have a reservation for seven o'clock there as well.

"If the two men you saw on his yacht are with him, the rest of the evening is yours to gamble, explore Brisbane, or whatever else you choose to do. If the men are not with him, they will probably meet with him in the Orchid private gaming room where he prefers to gamble. It's exclusive for members with Diamond-Level membership cards, so we won't be able to get in there, but we'll be able to see who he meets there. If it's the two friends from his yacht, mission accomplished. If we're not successful, I'll think of something else.

"I won't ask you to stay another day. Just let me know when you want to leave tomorrow, and I'll get your tickets to return to Hamilton Island," Barrett said.

Chapter Six

SAMUEL XUEPING MADE his entrance into the Black Hide restaurant noticeable by passing the hostess without a glance when she asked him if he had a reservation and walking directly to his reserved table. Two young men, who did their best to look menacing, followed him as they walked past patrons sitting at their tables.

Xueping was a short man wearing a flamboyant red paisley silk tuxedo and a charming smile. His bodyguards wore simple black suits and stood stiffly on either side of him as he looked around the restaurant before sitting in the chair pulled out for him.

"So that's what a triad boss looks like," Drake said. "He's not what I expected."

"Don't let the smile fool you," Barrett said. "He's the grandson of one founder of the Big Circle Gang that emerged after Mao purged the Red Guards from the communist party in the 1950s. They banished the survivors to re-education zones and eventually fled to Hong Kong to become the most violent of the triad criminal syndicates. They still are."

"I don't recognize the two men with him," Liz said, "But he was on the yacht when it passed us."

"I didn't think those two men looked like the high-stakes gamblers he likes to travel with," Barrett said.

"They're his bodyguards," Drake said. "Their Thai. My guess is they're Muay Thai trained fighters. In Thailand, they train kids as young as five or six and have their first fights by the time they're seven or eight. It's a way out of poverty, if they're good. Those two can't be over fifteen or sixteen years old yet."

"Let's order dinner," Barrett said. "I'm not passing up a Wagyu steak, courtesy of my government. Xuepeng likes to gamble later in the evening, after he stops at one of the bars with entertainment. We should have plenty of time to get to his private gaming room before he does."

While they waited for the Wagyu steaks they ordered, an Eye Fillet for Liz, and Rib Eyes for Drake and Barrett, they shared a bottle of Pinot Noir Barrett insisted they had to taste, Liz kept a light conversation going, asking about Barrett's family, his service in the military and any stories he cared to share about Drake she wasn't likely to hear from anyone else.

Before Barrett got started telling stories, Drake intervened and told Barrett that Xueping had been watching him. "Xueping stopped smiling when he noticed you. Have you two met before?"

"No," Barrett said. "He might know my name, but he shouldn't know what I look like. CDPP protects the identity of its special investigators. Maybe he's disappointed a beautiful woman like Liz is sitting with us and not at his table."

"Maybe your informant described you to him?" Drake said.

"If he did, it would explain why he's missing."

"Why?"

"Because the only way he would do that is if he was being tortured."

When their wine steward opened a second bottle of Australian Pinot Noir, Drake studied Xueping. If the man was the head of a transnational criminal syndicate involved in a plan to cripple America, he needed to know as much about the man as possible.

"What do you know about Xueping that would cause him to be involved in a plan targeting America?" he asked Barrett.

"Nothing. His triad is involved in illegal drugs, prostitution, human trafficking, gambling, and money laundering. The syndicate exists to make as much money as possible. It's not political. As far as we know, they're not into terrorism. There are cartels that move drugs for terrorist groups, but we don't have intel that Xueping does."

"Do you mind if I see what my government has on Xueping, or his syndicate?"

"Drake, if you do, my government will hear about it. I haven't briefed my agency about what my informant overheard. Can you await until we identify the other two men on Xueping's yacht? That will give us a better chance to determine if there is a genuine threat to your country."

"I'll agree to wait until you brief CDPP, if you'll agree to do it before we leave for home on Wednesday?"

"Agreed," Barrett said and smiled when he saw their server pushing a cart with their dinners coming toward them.

The steaks were the best they'd ever eaten, Drake and Liz told Barrett, and the Pinot Noir was- almost as good as what Oregon produced, but they declined an offer to join him for dessert.

Xueping and his bodyguards left the restaurant while Barrett was still waiting for his dessert.

"Do we need to leave you to enjoy your cheesecake and go ahead to his private gaming room?" Drake asked.

"I think we have plenty of time, but if you don't mind, sure," Barrett said. "Remember, all we're doing tonight is seeing if the men he's gambling with were on his yacht when it left Hamilton Island. Just get close enough to get a good look at them."

"Don't worry, Lucas," Drake said. "We know how to be careful."

When Barrett caught up with them twenty minutes later, Drake and Liz were talking with the floor manager in the hallway outside the entrance to the casino's Orchid private gaming room.

"Thank you so much for taking the time to explain the

Diamond membership requirements to get into the Orchid room." Liz said, shaking the man's hand. "When we come back, I hope we'll be able to play here."

"Sorry," Barrett said when the manager returned to his duties. "I think they had to make my cheesecake from scratch. Did you see Xueping and his friends?"

"We arrived just before they did," Liz said. "His two friends were the ones on his yacht."

"Was there anyone else with Xueping?" Barrett asked.

"Just his bodyguards," Drake said. "Will you be able to identify the two men with Xueping?"

"We have access to the casino's security CCTV footage. We'll find out who they are."

"How soon will that be?" Drake asked.

"I should be able to get you an answer by tomorrow morning. Why don't I pick you up and take you to the airport? There's one flight a day from Brisbane to Hamilton Island and it leaves at noon. We'll have breakfast and have plenty of time to get you to the airport."

"That sound fine to me," Drake said. "That okay with you, Liz?"

"Yes, but it means I have to get up early to do the shopping Lucas promised to pay for."

"By all means," Barrett said. "A promise is a promise."

Chapter Seven

THE NEXT MORNING, Liz left Drake in their room to call Mike Casey, while she visited the hotel's luxury shops before breakfast.

Casey and a team from Sound Security Information Solutions, the new intelligence contractor division of Puget Sound Security, were in New Zealand to finalize a penetration testing contract with the New Zealand Defence Force (NZDF).

Mark Holland, the former chief of the NYPD's Counterterrorism Bureau, was the director of the new PSIS division, in charge of developing it and growing its client base. Drake and Casey had gone after Holland to head the new division as soon as they decided to expand the services of Puget Sound Security.

"Morning mate, how are you getting along in Wellington?" Drake his friend and CEO of Puget Sound Security asked.

"You should be here," Casey said. "The top brass are taking us out deep sea fishing. Enjoying your honeymoon?"

"Every moment."

"Glad to hear that you'll be rested when you get back."

"Mike, do you remember Lucas Barrett from the SASR?"

"Sure, why?"

"We met him yesterday. He's with the Australian Public Prosecutions office, looking into an informant's tip about some plot to cripple America."

"A plot to cripple America? How?" Casey asked.

"That what he's trying to find out. We're meeting him for breakfast. If he turns up anything, I'll let you know."

"We're scheduled for meetings and demonstrations all next week, with each branch of the Defence Force. Do you want to extend your honeymoon a couple of days and fly back to Seattle with us?

"Thanks, but we're flying back to Portland first to pick up Lancer at the vineyard. How's Mark Holland doing?"

"We found the right man for the position. His stories about what the NYPD Counterterrorism Bureau accomplished and his vision for what we want to build will have companies begging to become our clients."

"Let's hope so. I'd better get going, Mike. I need to find Liz and meet Lucas for breakfast. Enjoy fishing."

Drake slipped on his beige linen blazer and walked to the door of their suite when his phone vibrated in his pocket.

"I'm finished shopping. Meet you at Ryan's?" Liz asked.

"Will Lucas be able to pay for lunch with all your shopping?"

"Lucas will, but his government might have to raise taxes."

Drake laughed. "Better Australia than me. See you at Ryan's."

He knew she was teasing him. Liz wasn't a shopper, as far as he knew, but then he still had a lot to learn about her.

She was waiting for him inside the restaurant with a puzzled look on her face. "Lucas isn't here, and they won't have a table open until eleven. That won't leave us enough time for breakfast to get to the airport by noon. What would you like to do?"

Drake looked around the crowded lounge bar, famous for its five-star breakfasts, and said, "Let's have a glass of champagne at the bar and wait for Lucas. He'll be here soon."

They walked to the end of the bar, where he pulled out a leather stool for her under an elegant two-tiered elk antler chandelier overhead and ordered two glasses of champagne.

"What did you buy?" he asked.

Liz held up her left hand and let the sleeve of her white summer jacket slide down so he could see the watch on her wrist. "Do you like it?"

Drake took her hand and pulled the watch closer. It was an oval Coach watch, with a gold case and white face on a brown leather strap.

"Simple and elegant. I like it a lot."

"Good, you bought it for me. I didn't feel good about Lucas or Australia paying for it."

He handed the bartender his credit card when their champagne arrived and lifted his flute to her. "Then here's to my beautiful wife and her good taste."

They sat quietly, sipping their champagne, wondering where Barrett was.

Drake took out his wallet and looked for the business card the Aussie had given him. "We'll need to call a cab if he isn't here soon. I'll call and see if he's on the way."

He entered Barrett's number on his phone and listened to it ringing for a minute before shaking his head. "We need to get our luggage and ask for a cab."

Liz nodded and took another sip of champagne before saying, "Why don't you see the concierge about a cab, and I'll have our luggage brought down."

Drake waited for his credit card and then walked with Liz though the lounge..

"This isn't like Lucas," he said.

"He said he'd have our tickets waiting for us at the airport. Maybe he'll meet us there."

"If he was delayed, he would have called. Something's happened."

They split up, with Liz leaving with a bellhop to get their luggage, while Drake talked with the concierge about a cab to get them to the airport.

When they arrived at the airport, their tickets were waiting for them at the Qantas counter, but Lucas Barrett wasn't.

"Should we take a later flight?" Liz asked.

"There's only one flight a day to Hamilton Island," Drake said. "Why don't you get us checked in? He might have stepped away to visit the restroom. I'll go check."

Liz returned to the Qantas counter with their rolling luggage and checked them in. Walking away, she heard the last boarding call for their flight.

If Drake didn't hurry, they'd be spending another night in Brisbane, and that wasn't what she had planned for their honeymoon. The Treasury Casino and Hotel was nice, if they could get a room there, but it didn't compare to their suite at the Qualia Resort and Spa.

Come on, Adam, she thought as she waited anxiously for him.

Chapter Eight

LIZ WAITED five minutes before she returned to the Qantas Service Desk and asked that the flight to Hamilton Island's be delayed until her husband returned.

"He'll be back in just a minute," she pleaded.

"We can't hold the flight, ma'am, but you might have enough time to find him, if you hurry," the Qantas agent said.

Liz turned and saw an Airport Police Constable across the terminal area near the exit to Level One and hurried over to him.

"Would you help me find my husband, constable? He went to the restroom and hasn't returned. His name is Adam Drake."

"Certainly, ma'am. Which restroom did he go to?"

"The one down by the Qantas lounge."

Liz watched the man walk across the terminal area and disappear in the men's restroom, and quickly come back out.

"There was no one in the restroom, ma'am," the constable said when he
   returned.

"I don't understand where he could be," Liz said. "We were supposed to meet one of your Public Prosecuting investigators here, but he didn't show up."

"Why don't I see if I can reach the investigator. Maybe they're here in the terminal somewhere. What's the investigator's name?"

"Lucas Barrett."

The AFP constable took the radio microphone from his shoulder and asked for someone to call the CDPP and locate investigator Lucas Barrett, as quickly as possible.

As they waited for a call from Barrett, Liz watched an AFP canine unit walk across the terminal and reached out to touch the AFP commander on the arm.

"I have a bad feeling about this, constable. I used to be with the FBI. Would you have Qantas pull our luggage from the flight to Hamilton Island? Maybe one of your canine teams can find Adam with the scent from one of his shirts."

"What's going on, ma'am?"

"I don't know. I think my husband's in trouble."

AFP Constable Jack Walker judged the worried look on Liz's face merited action and ordered the luggage belonging to Mr. and Mrs. Adam Drake pulled from the flight to Hamilton Island.

"Ma'am, please come with me. We'll let Commander Taylor help you find your husband."

Constable Walker escorted Liz across the terminal and down a hallway to the offices of the Australian Federal Police. AFP Commander Taylor was waiting for them.

"Mrs. Drake, please come in," the commander said, stepping aside to let her enter the conference room next to his office. "I will bring your luggage here and we'll see if one of our canine teams can find your husband."

"Thank you, commander. Are you able to reach Lucas Barrett?"

"Tell me how you know Mr. Barrett and why you were meeting him here?"

"He asked us to help him identify some men he's investigating, commander. He was supposed to drive us to the airport after breakfast but didn't show up. My husband went looking for him in the airport and hasn't come back."

Constable Walker stepped into the conference room and asked Commander Taylor to step outside.

When the commander returned, he sat down and looked across the table at Liz. "The CDPP hasn't been able to reach Mr. Barrett. He hasn't checked out of the Treasury Hotel and he's not in his room. Do you have any idea where he is, Mrs. Drake?"

"He was supposed to meet us here, commander. That's all I know. Have you checked your security cameras to find my husband?"

"Not yet, but we will. Why do you think your husband might be in trouble, Mrs. Drake?"

Liz looked down at her hands resting in her lap, and her wedding ring on her finger, before looking up and answering. "My husband is a former Tier One Special Forces operator. He can take care of himself. Lucas Barrett was investigating a missing informant, and Lucas thought the triads might be involved. That's why I'm worried, commander."

"I see. Let me find your luggage, Mrs. Drake. We'll get a canine team to look for him."

When Commander Taylor left Liz, she called Mike Casey.

"Hi Liz. Are you back on Hamilton Island?"

"Mike, Adam's missing. I need your help."

"Are you sure he's missing? Where are you?"

"The Brisbane airport."

"We can be there in three hours. Keep talking, while I pass a note to Mark Holland to get the G650 ready to fly. What's going on?"

"Have you talked with Adam lately?"

"He called this morning."

"Did he tell you about Lucas Barrett and why we're in Brisbane?"

"He did, something about a threat to cripple America. He thought Barrett might know something about it by this morning. Who do you have looking for Adam?"

"Right now, the Australian Federal Police at the airport. They're going to use a canine team to look for him."

"Liz, we can track his GPS chip. We'll find him. Just hold on until we get there. If he left the airport, we'll need to decide if we want the Federal Police to go after him or handle it ourselves. Evaluate their capability and let me know when we get there."

"This is not the way I wanted to end my honeymoon, Mike. Please hurry."

Chapter Nine

WHEN SAMUEL XUEPING'S chartered jet landed at the Macao International Airport a new BAIC BJ80 luxury SUV was waiting there to take him to a meeting with People's Liberation Army (PLA) General Da Wang.

Xueping smiled at the general's choice of transportation; the BAIC BJ80 was China's clone of a Mercedes G-Class luxury SUV.

"Where am I meeting General Wang?" Xueping asked the general's aide-de-camp.

"He at the Parisian Macao. He's waiting for you in a private dining room at the Lotus Palace restaurant."

"Of course," Xueping said and ran his hand over the soft, tan tufted-leather seat next to him. The general, he knew, was retiring soon and didn't care what anyone thought about him using his rank and privilege to enjoy fine things.

General Wang was the man directing China's unrestricted warfare plan to destabilize and weaken America by flooding the country with illicit synthetic fentanyl derivative drugs.

China would never forget the humiliation it suffered from the British-led Opium Wars in the 1800s, when the scourge of Western-supplied opium caused the demise of Chinese society and losing Hong Kong in 1841. The Treaty of Nanking formally ended the First Opium War, but China never stopped thinking it was still at war with the West.

China wanted to launch its own opium war against its most powerful enemy, America, and Xueping was the man the People's Liberation Army had selected to carry it out.

They had used patriotic triads and secret societies in China to support ruling regimes as far back as the Ming Dynasty, when secret societies had supported the dynasty's restoration. Even the British had also used them when it was convenient. It did not surprise Xueping when he'd been approached.

But it wasn't patriotism that caused him to agree to work with General Wang. It was self-preservation and greed, and both he and the general knew it. As long as his syndicate could operate from Hong Kong and continue to be supplied with fentanyl precursors from Chinese companies for labs in Mexico, Xueping was willing to be used by China.

The drug warfare he was helping China with, though, wasn't the reason for his urgent request to meet with General Wang. It was the American his men were holding in Brisbane.

General Wang was waiting in a private room in the Lotus Palace restaurant sitting on one side of a round table that was normally set for ten or twelve people. There was only one other chair at the table now, and it was across the table from the general.

General Wang told his aide-de-camp to leave and pushed a plate across the table to Xueping.

"Try the pork floss rolls, with foie gras and some caviar," General Wang said. "If you're bringing me news that I don't want to hear, at least my meal won't be a waste."

Xueping ignored the remark and tried the pork floss roll. "I suppose I'm paying for lunch?"

"You are. With the profit you're making with my help, you can afford the bill for my meals and my room when I leave the tomorrow."

"Will there be anything else I'll be asked to provide you while you're here?"

"I thought I might visit one of your casinos tonight. I feel I might be lucky for a change."

"General, we both know you are always lucky when you gamble at one of my casinos. Are we ordering lunch, or are you just here for an appetizer?"

"That depends on whether I'll have an appetite after I hear why you requested this meeting. Is there a problem I should know about?"

"Not a problem, perhaps an opportunity. I've been in Brisbane to eliminate a potential problem. A CDPP investigator heard from an informant about a whispered plan to take the war to America. Both the informant and the Chinese gambler the informant overheard are dead.

"I also had my men grab the CDPP investigator to learn how much he knew and who he talked to about it. Before he died, he admitted he talked with an American. I also had my men grab the American. I have him in Brisbane."

"Is he dead or alive?"

"He's alive. How long he stays alive is up to you."

"Tell me why this is something you want me to decide," General Wang said.

"The CDPP investigator also told my men his friend, the American, had recently exposed a Chinese espionage operation in America. You might want to interrogate the American and find out how much he discovered about the operation."

"What is this American's name?"

"His passport says he's Adam Drake. He was on Hamilton Island in the Whitsundays for his honeymoon," Xueping said.

General Wang nodded and called to his aide-de-camp, posted outside the door.

"Find out everything you can about an American by the name of Adam Drake. I need the information by the time we finish lunch."

"Would you like me to have the American brought here?" Xueping asked.

"Let's wait to see if it's worth the risk of kidnapping an American. He might know nothing. You did the right thing, Samuel, bringing this to me. Our little drug war is too important for the enemy to hear about."

"As you wish, General. I'm not familiar with the menu here. What would you recommend we order for lunch?"

"I'm told the Jiang Nan Hairy Crab specials are very good," General Wang said with a smile.

Chapter Ten

MIKE CASEY WAITED for Liz to meet him at the Qantas Service Desk. When she came through a door marked "Restricted Area" in the Domestic Flights terminal area, he waved and jogged over to her.

Casey opened his arms and hugged her. "We know where he is. It's not far. Let's go."

"Is he okay?" she asked, as they hurried to the Level 1 escalator.

"We'll know soon. Morales and Norris are driving there with a Black Hornet drone. He's in a warehouse in the Airport Industrial Park."

Riding down the escalator, Liz told Casey the airport security constables from the AFP wanted her to call local law enforcement for help. "We're on our own, Mike."

"Better that way. With Dan Norris's HRT training and our combined experience, we're better prepared than local law enforcement."

When they walked outside the terminal building, a white Toyota Land Cruiser was curbside with Mark Holland, the new head of Sound Security Information Solutions, behind the wheel.

Casey held the door open for Liz to ride shotgun and climbed into the seat behind her.

"Mrs. Drake, nice to see you again," Holland said, and reached over to shake her hand.

"Thank you for coming, Mark," Liz said.

Casey took a Sig Sauer P320X out of the duffel bag at his feet. "We didn't bring a lot of firepower to New Zealand, Liz. Norris put together war belts for his HTR team and we brought four of them. We have four Sigs, Taser 7s and body armor. The body armor won't fit you, so I want you to sit this one out."

"That's not going to happen, Mike. I don't need a Sig. I have pepper spray and my yellow Dragonfly knife in my purse. That'll have to do. What do we know about the warehouse?" Liz asked.

"It's new. Kevin found the blueprints that were filed with the industrial park developer," Casey said. "It's a big open floor with an office and supply room at the back. One front entrance, one back entrance out of the office, and a loading dock on the east wall. Morales will try to get the Black Hornet inside and scope it out."

"Who owns the warehouse?" she asked.

"Kevin traced it back to a holding company in Hong Kong," Holland said. "That's as far as he got before we landed. The company distributes casino gambling supplies."

"That must be the billionaire Lucas Barrett was interested in. He owns hotels and casinos. Casino gambling supplies would tie in with his businesses."

Casey's phone buzzed, and he put it on speaker.

"We're parked on the street behind the warehouse," Norris said. "Morales has the drone up, looking for a way in."

"Anyone around?" Casey asked.

"Not that we see."

"Are you back by the loading dock?"

"Fifty yards from it."

"Security cameras?"

"Two on each corner of the warehouse," Norris said. "We spotted two more in front when we drove by."

"Dan," Holland said, "Where do you want us?"

"Depending on what Morales sees, out front. Stay down the street."

"Let us know."

"Roger that."

Liz turned around and asked Casey for his Taser. "If I go in asking if I can buy poker chips or something, I should be able to get close enough to disable one of them."

"Liz, I…" Casey said, when Norris called back.

"Morales couldn't get the Black Hornet inside. It's a metal building. The IR and thermal imaging wouldn't penetrate, and the windows are tinted."

"Is there parking for employees at the rear of the building?" Casey asked.

"Yes, four spots and three cars parked there."

"What do you think, Dan?"

"We might be outnumbered, but they don't know we're coming. We don't have a choice. We'll have to go in blind."

"Dan, what if I go in," Liz said, "With my phone on speaker, like Mike has his on now, I can tell you where there are?"

"It would help, Liz, but if all the doors are locked and we can't get in, you'll be alone in there."

"Then we'll regroup and find another way to get Adam out of there," she said.

"Mike, what do you think?" Norris asked.

"Dan, it's not up to Mike! I'm going in," Liz said.

Casey knew he couldn't stop her. She was former FBI and been in dangerous situations before. "Okay, tell us what you want us to do, Dan."

"Drive Liz to the front entrance and let her go in," Norris said. "When she tells us what she sees, Morales and I will move to the two doors by the back office and the loading dock. You and Holland stay in the car until I give the signal, and then join Liz inside."

Mark Holland shifted the Land Cruiser in gear and pulled away from the curb, a block away from the warehouse.

"Liz, remember, until Norris gives the signal, no one in the warehouse will know who you are," Casey said from the seat behind her. "You can say something like 'I'll come back later' and we'll regroup. We're not leaving without Adam."

"Relax, Mike. I've worked undercover before. And you're right, I'm not leaving here without my husband."

Chapter Eleven

WHEN THE LAND Cruiser rolled to a stop in front of the warehouse, Liz stepped out wearing her white Pantagonia puff jacket, blue jeans and ice blue running shoes.

To anyone watching her walk to the front door, she looked like another rich trophy wife running errands on a weekend, while her husband stayed behind in the car. Except the man behind the steering wheel of the Land Cruiser wasn't her husband, and Elizabeth Drake was more than just a beautiful woman used to getting her way because of her good looks.

She was used to getting her way because she was better than the men she competed against at Quantico when she joined the FBI. Better than the men she was about to teach a lesson. Hurt my man and you'll pay a heavy price for doing it.

Liz smiled up at the security camera and opened the door. The expanse of concrete flooring had rows of tall metal shelving, with signage that identified the products in each of the rows; gaming tables, roulette wheels, slot machines and casino furniture.

At the far end of the aisle, two men started walking toward her with their hands raised, signaling her to stop.

"Not open," one man said. "You must leave."

"I'm looking for blackjack tables for Casino Night," she said. "I'm in charge of our Hospital Guild. Can you two men help me?"

"Come back tomorrow," the other man said.

"I'm leaving Brisbane today," Liz said, veering away from the men and heading to the aisle nearest the loading dock overhead door. "If I can just take a quick look at what you have, I can order what I need over the phone."

The men started running down the aisle, waving their hands.

"There are two more men at the back, standing near the office and supply room," she said. "I don't see anyone else."

"Abort, abort," she heard Norris say. "The doors are locked."

"Hold on, I'll see if I can get the overhead door up."

Liz sprinted across the warehouse toward the loading dock.

"Stop, you must leave!" a man shouted. "Leave now!"

She kept running and turned down the loading dock as she heard more shouting from the back of the warehouse.

"Almost there," she gasped and turned down the outside aisle and ran along the east wall to the overhead door and slapped at the red button on the control panel.

Liz turned and saw the nearest man chasing her was twenty yards away and drawing his gun from a crossbody shoulder holster.

When the overhead door was two feet off the floor, Marco Morales slid under it six feet away from her.

"Gun behind me!" she shouted and dropped to the floor.

Morales fired two shots from a prone position and hit the first man center body.

The second man running behind him got off a shot that ricocheted off the floor near Liz before Morales fired again and stopped him.

Liz got up on a knee and shouted, "Two more, hard right," as two more men came around the aisle at the back of the warehouse and ran toward them.

Morales fired once down the aisle to drive them back and

jumped up. "Take cover," he said, and pulled Liz back to the front of the warehouse.

Casey and Holland rushed in from the loading dock and met them at the end of the middle aisle.

"Norris, come in," Casey asked, with his phone held to his lips.

"I'm at the loading dock," Norris answered.

"Flank right," Casey said. We'll flank left and meet you at the back."

"Roger that."

Casey put his hand on her shoulder and handed her his Taser. "Nice work, Liz. Let's go get Adam."

Casey motioned Mark Holland to an aisle to his left and stepped in front of Liz. "Use me as a shield if you need to."

They started down the aisle and heard shots fired at the back of the warehouse.

"Let's go," Casey said, and ran forward.

When they reached the end of their aisle, they heard two double taps and Norris shouting, "Clear!"

Two triad thugs, with tattoos up and down their necks and both arms, were lying in the open doorway of the supply room.

"I checked, he's alive," Norris said,

Liz ran to the open door and saw Drake duct taped to a chair. His face was caked with dried blood and his eyes were swollen shut.

"We need to get him to a hospital," she said, taking her knife out to cut the duct tape from his arms and legs.

"No hospital," Drake whispered weakly through his cracked puffy lips.

"How badly are you hurt?" Liz asked, leaning down to hear him.

"Hurts to breathe, ribs. Hospital won't help. Need to leave."

"He's right," Casey said. "He's hurt like this before. Search the men and bring the security camera and recordings, if you find them. I'll help Liz get him to the Land Cruiser."

When the duct tape was off him and he could stand, Liz and

Casey walked Drake slowly, with his arms draped across their shoulders, toward the front of the warehouse.

Halfway there, Mark Holland came around the end of the aisle and said, "Let me take your place, Mike. Go look at the shrink-wrapped pallets of 5-gallon buckets at the loading dock and tell me what you think."

Casey stepped aside and jogged to the end of the aisle and disappeared.

Dan Norris and Marco Morales ran up behind them and Norris said, "Liz, let me take your place."

"I'm fine, Dan. Pull the Land Cruiser parallel to the front door to provide cover when we come out. Marco, bring your Land Cruiser around front. I want to be out of here and in the air as soon as possible."

"Roger that, Liz," Morales said and ran toward the half-opened overhead door at the loading dock.

Chapter Twelve

WHILE THEY WAITED at the Great Pacific Aviation Services terminal for the PSS Gulfstream G-650 to be fueled, Liz cleaned Drake's cuts and made sure he was comfortable at the rear of the plane. When she was sure that he was okay, she asked him about his abduction.

"They followed me into the men's room," he said. "When I walked by them on my way out, they jabbed a needle in my arm. That's the last thing I remember until I came to in that supply room."

"Did they tell you why they grabbed you?" Liz asked.

"They knew Barrett told me about his informant and they wanted to know if I'd told anyone about it."

"They were going to kill you, weren't they?"

"I don't know," Drake said. "They were waiting for a call from someone to tell them what to do."

Casey had been listening from the galley and asked, "Did they mention Xueping? Is he responsible for grabbing you and probably killing Barrett?"

"I didn't hear Xueping's name mentioned. He could be, but it could be the men he met in the private gaming room, or all of them."

"What do you want to do?" Casey asked.

"Get our things and leave Hamilton Island. They'll find out that's where we were staying. Then we'll decide what we're going to do."

"What about your meetings with the New Zealand Defence Force?" Liz asked.

"Our final meeting is tomorrow," Casey said. "We could fly there tonight, after stopping on Hamilton Island, and take a day in Wellington to decide where we go from there."

"Let's do that, Mike," Drake said. "Have Kevin access the casino's security system and find out who those triads are. If they're willing to torture and kill a CDPP investigator, something Barrett said they never do, and come after me, they're playing differently, and we need to know why."

"I'll get Kevin on it," Casey said. "Get some rest."

Drake watched Casey walk down the aisle and turned to Liz. "Sorry about having to cut our honeymoon short."

"It's not your fault. Besides, I've seen the Great Barrier Reef and enjoyed every minute of our honeymoon. This is just the first of many wonderful things I have planned for us."

He smiled and closed his eyes. "I can't wait to hear what else you're planning."

She watched him sleeping for a moment and left to talk with Casey.

He was coming out of the cockpit and said, "Wheels up in ten minutes. Is he resting?"

"Sleeping. Can we talk?"

"Sure," Casey said. "I'm going to get something to drink before we take off. Want something?"

"Something strong. Vodka tonic, if you have it."

"Be right back."

Liz walked back and sat in a rear-facing seat where she could see Drake in his seat across the aisle behind the galley. He was beaten and bruised, but that wasn't what she was worried about.

Casey returned and handed her a highball glass with a twist of lemon on top.

"Cheers," he said and raised a tumbler full of amber liquid and ice.

"I'm worried about him, Mike."

"He'll be okay. The ribs will heal."

"He's going after them. You know that."

"They came after him and made it personal, Liz."

"That doesn't mean he has to take them on. They walked him out of the airport in broad daylight!"

Casey took a drink and sighed. "Do you know the Special Forces Creed? A part of it reads, "I will never surrender, though I be the last. If I am taken, I pray that I may have the strength to spit upon my enemy." We talked about that in Afghanistan, where we knew what terrorists did to the soldiers they captured. He won't back down until he spits on this enemy."

"What can I do?" I can't lose him."

"He won't be going after them alone, Liz. He put together a good team for our Special Projects section. If it gets too big for us, I'll make sure we call in the cavalry."

"Do you have any idea what this triad's plan might be?"

"Not really," Casey admitted. "The triads are criminal organizations. They're about making as much money as they can. Al-Qaeda and ISIS learned you won't be around for long if you take on a world power. The triads have been around since the seventeenth century in China. They know how to survive. Being involved in some grand scheme to take down America makes little sense."

Liz got up and walked back to check on Drake when she saw he was jerking around in his seat. Leaning down, she smoothed his hair and kissed his forehead, and returned to talk with Casey.

"He's back in the warehouse," she said, "Flinching in his sleep, like he's taking punches."

"We'll be landing soon on Hamilton Island," Casey said. "Do you want me to check you out at Qualia so you can stay here with him?"

Liz looked back at Drake. "No, I'll do it. Would you like to come and see where he's been keeping me? It's rather fantastic."

"Yes, I would. I'd like to bring Morales and Norris with us, in case there's a welcoming party waiting."

"They couldn't be here ahead of us," Liz said. "We just left their warehouse."

"The triads are everywhere, Liz. One phone call and your smiling resort employee becomes a triad assassin. We just killed four of their men. We're not taking any chances until we're on our way again."

Casey left to talk to Morales and Norris, leaving Liz wishing they'd never run into Lucas Barrett and helped him identify the men on Xueping's superyacht.

Chapter Thirteen

SAMUEL XUEPING LEFT the corporate headquarters of Xueping Properties Limited in the Sun Hung Kai Centre, an office skyscraper in Hong Kong. He was walking west on Harbour Road to the Harbour Road Garden with his jaw tightly clenched.

He ignored the children roller skating in the garden and stood beside a fountain, using white noise coming from its splashing water to cover his call to General Wang on his Iridium Extreme satellite phone.

His 426 triad leader in Australia had called to tell him the American escaped and four of his soldiers were dead.

"Yes?" General Wang barked.

"The American escaped."

"How?"

"He had help. They killed four of my men guarding him in the warehouse."

"Saves you from having to kill them yourself. Where is the American now?"

"I don't know. His company's Gulfstream left Brisbane right after he escaped. It didn't file a flight plan, so it had to fly VFR to somewhere nearby, like Hamilton Island, where he was staying. I have a man checking to see if he's there."

"He won't be," General Wang said.

"What do you want me to do?"

"What you usually do when someone interferes with your plan and kills your soldiers? Find him, and the ones who helped him escape, and kill them. Did he escape from the warehouse where you store the 4-AP precursors I send you?"

"Yes, but they're repackaged as Gambling Chip Disinfectant in five-gallon buckets and shrink-wrapped before they're shipped to Mexico. They couldn't know what's in the buckets."

"We can't risk it. Ship the remaining supply of 4-AP as soon as possible. When the blue pills are on the way north to America, it will be too late for them to do anything about it."

"About the American. Can you find him?" Xueping asked. "Your resources are better than mine."

"I have a friend in the MSS who might be able to help. When my aide tried to find out about the American, he was told to contact our Ministry of State Security for information. When he did, he was told the MSS knew nothing about a man named Adam Drake. That means they know him but aren't willing to share what they know. I will find out what they have and let you know."

"Thank you, General Wang," Xueping said.

"If you want to continue your relationship with us, make sure our plan does not fail. You are responsible for those you chose for this mission. If they fail you, like the men guarding the American did, you are the one who will pay for their failure. I will be the one who makes sure that you do."

Xueping left the garden determined to find out why the MSS knew about the American. It was bad enough an investigator for the Australian CDPP became interested in what they were doing. It would be worse if someone involved from America became curious as well.

On the way back to his office, the soldier called that he sent to the resort where the American was staying. "The American had checked out. The car his wife and another man left the resort in was from a Hamilton Island airport car rental agency, rented by Sound Security Information Solutions, a company from Seattle, Washington.

"Go to the airport and find out if the plane is still there," Xueping ordered. "If it's a Gulfstream G-650, find out where it's going and report back."

He knew the risks when he agreed to work with General Wang. He was worrying the tea leaves at the bottom of his cup right now would not encourage him, as they had before.

Xueping did an about face and returned to the Harbour Road Garden. He had to know about the American and his company, and he knew someone who could find out.

He checked the time on his Patek Phillipe Nautilus watch and calculated that with the sixteen-hour difference in time between Hong Kong and Vancouver, B.C., it was almost midnight. Frank Zheng would either be gambling or with his mistress. Xueping didn't care which it was.

"To what do I owe the honor of being interrupted this evening, Sam?" Zheng grumbled.

"The honor is that you're someone I help make a lot of money, Frank."

"What do you need? I'm in the middle of something."

"I have no doubt," Xueping snapped. "Frank, I need to know as much as you can find out about a man named Adam Drake. His company is Puget Sound Security in Seattle."

"Who is he?"

"That's what I want you to find out. Remember the man who went swimming from the back of my yacht the other night? This man may know something about him and the person he was talking to."

"Do you need me to take care of him?"

"Just have one of your men find out who he is and what he does."

"I'll send someone to Seattle tomorrow," Zheng said.

"Now would be better."

With a meeting of the three principals next week to coordinate the schedule for the final stage of General Wang's drug war, he Wang's plan relied on the element of surprise for success. Once the flood of cheap fentanyl, with a deadly dose of three milligrams in each little blue pill, reached America, their preemptive strike would have dealt a fatal blow to the enemy.

The world would blame the overdose deaths on America's insatiable appetite for illegal drugs, with no mention of China in the media.

If anything implicated China in the deaths, his triad would not survive. General Wang would make sure of that.

Chapter Fourteen

WHEN THE PSS Gulfstream G-650 landed at the Wellington International Airport in Wellington, New Zealand, Drake and Liz were escorted to the Copthorne Hotel Wellington on Oriental Bay, north of the airport.

Mike Casey insisted on Dan Norris and Marco Morales staying with them and checked both men into harbor view rooms next to each other.

"I'll see if I can get one of the docs from the Defence Force to look at your ribs," Casey told Drake in his room before leaving for New Zealand's Defence Force Headquarters. "If there's anything you or Liz need, don't go out. Send Morales for it. Norris will stay here to keep an eye on you. I don't think your friends have followed us here, but if they did, Marco will spot them."

"All I need is ice to get the swelling down and something to put in the whiskey Liz is calling room service for," Drake said. "If Kevin isn't too busy at the base tonight, have him access the security cameras at the Treasury Casino and ID the two Chinese men in the Orchid private gaming room with Xueping. Lucas Barrett thought they might all be involved in the plot his informant told him about."

"The three of them entered the private room a little after nine o'clock," Liz added. "Kevin will see us at the door, talking with the gaming room's manager when they walk in."

"Anything else?" Casey asked.

"We need to let the CDPP know what Barrett was investigating, in case he didn't report in before he disappeared," Drake continued.

"They might not know he's missing," Casey said. "If he isn't, do we want to get in the middle of that?"

"He's missing, Mike. They asked me about things they could have only gotten from him, unless they beat it out of him, but he didn't tell them my name."

"What did he tell them?"

"That we were involved in exposing a Chinese espionage operation."

"How did Barrett know about that?"

"When we met on Hamilton Island, he asked me what I was doing these days. I told him why we were encouraged to do intelligence contractor work for the government."

"Why doesn't Liz call the CDPP and ask to speak to Barrett," Casey suggested. "She can tell them he didn't meet you for breakfast and you just wanted to know if he was okay. You should be able to tell if they know what he was investigating, by the things they ask you about. If it seems they don't know that Barrett's missing or about his informant, we'll decide when to tell them."

"I can do that," Liz said.

"All right, I'm out of here," Casey said.

"Have Kevin call me, if he finds anything about Xueping and his friends," Drake said, as Casey walked out and then raised his hand to acknowledge that he'd heard him.

Drake stretched out on the bed and closed his eyes.

"I'll go get some ice," Liz said.

"Call room service first. Wouldn't want the ice to melt before my whiskey gets here."

"No, we wouldn't want that," Liz said. She knew if he still had his sense of humor, he was going to be okay. She called room service and ordered the best bottle of Japanese whiskey the hotel had and quietly slipped out of their room.

She stopped at the door of the room next door and knocked twice.

Dan Norris opened the door wide and invited her in. "How's he doing?"

"I'm going down the hall for ice for the whiskey he had me order. I think he'll be asleep before I get back."

"How are you doing?" Norris asked.

"Better, now that he's back. I panicked at the airport, but I'm okay now."

"All the training in the world doesn't protect you when it's someone you love. You had it under control by the time we hit the warehouse."

"Not completely, Dan. It's probably a good thing I didn't have a gun. I'd better get back. You want me to bring you some ice?"

"We're okay, thanks."

When she got back to their room, Drake was sitting up in bed with a bottle of whiskey on the nightstand.

"What role could the triad have in a plot against America," he asked. "I've been trying to think of one that makes sense."

Liz unwrapped two glasses from the shelf above the small refrigerator and put ice in them from the ice bucket she brought back. "Mind if I join you?"

"Of course not," he said. He broke the seal on the bottle of Hibiki Harmony and held it up. "You remembered."

"I did."

Drake poured two fingers of the amber liquid for each of them and said, "Kanpai!"

"Kanpai!" she repeated and sipped the whiskey. "Not bad."

"The triads are into drug trafficking, gambling, prostitution, the sex trades. None of those will cripple America. We've been dealing with those problems for decades."

Liz sat down on the end of the bed. "Maybe they're going after government leaders? They've certainly proven to be susceptible to some of those temptations."

"Agreed, but to cripple America, they'd have to take out the entire top-level of our leaders. I don't see that happening."

"Al Qaeda wanted to do that when they hit us on 9/11. Maybe it's going to be a terrorist attack in Washington by samurais dressed as geisha prostitutes."

Drake laughed so hard he spilled his drink. "That hurt. Please, don't make me laugh! Samurais and geishas are Japanese!"

"And whiskey is from Scotland, not Japan. You never know."

Drake tried not to laugh. "No, you never know."

Chapter Fifteen

WITH THE REPEATING dream of his capture playing in his mind throughout the night, Drake woke up with a throbbing headache and an aching body.

When he tried to sit up, a spasm of pain made him fall back in bed.

"Are you ready to take a pain pill now?" Liz asked, sitting in a reading chair beside the window that looked out to Oriental Bay and the sailboats anchored there. "The doctor told you last night the pain would get worse if you didn't stay ahead of it."

"I need to have a clear head when we meet Mike," Drake said.

"Then you didn't need to drink as much whisky as you did. There's nothing that needs to be decided right now. We'll have plenty of time on the flight home."

Drake rolled to his left side, used his arm to raise up and swung his legs out to sit on the side of the bed. "When is Mike coming by?"

"He's having breakfast with the generals, then coming to pick us up. Would you like something to eat before he gets back?"

"Probably a good idea. Scrambled eggs, toast, and a pot of coffee would be great."

Liz picked up the phone on the end table beside her chair and ordered Drake's breakfast from room service.

"Aren't you going to have something?" he asked.

"Morales brought me yogurt and fresh fruit from the restaurant when they came back from breakfast."

"I didn't hear a thing."

"I ate in their room next door. I didn't want to wake you."

Drake got up slowly and walked to the window. "What do you think we should do, Liz?"

She joined him and gingerly put her arm around his waist. "Get you healed up before you do anything."

"We don't have time for that. If they're bold enough to come after me in a crowded airport, their plan is already in play."

"If Lucas let the CDPP know about the informant, Australia could have passed it along to the CIA. Do we want to go after Xueping and his friends, if the CIA's already on it?"

"That wouldn't keep me from making Xueping pay for interrupting our honeymoon," Drake said as he continued staring out the window.

He turned and walked to the nightstand to get his wallet. "Here's the business card Lucas gave me. Let's call the number on it and ask to speak with him. Let's make sure there's isn't a good reason he didn't show up."

Liz took the card from Drake and opened her phone to make the call. She listened for a moment and shook her head.

"It went to voicemail," she said. "Now what?"

There was a knock on the door. "Room service."

"Have breakfast and wait until Mike's here," Drake said.

Liz tipped the young server and rolled the cart over to the small table on the far side of the window. "While you're eating, I'll go check with Norris and Morales and find out if they have an ETA for Mike."

Drake sat down, took the lid off the plate, and stared at what was on it; a mound of scrambled eggs with chopped herbs, two pieces of thick toast with pads of butter, marmalade, and three pieces of bacon.

Liz had known how hungry he was and ordered the perfect breakfast to get him going again.

He was putting marmalade on a second piece of toast when Liz came back.

"Mike's on his way, Liz said. "Kevin identified the men with Xueping in the casino," she said. "One is from Mexico, the owner of a large pharmaceutical company. He's believed to be affiliated with a Chinese cartel trafficking fentanyl. The other man is a Chinese Canadian from Vancouver, B.C. The DEA has a classified file on him, but Mike told Kevin we'll get the information without hacking the DEA's system."

"That's what Barrett was investigating, cartels laundering fentanyl profits through Australian casinos. Knowing who these guys are doesn't get us any closer to knowing what they're up to. Does Kevin know where these guys are now? Drake asked.

"Mike didn't say, and I didn't ask."

Drake held up the piece of toast and said, "Great marmalade, want a taste?"

"No, thanks. Why do you want to know where Xueping and his two friends are?" Liz asked.

"The only way we're going to find out if Barrett's informant was on to something is by finding out what those three men are up to. They're not going to have anything on their computers or phones about it. The Chinese triads and transnational criminal syndicates are smarter than that."

"If we're going to find out what this plan is, and if it's real, we'll have to find out about it from one of these three men," he finished and poured himself another cup of coffee.

Liz saw the steely look in his eyes and asked, "What are you planning on doing when you find them?"

Drake raised the coffee cup to his mouth and tilted his head to one side before taking a sip. "It depends on whether I like what they say."

"Is there any way you're going to like what they say?"

Drake smiled. "Probably not. Liz, I'm not going vigilante on these guys, but I do plan on seeing that they get what's coming to them."

"Because of what they're planning or what they did to you?"

"Both are good reasons, but one is enough."

Chapter Sixteen

MIKE CASEY RETURNED to the Copthorne Wellington Hotel just before noon, with Mark Holland and Kevin McRoberts.

While Morales and Norris checked them out of the hotel for the rooms they'd rented and loaded luggage into a van from the airport, Casey walked the PSS group across the street from the hotel to Coene's Bar and Eatery.

"General Warner said to have lunch on the outdoor deck with the best view of Oriental harbor, before we left," Casey said. "I'd like to hear from everyone, before we file a flight plan to wherever our next stop is going to be. Outside on a beautiful day, like today, seemed like a good place to do it."

Drake was walking between Casey on his left and Liz on his right and asked, "Did we get the contract we wanted for the penetration testing?"

"Every last detail," Casey said. "They signed the contact you drafted without a single change. They're excited to see how they do when Kevin has a go at them."

"They won't be after he exploits the weaknesses in their system."

"How are you doing?" Casey asked. "If your body feels as bad as your face looks, you're hurting big time."

"Thanks Mike. I'm fine."

"Liz?"

"He's hurting, but he ate an excellent breakfast."

When they got to Coene's front door, Kevin darted around them and held the door open. "Glad you're okay, Mr. Drake."

"Am I ever going to get you to call me Adam, Kevin?"

"No, sir."

Casey asked the hostess for outside seating for eight and she led through the restaurant to the deck. With the help of a server, she pulled two tables together and laid down menus for their party.

"Michele will be your server today," the hostess said. "Enjoy the best food on Oriental Bay."

They ordered a round of drinks, while they waited for Morales, Norris and Steve Carson, the PSS pilot, to join them.

After a quick look at his menu, Casey asked if anyone objected to him ordering platters for all of them. "The Fried Platter and the Veggie Platter look good for starters. If anyone has something they want to try, add it to the order."

No one did. When their drinks were served, Casey proposed a toast to the New Zealand Defence Force for the wise decision it made in hiring them, and for Drake's safe return.

"Before we leave here, we need to decide what to do next," Casey said. "Through no fault of his own, Drake has presented us with a conundrum. We don't know if there is a plot, as Lucas Barrett's informant overheard someone mention, and, if there is, what do we do with that information?"

"If we decided to go it alone, without letting the ASIO, the Australian Security Intelligence Organization, or the CIA handle it, I believe there's a good chance it will put us and the company at greater risk than ever before. When you take on a Chinese triad, they come after you and your family. When you take on a transnational criminal syndicate, like the Mexican cartels, they come after you, your family, and the entire village.

"That's why I want to hear from all of you," Casey said. "Drake and I have made decisions like this before, without asking for your input. But this is different. If China is involved, we'll also be taking on an enemy that's willing to risk war, if it's backing whatever Xueping and his friends are planning."

"Do we know if Barrett's people know about his informant?" Marco Morales asked.

"We don't," Liz said. "I called the number he gave Adam and my call went to voicemail. He hasn't called back. I didn't call the CDPP. I didn't know who he works with there."

"I think it's better that you didn't, Liz," Mark Holland said. "In 2019, the ASIO arrested a Chinese spy who revealed the Chinese government was seeking to takeover Australian politics, by infiltrating and disrupting democratic systems in the country. China may have infiltrated the ASIO."

"Is there someone in the FBI or CIA we trust enough to tell them what we know?" Dan Norris asked. "Like Kate Perkins. We've worked with her before."

"I don't think we have time to bring someone in on this," Drake said. "Taking action against Lucas Barrett and me like they did shows they're serious about not letting anyone stop them. It also may mean they don't have time to change their plan, in case Barrett tipped off his agency."

"We don't have much to go on," Kevin McRoberts pointed out. "I was able to identify the two men with Xueping, but we don't know where they are now."

Casey looked across the bay, with his pilsner glass to his lips, and paused before saying, "We might have an idea, though. Dan, do you remember those shrink-wrapped pallets in the warehouse? They had packing labels that said they contained cleaning detergents for casino gambling chips. The label had a picture of a gambling chip on it. Do you remember which casino it was?"

Norris smiled and took out his phone. "No, but I took a picture. Let me check."

"How will that help?" Steve Carson said.

"It's bothered me since we left Brisbane," Casey said. "Why

would a company that sells gambling equipment bother to sell cleaning detergents? A casino could buy those supplies anywhere. Xueping owns hotels and casinos. What better way to move fentanyl precursors from China to Mexico than shipping them to a casino he owns disguised as cleaning detergents?"

Norris found the picture he'd taken and pulled it apart to enlarge it. "The chip shown on the packing label is from the "*Casino Cortez*". I know where that is. I've been there. It's in La Paz, Baja California."

"You think that's where Xueping might be?" Drake asked Casey.

"It's worth a trip there to find out. Dan, since you've been there, why don't you and Morales go check it out? I'll buy you first-class tickets and let you use a company credit card. Be rich Americans looking for a good time and some high-stakes gambling. See if Xueping or his friends are there. We'll return to Seattle and wait to hear from you."

"Muchas gracias, jefe," Norris said.

"Si, muchas gracias, jefe," Morales chimed in.

Chapter Seventeen

SAMUEL XUEPING TURNED the sound down on the flat screen monitor to take the call from General Wang. He'd been watching the news on CNN in the rear suite of his new BomBardier 8000 executive jet on his way to Mexico.

"Have you found him?" General Wang asked.

"I have someone watching the townhouse where he lives, and his company's headquarters. He hasn't been seen at either place," Xueping reported.

"When you find him, kill him as soon as possible. He's a dangerous man."

"What have you learned?"

"MSS has a file on him because he embarrassed them recently. He's a lawyer, who was in Afghanistan and Iraq with the U.S. Delta Force. His father-in-law is a U.S. Senator, and he's a friend of the American President. We can't let him tell anyone about what the CDPP investigator told him."

"Does it matter how he dies?"

"What do you mean?"

"If he's killed as soon as he returns home, they might become suspicious. Do you want me to make it look like an accident, or do you care?"

Xueping rolled the remaining whisky in his tumbler and waited for the general to answer.

"If you find him today, make it look like an accident," General Wang ordered. "If it takes longer, we'll make it look like someone else did it. The party is working to weaken the alliances Russia has in the Middle East. We have some of Russia's LPO-97 the grenade launchers developed for use with thermobaric grenades. They supplied them to Syria, and they wound up with ISIS. I'll have a couple of them delivered to you tomorrow. We can make it look like Russia and the terrorists killed the attorney."

"As you wish, general," Xueping said.

He finished his drink and refilled the tumbler. Playing the pawn for China in another of its geopolitical maneuvers wasn't what he signed on for. Keeping a lucrative arrangement in place was.

Even it meant killing someone who was a friend of the American President. But watching the skies for the rest of his life for a killer drone flying overhead wasn't something he wanted to live with.

China couldn't risk getting blamed for the death of the attorney. It would deny responsibility, and General Wang would make sure someone else was blamed.

But the triads who escaped to Hong Kong had learned how to survive and so had Xueping. He had his own survival plan in place. His triad, and the other Hong Kong triads, kept records of all of their dealings with Chinese officials, who were foolish enough to think they were above the corruption laws China used to punish officials who went too far.

Xueping had a treasure trove of recorded conversations, videos of Wang's indiscretions, and copies of wire transfers to Wang's secret offshore bank accounts. If Wang tried to make him responsible for any part of his plan, he would make sure General Wang and his cronies paid for it. That was his long game, and he'd played it with skill so far.

He took the sat phone out of the leather laptop carrier bag next to his feet and called his best man in Mexico.

"Take a plane and fly to Seattle," he ordered. "There's a man there who has to be silenced. A friend from Vancouver will contact you. He'll tell you where you can find him. If you have him in sight tonight, make it look like an accident. If you can't find him tonight, call me tomorrow. The general is sending something he wants us to use to kill him."

"Do I need to be concerned about collateral damage?"

"Tonight, yes. We'll talk about whether it is tomorrow."

"I'm on my way."

Xueping closed his eyes and massaged his forehead with his fingers. He planned to be in Viareggio, Italy, early next week to finalize an order for another Benetti Oasis 40m for his fleet of superyachts. If it took longer than a few more days to kill this attorney, he'd have to postpone the trip.

That would cause a delay in the delivery of the new Benetti his high-stake gambling Saudi princes had booked for next year. There was too much money at stake to let that happen.

Li Kuan was his best enforcer, but he was only one man. If he needed backup tomorrow, there wasn't enough time to get more of his men to Seattle. As much as he disliked asking Francis Zheng for another favor, he didn't have a choice if he wanted to be in Italy by the weekend.

Xueping entered the numbers for Zheng on his sat phone and waited for him to answer.

"Did I wake you?" he asked, knowing it was 10:00 a.m. PST in the Pacific Northwest.

"Very funny. What can I do for you this time, Sam?"

"Since you couldn't find the attorney, I want you to send men to Seattle as backup for a man I'm sending there."

"We didn't find him because he's not there."

"Did you confirm that?"

"The townhouse belongs to his wife, and her neighbor said they're still on their honeymoon. His company said the same thing when we called there. Yes, we confirmed it."

"All right," Xueping said. "Then I need another favor. I'll make it up to you when you get to La Paz. I need four of your best soldiers that you can spare for a day or two. Have them in Seattle tomorrow morning and call me when they're in place. I'll text you a number for them to call to meet my man."

"How do you plan to make it up to me?"

"Don't worry, I know what you like."

Chapter Eighteen

THIRTY-EIGHT HOURS after leaving New Zealand on an overnight commercial airlines flight from Wellington, Marco Morales and Dan Norris landed in La Paz, Mexico, Wednesday morning at 7:30 A.M.

They traveled separately as two high-stakes gamblers, looking to enjoy the sun of Baja California and the hospitality of the Casino Cortez, owned by Samuel Xueping.

After clearing customs at the Aeropuerto Internacional Manuel Márquez de León, they each took taxis directly to their individual destinations; the casino for Morales and the Casa al Mar luxury hotel for Norris.

The Casino Cortèz was next to Marina Palmira on the western shore of the Sea of Cortèz.

Morales had laughed at Xueping's lack of originality in the names chosen for his casino and marina. For a man as flamboyant as the man Drake had described seeing in the casino in Brisbane, the names of these properties didn't have the allure of a casino wanting to attract high-stakes gamblers from around the world.

The casino itself made up for the glamour its name lacked. Designed in the style of Mexican contemporary architecture, its sprawling two-story geometric exterior of Italian rose marble and privacy mirror windows promised exclusivity and privilege for all those who entered.

Morales walked into the air-conditioned lobby and continued past a waterfall flowing from the top of a tall slab of black granite on his way to the cashier's window. He'd picked up an American Express Black card in his own name, courtesy of Sound Security Information Solutions, when he stopped at Los Angeles International Airport on the way to La Paz.

When he left the cashier's window, he had a marker for fifty thousand dollars he didn't intend to use, unless he had to. He was at the casino to look for Xueping or his friends later in the day or that night.

As early as it was, he didn't expect any of them to be at the casino but decided to check out the private gaming rooms on the second floor, just in case.

Casino Cortèz had two private gaming rooms. Both rooms allowed the members of its invitation-only, high-stakes gamblers to play there, Morales was told. When he told the private room's manager that he was interested in becoming a member and slipped him a fifty-dollar bill, however, he was given a tour of the rooms by the manager.

Xueping or his friends were not gambling in either of the two rooms.

Morales took the escalator down to the casino's restaurant on the main floor to have breakfast. When he had a cup of coffee in his hands and an order of steak and eggs on the way, he called Norris.

"Any luck," Norris asked.

"Sí amigo. I'm enjoying a cup of Jamaican Blue Mountain coffee and waiting for a breakfast of steak and eggs."

"Where are you?"

"At the casino."

"Did you have time to look for the men they sent us here us to find?"

"They're not here. Did you get us a room?"

"I did," Norris said. "Wish you were here. I'm on the room's balcony with a plate of fresh fruit and croissants the hotel provided."

"Touché. What now?"

"Go to the marina next to the casino and look for a Benetti Oasis 40m superyacht. Kevin says Xueping has one moored there. It shouldn't be hard to find, there are only fifteen of them in the world."

"Where are you going to be?" Morales asked. "I'd like to get a key card for the room and take a shower."

"Call me when you leave the marina. Kevin found the address of a villa one of Xueping's friends has here in La Paz. It's not far. I thought I'd see if anyone's home."

"Roger that. See you when I see you."

Morales put his phone away as his server arrived with his breakfast and stared at the plate set before him. Fifteen ounces of New York Strip Steak cut in one-inch thick strips, three eggs and roasted potatoes, and a pitcher of fresh-squeezed orange juice.

A man's breakfast, he thought. *I hope Norris is getting enough nourishment to get through the day.*

After he finished off his steak and egg breakfast a half an hour later, he left the casino and walked the short distance to the marina to look for Xueping's yacht.

When he approached the ramp leading down to the marina's docks, he saw the gate at the head of the ramp was locked and needed the code for a keypad to enter.

He walked on past the gate and looked for Xueping's yacht. He wasn't a boat guy, but there were fifteen or twenty boats big enough to be considered a superyacht. Only one was big enough to be a hundred and thirty-one foot long.

Morales stopped and studied the yacht through the marina's chain-link fencing. Towering above the other yachts moored nearby, the champagne-colored yacht with its elongated rear swim deck was an impressive sight.

Two young women wearing bikinis were sunning themselves on orange chaise lounge chairs on the swim deck. At the top of the stairs from the swim deck to the main deck, a crewman was standing facing inside, where three men sat around a table.

The men were facing away from his position, but from the descriptions he had, Morales knew he'd found the men they were searching for.

Chapter Nineteen

DAN NORRIS DROVE AWAY from Casa al Mar in a white Jeep Rubicon with half doors and a black sunshade top he rented. He wasn't planning on off-roading in the desert, but the vehicle's capabilities matched his feeling that he needed to be prepared for anything.

Unarmed as he was, except for the Benchmade Vector folding knife in his pocket, the jeep gave off a vibe that he was a man of adventure you might not want to mess with. If that gave him an advantage, if he encountered triad thugs, terrific. If it didn't, at least he was going to enjoy driving it.

The address Kevin McRoberts gave him for Ramon Ying's villa was in an exclusive gated community of Pedregal de Cortes, on the hillside north of the center of La Paz. A search on Google Earth located the white contemporary two-story structure at the highest part of Pedregal de Cortes on the hillside.

With direct access to the villa denied to him, Norris pulled off Pedregal de Cortes Avenue onto a dirt road just below the gated community. He drove higher up the hillside until he had an unobstructed view of the villa.

Norris parked the Jeep, pointed downhill two hundred yards

from the villa, and set the parking brake. Focusing a pair of compact Leupold BX-1 Rogue binoculars on the open garage in the villa's front, he saw there were no cars parked inside. The pool area at the side of the villa closest to him was being cleaned by a pool boy, but there was no sign of Ramon Ying on the premises.

He put the binoculars away and sat back to admire the view of the shimmering waters the off the Sea of Cortèz and a ferry moving across it to the Mexican mainland. In its brown and barren way, Baja California had an exotic attraction that he promised he would explore someday.

His phone buzzed in his pocket as he was about to start the jeep and pull back onto the dirt road.

"Come to the marina," Morales said. "They're here, on Xueping's yacht."

"Xueping's friends?"

"And Xueping."

"What are they doing?"

"Sitting around a table playing some game."

"Do they have their bodyguards with them?"

"I haven't seen any. Doesn't mean they're not on the yacht somewhere."

"I'll be there in fifteen minutes," Norris said.

Crawling through the noon traffic on the way to the marina took longer than fifteen minutes. When he pulled into the parking lot, Morales was waving to him by a chain-link security fence.

Norris parked the Jeep as close to Morales as possible and walked across the recently paved asphalt parking lot.

"Glad you brought binoculars," Morales said. "It's the big yacht at the end of the dock on the left."

Norris lifted the binoculars to his eyes and turned the focus wheel until he had a crystal-clear view of the yacht.

"When you said they were playing a game, I didn't think it would be mahjong. Xueping's the one laughing. He must be winning."

"Other than the two lovelies sunning themselves, can you see anyone else?" Morales asked.

"Two men up top in the pilothouse. One man, leaning on the forward sundeck. I can't see through the darkened private windows of the main salon." Norris answered. "How big a crew does it take to sail something like that?"

"I checked while I was waiting for you. The Benetti Oasis 40m accommodates ten guests and has five staterooms. It usually sails with seven crew members, sleeping in four staterooms."

"Wonder if they're on shore leave or below deck sleeping?"

Morales turned away and watched four men getting out of a black Mercedes Sprinter van in the parking lot and walking toward the marina security gate. When they passed by, he saw they all had tattoos of dragons on their necks, one of the favorite tattoos of Chinese triad members.

"I think Xueping has visitors headed his way," Morales said quietly. "Check out their tattoos."

Norris lowered his binoculars and turned to watch the four men at the security gate. "Triad."

"That's my guess. The way they're dressed, you don't get to see their full body tats. But those don't look like the tattoos Mexican cartels brand their members with."

"I'm surprised Xueping would let them get anywhere near his yacht," Norris said. "He publicly denies being a triad dragon head."

"He does. Maybe these aren't friendlies headed his way."

"Guess we'll know soon enough."

The leader of the four punched in a code from a card he was reading and led his men down the ramp to the main dock.

Norris turned back to Xueping's yacht and focused the binoculars on a crew member standing at the rear of the lower rear deck watching the four men approach.

The leader raised his hand in greeting, and the crew member returned the gesture.

"Looks like they're friendlies," Norris said. "Xueping must have expected them."

Morales held out his hand for the binoculars and took them from Norris. "Let's see who comes out to meet them."

He trained the binoculars on the lower rear deck where the three men had been playing mahjong. All three were standing, watching the four men walk down the dock toward them.

When the four men reached the end of the dock, one Chinese man left the other two and stepped to the edge of the lower rear desk.

It was Ramon Ying, the owner of the villa Norris had been watching.

Morales watched as Ying turned to say something to Xuepeng, who nodded for Ying to come aboard and joined him.

"What now?" Norris asked.

"Now we follow Ying and see what he's doing here."

Chapter Twenty

THE MERCEDES SPRINTER van left the marina and drove north on Highway 11.

"Any idea where they're going?" Norris asked.

Morales studied the Jeep's GPS navigation screen and made the image smaller to see what was up ahead on Highway 11.

"There's one small town, Punta Prieta, and then the Port of Pichinlique, where the ferries leave for the mainland of Mexico," Morales said.

"If they take a ferry, I'm not sure I want to go with them. That's Sinaloa cartel country over there. I've dealt with those guys in my FBI days. I won't do it again, armed with only a pocketknife."

"We're only here to locate Xueping and his two friends, and find out what they're up to," Morris reminded him. "Besides, these guys are triads, not *narcotraficantes*."

"Thanks for clarifying that. I feel so much better being reminded that the men in the van are just members of the oldest transnational criminal syndicate in the world."

Morales turned to see if Norris was being serious. "I thought you HRT guys were fearless. They're just five guys with ugly tattoos."

"Right."

Morales let it go, wondering what Norris had experienced that made him so wary of triad gang members.

They drove on, without either man talking, past the town of Punta Prieta and continued on the coast road to the port city of Pichilingue.

Norris dropped back as the black van slowed to enter the city and broke the silence. "I read our navy used Pichinlique as a base of operation during the Mexican American war of 1846. Wonder if there's anything interesting left around from it."

"Probably not," Morales said. "Mexico fought that war because we annexed Texas. I wouldn't expect them to leave memorials around to remind them of it."

They watched the van drive past the LNG terminal and then the ferry terminal.

"We're not going to the mainland, it seems," Norris said.

"Not on a ferry, anyway," Morales said, when the van signaled it was turning left onto Avenue Pichilingue toward a marina.

"Maybe they have a boat?"

"Then you won't have to worry about going with them."

Norris sighed and said, "I didn't say I was afraid of them, Marco. I led a hostage rescue into a warehouse in Maryland. Our intel said they were holding hostages there. They knew we were coming and butchered seventeen trafficking victims, young women and men, in ways you should never witness. If I ever come across men like the ones who killed them, I'll shoot them all without worrying about what happens to me. That's why I don't want to get too close to any of them."

They both watched as the black van turned left again and drove along the eastern side of the marina, past warehouses and then a Cemex plant. A hundred yards past the plant on the other side of the road was a newer warehouse, surrounded with a security chain-link fence topped with coils of barbed wire.

The name on the side of the manned security post was UniMex Pharm, S.A.B.

"Off the beaten path for a pharmaceutical company," Norris said.

"Especially UniMex. It's one of the largest pharma companies in Mexico. Its CEO is Ramon Ying, the man we're following."

Norris drove past the manned security gate. "I'd sure like to see what's in that warehouse."

"That makes two of us. Let's turn around and find a spot where we can see who's coming and going. I'll call Casey and ask him what he wants us to do."

Norris drove to the end of Avenue Pichilingue, turned the Jeep around and parked on the side of the road.

The UniMex warehouse was a sand-colored structural steel building with a red roof two hundred yards away. There were no windows on the side of the building facing them and only one small window at the side of the main entrance. At the rear of the building, a dozen cars were parked in a row. By the age and dilapidated condition of the cars, they probably belonged to employees working in the warehouse.

"It doesn't have the ventilation you'd expect for a manufacturing facility," Morales said. "Must be a shipping depot for the company."

"Strange place for one, this far from La Paz."

Morales leaned out and looked up in the sky. "Hear that?"

"Sounds like a Black Hawk. Maybe Ying's going somewhere and didn't want anyone to know about it."

They watched a drab olive green colored Mexican army helicopter descend slowly from the east and hover briefly before setting down. Before the dust had time to settle, a two-star Mexican general in dress uniform got out and hurried toward the building, holding onto the bill of his hat.

Norris had his binoculars trained on the general and watched him walk across the sandy earth. "I didn't get a good look at his face," he said to Morales.

"I might have. I kept the video on my Samsung running from

the time the door slid back and he jumped out. We should be able to pull out a high-res photo from the video in one of them that captures his face."

"Do we wait for Ying to leave or follow the general?"

"I'll call Casey and find out what he wants us to do," Morales said.

Before his call had time to reach the PSS CEO on Seattle, Ying and the Mexican general walked out surrounded by the four triad goons and got in the black Mercedes Sprinter van.

"There's your answer," Norris said. "We follow both of them."

Chapter Twenty-One

DRAKE SAT in the passenger seat of Liz's Cadillac CTS-V on the drive back to Seattle from Oregon and tried to relax. It wasn't that Liz was a bad driver. She loved driving the six hundred and forty horsepower sports sedan hard and sometimes took corners a little faster than he would have. But she always drove within the car's limit, even if she exceeded the posted speed limit by twenty or thirty miles an hour when doing so.

He had trouble relaxing because he was still dealing with the damage the triad caused when they beat him in the warehouse. They were out there somewhere, and he wouldn't fully relax until he found them.

"Would you like to stop and walk around a bit?" Liz asked.

"I don't think that would help, but thanks for asking. Lancer might need to stop sometime."

Liz turned to look at Lancer stretched out across the rear seat. "Lancer's sleeping, like you should be. Would you rather drive for a while before your nap?"

Drake grimaced and tried to keep from laughing. "You're a devil, you know. I keep asking you to let me drive your car and you wait until even holding my arms up to the steering wheel would hurt like hell."

"Will you see a doctor when we get to Seattle?"

"There's nothing a doctor can do for cracked ribs and sore muscles. I'll be fine."

"I wonder how many of our wedding gifts in the trunk were purchased in Oregon to keep from paying the Washington sales tax," she said to change the subject, as they drove across the I-5 bridge over the Columbia River from Portland, Oregon, to Vancouver, Washington.

Drake took his phone out of the pocket of his black bomber jacket to call Mike Casey.

"If you're calling Mike, I called him just before we left the vineyard," Liz said.

"You didn't mention it. What did he say?"

"He wanted to know how you were feeling and when we'd be back."

"Did he say he'd heard from Morales and Norris in Mexico?"

"He said they hadn't called him with anything new."

"Maybe they have by now," Drake said and hit speed dial to call his friend.

"How are you feeling?" Casey asked when he answered.

"I'm fine, Mike. I wish everyone would quit asking. Have you heard from Morales and Norris?"

"Morales just called to say they have eyes on our two guys. They followed Ramon Ying to a warehouse where a Mexican general landed in a Blackhawk. Now they're following Ying and the general."

"Do we know anything about the general?"

"Morales said he's putting together some photos he took on his phone and sending them to Kevin to work on."

"You said they have eyes on our guys. What are they doing?"

"Morales says they're playing mahjong on Xueping's yacht."

"He hasn't had time to get it across the Pacific. Are they sure?"

"Same make and model, different name on the stern."

"Mike, we need to find out what they're doing on that yacht."

"How do you suggest we do that?"

"Does Morales have the Black Hornet Nano? Have him look."

"I'll ask him if he still has the drone. When do you think you'll feel like getting back to work?"

"Tomorrow."

"See you then."

Liz turned to look at him and saw him clenching and unclenching his jaw muscles. "I thought you agreed to see a doctor before going back to work?"

"I remember saying I would see a doctor. Before going back to work is an amendment to my agreement," Drake said with a smile. "Liz, I said I'll see a doctor. But my ribs will heal just as fast if I'm working at headquarters, as they would if I'm sitting around in the townhouse all day."

"All right, I'll make you a deal. We have two hours before we reach Seattle. You close your eyes and rest and I'll stop nagging you."

"Deal," Drake said, and leaned his head back onto his seat's head restraint. He didn't intend to sleep. He intended to come up with a way to settle the score with Xueping and he could do that with his eyes closed as well as open.

Two hours later, Liz patted his leg. "Wake up sleepy head."

Drake opened his eyes and looked around. The Cadillac was parked in her reserved space in their townhouse's underground parking.

"Huh," he said, rubbing his eyes. "Looks like I needed a nap."

"Why don't we take our luggage upstairs and get the wedding gifts later. Lancer might like to go for a walk."

"That right Lancer?" Drake said and opened his door to get out. Lancer squeezed through the space from the back seat and stood next to him, wagging his tail.

"Looks like Lancer would like to go for a walk sooner rather than later. You go ahead. We can unload the car later."

Drake snapped a leash on Lancer's collar and walked up the ramp from underground parking with Lancer at heel on his left side.

It felt good to be out of the car, walking his dog on a warm fall day with feathery clouds high overhead. Liz's townhouse was uphill, a block away from a small city park with old maple trees and walking paths.

The maple trees' leaves were just beginning to turn yellow and orange, promising the beautiful change of seasons Drake loved.

They continued walking down the sidewalk to the park and veered left onto a walking path that cut diagonally across the park. Ten feet down the path, Lancer stopped and turned to look back at the street.

"What is it, Lancer?"

Drake didn't see what got Lancer's attention but noticed the hair on the back of his dog's neck was standing up. His nose was pointed at a late-model black Chevrolet Impala with tinted windows parked at the sidewalk on the other side of the street.

Drake watched the black car for a moment and pulled gently on Lancer's collar. "Come on, boy. No one's going to hurt me with you around. We need to get back and help Liz unload the car."

Chapter Twenty-Two

THEY CONTINUED across the park to the other side and turned back. Lancer was still looking toward the Impala at a forty-five-degree angle off to their right.

Lancer had performed at the highest level in his Schutzhund training and won top awards all over the Northwest in Schutzhund trials with Drake, as his handler, before they stopped competing. He always passed the tracking and obedience tests with high marks, but he was at his best in the protective phase of the trial that involved finding and warning his handler of hidden danger and aggressively stopping a menacing intruder wearing protective clothing.

He'd saved Drake's life twice in the past, and Drake knew he could count on him to do it again. Thinking about that made him wonder if this was another of those times.

As they approached the sidewalk to turn left and walk back uphill to Liz's townhouse, Drake couldn't see if there was anyone in the Impala. But Lancer sensed there was and kept his head turned back to the black car.

Halfway up the block, Drake heard the Impala's engine start and reached under his bomber jacket to wrap his hand around the checkered rosewood grips of his Kimber Ultra Carry II.

Lancer squared around to face the Impala as it pulled away from the curb and started up the hill. When the driver's tinted window started coming down, he started barking.

Drake turned and moved into a two-handed stance, with his Kimber aimed at the driver's side window. When he saw the barrel of an AK-47 pistol come out pointed in his direction, he fired three times into the half-open window.

A burst of 7.62 x 39mm NATO rounds fired over his head and the Impala accelerated wildly across the street, crashing into a tan Volvo and setting off its alarm.

Drake approached the black car slowly with Lancer at his side. The driver's bloody head was pinned between the deployed airbag and his seat's headrest. A dragon tattoo was visible beneath the blood flowing down from his head.

Stepping away from the car, he holstered his Kimber and took out his phone.

"911, what is your emergency?"

"There's been a shooting. One man is dead. I'm at the scene. Please notify the police"

"Is the shooter still there?"

"I am the shooter. My name is Adam Drake."

"Is anyone hurt?"

"Only the other guy. He's dead."

Drake looked up the street and saw Liz running toward him. He waved to let her know he was okay.

"911, I have to help keep traffic away from the scene. I'll wait here for officers to arrive. Let them know I'm armed, have a carry permit and an armed security guard license."

Drake stepped out into the street, holding out his hands to stop two cars approaching, as Liz ran to join him.

"Are you okay?"

"I'm okay. The triad guy isn't. I called the police. Before they get here, take my Kimber over to the sidewalk where they can see it and keep an eye on it."

Liz took the gun and held out her hand. "Better let me have your jacket too."

Drake unzipped his jacket and handed it to her. "Call Mike. Let him know what happened."

As traffic began backing up on the street, he walked to each car in both directions and asked them to remain there until the police arrived. He didn't think anyone in the cars had seen the shooting, but he wanted the police to have their names and contact information to confirm it.

Before he finished talking to the last car on the downhill side of the street, he heard sirens approaching and walked back to stand in the middle of the street behind the black Impala. His hands were out at his side, open and palms facing toward the first patrol car as it rolled to a stop.

Liz remained on the sidewalk with Lancer, with her phone held up to her ear.

Both doors of the patrol car swung open and the two officers stood behind them with their weapons drawn and pointing at Drake.

"Are you Adam Drake?" the first officer shouted over the noise of the Volvo's car alarm.

"Yes. I'm not armed. My gun is on the sidewalk over there," Drake shouted back, with a nod in its direction.

The officers walked out from behind the patrol car's doors and moved closer.

"Care to tell us what happened, Mr. Drake?" the other officer asked.

"The man in the Impala started shooting at me with an AK-47 pistol. I returned fire."

"Do you know him?"

"No, I don't know him."

A second patrol car arrived and parked next to the first car. Its two officers got out and walked cautiously to each side of the Impala. When the officer looking in at the dead shooter shook his head, he walked around to the far side of the Volvo and tried to open the door. The door was locked, and the car's alarm continued to shriek.

Drake stayed in the middle of the street while the four officers huddled ten feet away. When they broke up, the first officer he talked with returned and told him the crime scene investigators were on the way.

"Is that your wife over there?" the officer asked. "Was she here when this happened?"

"We live up the street. She came when she heard the shooting."

"The detectives will want to take you to the station for questioning. Take a moment, let her know it might be a while before she sees you again."

Chapter Twenty-Three

IT WAS nine o'clock that evening before the Kirkland Police Department detectives finished questioning Drake and let him leave.

Mike Casey's black Range Rover was idling at the curb when he walked out of the police station.

"Where's Liz?" he asked Casey when he opened the passenger door and looked in.

"She's at the townhouse with the rest of Carol's team," Casey said. "Say hello to the leader of your close-protection team."

Drake got in and saw Carol Sanchez sitting in the rear seat behind Casey.

"Mike, I don't need a protection team."

"We don't know that," Casey said as he pulled away from the curb. "Just say thank you and congratulate Carol Sanchez on her new position."

Drake forced a smile and reached back to shake the hand of his new bodyguard. "Congratulations, Carol. Mike mentioned he was thinking of giving you a team. I didn't know he'd already done it."

"You were on your honeymoon. It just happened last week," Sanchez said. "How was Australia?"

"Relaxing until the last couple of days."

"Did the detectives ID the shooter?" Casey asked.

Drake shook his head. "They said they've seen his tattoos on members of a Chinese cartel operating out of Mexico called Los Zheng. They don't know who this guy is or where he's from."

"But we do, don't we?"

"Why would Xueping want me dead? He must assume I reported being kidnapped and mentioned the rumor about a plan to attack America. It doesn't make sense for him to come after me now."

"But you didn't mention the rumor to the Aussies or the Kiwis, did you? Maybe Xueping has sources in both governments and knows you didn't say anything."

"If he's that well connected, he's more dangerous than I thought."

"All the more reason for Carol and her team. They'll guard you tonight. We'll find a place for you tomorrow that Xueping won't know about."

Drake stared straight ahead, thinking. "I'm not hiding out somewhere, Mike. If Xueping wants a shot at me, let him take it in Mexico. That's where I need to be."

"Where you need to be tonight is home with Liz," Casey said. "Carol, tell him what you've set up."

"With the townhouse having three floors, I put Leeland on the roof with a M110A1 sniper rifle. I put Ken and Tommy outside with Sig P320s and MPX Copperheads. I'll be inside with the new Smith and Wesson M&P 12, the new bullpup duel-tube 12-gauge shotgun. No one is getting close to you, Mr. Drake. You have my word," Sanchez said.

Drake knew her word was good. She was an undercover cop in Denver, Colorado, when her cover was blown, and she'd applied for a job with PSS. He'd put her undercover again in Portland, Oregon, when they were protecting the Catholic Diocese from a terrorist threat. She'd been captured and tortured by female terrorists and then instrumental in taking down the group's leader. She was now one of the best operators in his Special Projects Division.

"That's a lot of firepower," Drake said. "Hope you don't have to use any of it in a firefight I'm responsible for."

Casey turned up the street to Liz's townhouse and passed the yellow tape still stretched around the crime scene and the black Impala.

The townhouse Liz bought when she moved to Seattle sat atop a crest with a view of Lake Washington to the west. The end-unit came with an underground two-car garage, a guest bedroom and office on the first floor, main living and chef's kitchen on the second floor, and the master suite on the third floor. A large private rooftop deck provided a panoramic view of the surrounding area and a perfect nest for a sniper.

Drake's gunmetal gray Cayman GTS was next to Liz's Cadillac CTS-V in the garage when Carol Sanchez opened the garage-door with the key fob Liz gave her.

"Park in our guest parking spot numbered 1, Mike," Drake said as he and Sanchez got out of the Range Rover. "We'll hold the elevator for you."

He followed Sanchez down the ramp to the garage and saw Liz standing in the elevator door, waiting for him.

"Welcome home, soldier," she said. "Would you like something to eat?"

"I think I'll have a drink first."

"Hell yes," Casey laughed behind him before belting the words to a Toby Keith song, "We'll raise our glasses against evil forces, singing whiskey for my men, beer for my horses."

Liz put her arm around Drake and pulled him into the elevator. "Did Kirkland's finest give you a bad time?"

"Let's just say they're very curious and want to know why a Chinese triad tried to gun me down this afternoon."

"What did you tell them?"

Drake shrugged. "Not much I could tell them. They'll be back when they find the Brisbane police report about me being kidnapped. They knew we just returned from our honeymoon in Australia. I let them think Brisbane was just a run-of-the-mill kidnap and ransom attempt by the Chinese triads that I was lucky to escape from. They weren't convinced and gave me the 'don't leave town' warning."

The elevator stopped at the second floor and Drake saw the kitchen island was covered with takeout food.

Casey saw Drake looking at him and said, "What? The troops have to eat."

"Mike, that's enough food to last a month."

"Plan for the worst, hope for the best. We haven't figured out what Xueping is up to. You may have to hunker down here until we do."

"That's not going to happen," Drake said. "Xueping took his shot and missed. He won't try again."

Chapter Twenty-Four

AFTER DRINKING the glass of Maker's Mark, Casey poured him and eating a brisket taco, Drake took the stairs to the townhouse's private rooftop deck. If they were going after Xueping in Mexico, he wanted to know he had the president's blessing.

President Ballard had said he wanted to use Sound Security Information Solutions for what he called his 'special projects'. If there was a Chinese plot Drake stumbled onto, using SSIS to track it down made sense.

If the president didn't see it that way, it wouldn't matter. He was going to Mexico, anyway. Having the government pay the bill for the venture would just be frosting on the cake.

He tapped in the number for the president from memory and…

"Drake," Casey yelled from the top of the stairs, "Get in here! Trouble outside!"

Drake ran across the deck and started down the stairs after Casey. "What's going on?"

"A plumbing company's van parked down the street at the curb, with its lights off and the engine running," Casey shouted over his shoulder. "Sanchez called the company. They didn't dispatch anyone to this part of town."

Sanchez stood at the window, watching the van with binoculars raised to her eyes. "Ken is approaching down the sidewalk to get a closer look," she reported. "Tommy is staying out front."

Drake crossed the kitchen area and stood at her side. Casey moved to the other end of the picture window where Liz was standing.

"Ken's almost there," she said.

Drake saw the dark-colored van pull away from the curb and start up the street with its lights turned off.

"Hand me your Sig," he said softly to Sanchez.

"They won't get in here, sir," she said. "We have this."

"I don't doubt it," but he kept his hand out for her pistol.

The van continued slowly up the street, a lion stalking its prey.

"Wait for them to show us why they're here," Drake said. "It's got to be obvious we're defending ourselves."

Sanchez lowered her binoculars and pushed the PTT button on her Motorola APX NEXT radio. "Leeland, what do you see?"

She listened and said, "Four men in the van. He can't see what weapons they have."

When the passenger door opened and the van's side door slid back, they all could see. The first man held an AK-47, and the second man jumping out from the cargo area held something even deadlier.

"Take the second man out," Drake said. "That's a pump action grenade launcher."

"Leeland, drop the guy with the grenade launcher," Sanchez ordered.

The man's head snapped back, and he fell against the side of the van.

The man beside him lifted his AK-47 and fired wildly up at the rooftop deck.

A second shot from the M110A1 sniper rifle dropped the shooter next to his compatriot.

"Are the other two still in the van?" Casey asked.

"Ken says they're huddled on the other side of the van, talking," Sanchez reported. "He's asking if we want him to engage?"

"Let's try to take one or both of them alive," Drake said, and moved away from the window. "We need answers. Tell Ken to move in behind them. I'm going out front with Tommy. If they see they're surrounded, they might choose to live to fight another day."

"If these guys are triad, that won't happen," Casey said. "I'll take the elevator and circle around behind them."

Liz caught up with Drake and grabbed his arm. "The police will be here soon. Let them take care of this."

"We have a better chance of ending this with fewer casualties. The police will trigger a response we might prevent. Tell Sanchez to have Leeland fire a warning shot if they move from behind the van before I get outside."

Drake ran down the stairs. The townhouse had two concrete raised flower beds on each side of a walkway leading to the street ten yards away. The flower beds were five or six feet away from the front of the townhouse and tall enough to provide cover from a shooter on the street.

Tommy was behind the flower bed on the right when he opened the door a few inches.

"They're still behind the van," Tommy said. "Come out whenever you want, sir."

Drake stepped out and knelt behind the flower bed on the left. "What's the plan, sir?"

"If they won't surrender before the police get here, we defend ourselves. Let's see how they want this to end," Drake said, and stood up.

"Xueping made a mistake sending you," he shouted. "You're surrounded. Put your weapons down. Come around the van where I can see you."

Police sirens racing toward them broke the silence of the night.

"Ken says get ready," Tommy said. "They've moved to the corners of the van. They haven't put their weapons down."

"Tommy, I'll take shooter left, you take shooter right," Drake said, and got behind the flower bed. "Let them fire first. Relay that to Sanchez."

"Roger that."

Drake steadied his pistol in a two-handed grip, resting his left hand on the top of the flower bed, and waited for a target to engage.

His man walked out from behind the van with his AK-47 held at his waist, firing from right to left, shattering the windows behind Drake. When he crossed the sidewalk and took one step onto the lawn in front of the townhouse, Drake fired two rounds into the man's forehead.

Tommy made sure the other shooter met the same fate, with a double tap to the man's head when he ran forward, spraying bullets wildly.

"We're coming forward," Casey shouted from the other side of the van.

Drake came out from behind the cement flower bed and made sure the two shooters on his side of the van were dead before walking out to meet Casey.

"Let me handle this with the police," Casey said.

"It's okay, Mike. They'll want to talk with all of us. I'd like to get to bed before the sun comes up."

Chapter Twenty-Five

IT WAS NOON the next day before Drake returned to the townhouse. The Kirkland Police Department detectives questioned him, Casey and the PSS protection detail through the night and the next morning before releasing them. The detectives' parting shot was telling them the FBI had been called in to investigate the triad's involvement, and not to leave Seattle before the FBI was finished with them.

He was not about to let the FBI keep him in Seattle when he needed to be in Mexico. Xueping and his friends were involved in something big enough that they'd tried to kill him twice. It was time to find out why.

But first, he had to get the FBI off his back and there was only one way he could think of to accomplish that.

"Mr. President, do you have time to talk?" Drake asked.

"Give me ten minutes and I'll call you back," President Ballard said.

Drake refilled his coffee cup and sat down at the small table in the breakfast nook across from Liz.

"Do you think he'll do it?" she asked.

"It might depend on how much I tell him. I'd like to know we have his support if there's trouble in Mexico. I don't plan on telling him everything over the phone. He might think he has a secure line when we talk, but I don't trust the NSA or the FBI when they tell him he does. I want him to hear it all in person from someone we both know and trust."

"That won't make the Seattle FBI office happy when the home office flies in and takes over," Liz said.

"She can handle it. She has before."

The opening notes from Credence Clearwater Revival's *Up Around the Bend* rang out on Drake's phone.

"Good afternoon, Adam," the president said. "Back from your honeymoon?"

"We are, Mr. President. Sooner than we planned."

"Is that what you want to talk about? Are you and Liz okay?"

"Is it all right if I put you on speakerphone? Liz is here and wants to say hello."

"Go right ahead."

"Hello Mr. President. We had a wonderful vacation and we're fine, although I'm in better shape than he is."

"Do I want to know why that is?" the president asked.

"That's why I called," Drake said. "I think we stumbled onto something that you need to hear about, but I'd like you to hear about it in person."

"This is a secure line, Adam."

"I'm sure it is, but there's another reason I'm asking you to trust me and send the Deputy Director of the FBI to Seattle so I can brief her on the matter personally. I'd like to keep the FBI here in Seattle on the sideline for the time being. That won't be possible unless Kate Perkins takes charge of the investigation."

"What investigation?"

"My abduction in Australia and two attempts yesterday by Chinese triad members trying to kill me. It's possible there's a plot to attack America that's behind this."

"What are you're asking me to do, Adam?"

"Get Kate Perkins involved on behalf of the FBI and allow me to develop intelligence about this plot."

"Do we know who's behind this rumored plot?" the president asked.

"From all indications, it's Chinese triads and possibly China itself."

"The possibility that China's involved is not something I wanted to hear," President Ballard said. "Find out about the plot, if there is one, and keep me informed. I'll have Kate Perkins jump on a plane and meet with you."

"Thank you, Mr. President."

Drake got up and walked to the end of the kitchen and back. "I should have asked for Kate to meet me today. Now I'm stuck here until she can "arrange" to come. That could be next week!"

"What's the rush? Mexico will be there next week."

"Xueping might not be. I need to get to the office."

"And I need you to see your doctor."

"I will, after I meet with Mike. I'm going to take a shower. You're welcome to join me."

"Maybe later, after you see your doctor and I know you're up to it."

Drake laughed, seeing the cheesy grin on her face, and headed upstairs to shower.

While he was gone, Liz called Mike Casey. "Adam's coming in to see you. Will you make sure he sees his doctor? He's trying to hide it, but his grimacing says he's hurting."

"I'll try. Will you be in today?"

"I'm coming with him."

"Good," Casey said. "We need to work out a few kinks in the New Zealand Defense Force agreement, and the Australian CDPP contacted us about their investigator, Lucas Barrett. They want to know why he paid for your stay at the casino."

"If they don't know, they don't know about what his informant told him," Liz said. "We might be the only ones he told."

"If we are and there is a plot, they won't want anyone hearing about it. That has to be why they came after you and Adam."

"They can't be stupid enough to try again, can they?" Liz asked.

"They might," Casey said. "Let's keep a close protection team assigned to you a little longer."

"He wants to go to Mexico. Send the team with him."

"He won't need it. Morales and Norris will be with him."

"You're assuming I'm not going with him, aren't you?" she asked.

"I need you here, Liz. We'll reach out to our contacts from here while he's turning over rocks in Mexico. The sooner we sort this out, the sooner we'll all be safe."

Chapter Twenty-Six

MIKE CASEY MET Drake and Liz in the conference room at PSS headquarters when they arrived.

"How are you feeling?" he asked Drake.

"Angry as hell."

"I mean your ribs."

"I'm fine, Mike. What have Morales and Norris found out?"

Casey saw Liz tilt her head and raise her eyebrows.

"I asked your doctor to stop by on his way home to check you out," Casey said and smiled. "We'll talk about it later."

"You know it won't make a difference," Drake said. "We've both been on missions in worse shape than this."

"We were younger."

"Is Xueping still in La Paz?"

"Before we get into that, did you call the president, like you said you were going to?"

"I did. He wants us to find out if there is a plot. I didn't tell him everything. I asked him to have Kate Perkins get involved on behalf of the FBI. We'll have a better chance of getting answers on our own without the locals handcuffing us."

"So, we have his backing, if we need it?"

"Yes."

"All right, here's what we know," Casey began. "Xueping and his friends are in Mexico. Xueping is on one of his super yachts in La Paz. Morales and Norris followed one of his friends, Ramon Ying, from the yacht to a UniMex warehouse close to La Paz. Ying is the CEO of UniMex. Some Mexican general flew in on a helicopter and was driven back to a casino in La Paz. Morales and Norris want to know if they should find out what's in the warehouse."

"What do we know about Ying?" Liz asked.

"Kevin says he's rumored to be connected to a Chinese cartel in Mexico," Casey said. "He lives in Mexico City and has a villa in La Paz."

"What about the third guy we saw on Xueping's yacht on Hamilton Island?" Drake asked.

"We haven't identified him," Casey said.

"How does a Chinese cartel operate in Mexico?" Liz asked. "The Mexican cartels can't be happy with that."

"If the Chinese cartel is a supplier of fentanyl precursors from China, they might not care as long as they get what they need for their own operations," Drake said.

"We know China hasn't done much to shut off the flow of fentanyl precursors to Mexico," Casey pointed out. "What does that have to do with some plot to cripple America?"

"Unless that is the plot," Liz said.

"There has to be more to it than that, Liz. The Chinese triad guys wouldn't have a reason to abduct me in Australia or come after me here in Seattle, if that's all this is about."

"But what if that is all that it is? Why shouldn't we let the DEA or the FBI deal with this, as just another drug trafficking case?" Liz asked.

Drake looked away and didn't answer her.

Casey gave him a chance to explain before doing it for him. "They made it personal, Liz. They brought a grenade launcher armed with a thermobaric grenade to bring down your townhouse. That's something you don't walk away from."

"I didn't know it was a thermobaric grenade," she said.

"I recognized the LPO-97 pump action launcher before I ran downstairs," Drake said quietly. "The Russians developed it to bring down buildings in urban street fighting. They didn't want to kill just me. They wanted to kill you and everyone in the townhouse. You don't go after a man's wife."

"The men who tried to kill you are dead, Adam. Isn't that enough?"

"Someone gave the order, Liz. When we know who that was and they're dealt with, then it's enough."

"What do you want to do, Adam?" Casey asked.

"I need to meet with Kate Perkins and get the FBI off our backs. When I do, I'll ask her for everything she has on Xueping, Ramon Ying and the third man. Then I want to go to Mexico and find out if Lucas Barrett's informant gave him credible intel that we need to take seriously."

"Do we do this as a Sound Security Information Solutions matter, or is this off the books?" Casey asked.

"The president asked us to look into it," Drake said. "It's SSIS all the way."

"Who do you want to take with you?"

"Morales and Norris are already there. That should be all the help I need."

"I'll let Morales and Norris know you're coming and ask them what they need," Casey said. "They flew commercial and didn't try to get something past security."

"Is there anything else we need to go over?" Casey asked.

Liz cleared her throat. "It's four o'clock. Did his doctor say when he might get here?"

"I won't leave until he gets here," Drake promised.

Casey pushed back his chair and started to get up when his assistant knocked and opened the conference room door.

"Mike, Kate Perkins from the FBI just landed at SeaTac and wanted to know if she can meet with Adam here, before he takes her to dinner," Rollie Edwards said.

Major Rollie Edwards was a disabled former Army Ranger

who served as Casey's personal assistant and PSS office administrator.

"I guess when the president says jump on a plane, you jump on a plane," Drake said.

"That may not be the only reason she got here so fast," Liz said. "She's going to be disappointed when she finds out Dan Norris isn't here. They've been talking about going somewhere to give their relationship another chance."

"Rollie, tell Kate Adam will meet with her here and he'll be happy to take her to dinner."

"Let's hope dinner is the only place she wants to go, when she finds out Dan's in Mexico," Liz said.

Chapter Twenty-Seven

FBI DEPUTY DIRECTOR Kate Perkins came down the hall to Drake's office looking very stylish, wearing a black leather blazer over a white high-collar blouse, black jeans and black ankle boots. Her all-business, 'this-better-be-worth-it' look softened when she saw Liz sitting in one chair in front of Drake's desk.

Drake stood and came around with his hand held out. "Hello, Kate. Thank you for coming."

Perkins nodded and sat down beside Liz. "Congratulations, Liz. I'm told you just returned from an interesting honeymoon."

"We did. Unfortunately, it ended sooner than we'd planned. How are you getting along with the boys at 935 Pennsylvania Avenue?"

"They're coming around," Perkins said. "It's still a 'good-old-boys-club' at headquarters, but they respect results. I've been fortunate to provide them with some, thanks to you two."

"Kate, can I get you coffee or anything?" Drake asked.

"You can tell me why the president called me and told me to catch the next flight to Seattle. That will do for starters."

Drake thought for a moment about where to begin. "Let me explain by telling you that yesterday, Chinese triad soldiers tried to kill me twice. I don't know why, but it's possible it has something to do with a rumored plot to cripple America we heard about in Australia."

"The president mentioned that, but I've seen nothing about triad activity here in Seattle."

"Your Seattle Field Office has been called in to assist the Kirkland Police Department, but they haven't talked with me yet. They just told me to not leave Seattle. That's what I'm hoping you can help me with. I need to be in Mexico as soon as possible."

Perkins held up her hand. "Whoa, you want me to fly in from headquarters and take over an investigation? I can't do that."

"Wait until you hear the whole story," Liz suggested.

"Alright, tell me everything," Perkins said.

For the next hour, Drake recounted events from the time he and Liz met with Lucas Barrett of the CDPP on Hamilton Island, to his abduction and rescue in Brisbane, and the two attempts on his life the day before.

"Why do you need to be in Mexico?" Perkins asked. "You didn't explain that."

"Xueping is in La Paz, Mexico," Drake said. "Marco Morales and Dan Norris are there watching him, and the two men we saw on his super yacht. One of his friends is Ramon Ying, the CEO of UniMex, a big pharma company. We haven't identified the third man. I believe Xueping is responsible for Lucas Barrett disappearing, my abduction and the triads trying to kill me. If there is a plot to harm America, I believe Xueping's involved in it."

"I know about Ramon Ying," Perkins said. "We believe he's connected to the Los Zheng Chinese cartel and fentanyl trafficking to the U.S. from Mexico. Do you have photos of the third man? I might be able to identify him."

"I'll ask Morales if he has a photo of him," Drake said.

"Also ask Marco if he has anything on the Mexican general who landed at the UniMex warehouse," Liz added. "If you're going down there, we need to know how well protected Xueping and Ying are."

Perkins was quiet, looking out the window of Drake's corner office.

"What exactly are you planning to do in Mexico?" she asked Drake.

"I want to know what's in the UniMex warehouse. Morales can use a Black Hornet nano drone to get inside. If we can find a way to hear what Xueping and his friends are talking about on his yacht, or at Ying's villa in La Paz, we might learn what they're planning."

"Are you equipped to do that?" Perkins asked.

"The president asked us to branch out and become a private intelligence contractor," Drake said. "We've done some work for Homeland Security and we're adding staff with security clearances. We were already strong on the technical side. Are there FBI or DEA assets in Mexico who might know about Ying and UniMex?"

"You mean U.S. foreign agents?" she asked. "You're aware that Mexico has a law that allows it to treat foreign agents as spies. So, no is the official answer. We might, however, have resources who know about Ying and UniMex. I'll ask around."

"Kate, does Mexico regard private intelligence contractors as spies?" Liz asked.

"I haven't heard that," she said. "That doesn't mean they won't, I suppose."

"I don't like the thought of you being arrested as a spy, Adam," Liz said. "You need a way to explain why you're in La Paz."

"I'll come up with something."

"How soon are you leaving for Mexico?" Perkins asked.

"As soon as his doctor says it's okay," Liz said, staring at her husband.

"As soon as you say the FBI won't arrest me at the airport," Drake said with a wink at his wife.

"Kate, let's go have a glass of wine at home before dinner. He'll make dinner reservations for us while he waits to see his doctor."

"I'd like that, Liz."

Both women got up and waved goodbye to Drake, who folded his arms and tipped his head to the sisterhood, walking out of his office.

Chapter Twenty-Eight

AFTER HIS DOCTOR reassured Liz that flying to Mexico would not impede the healing of his cracked ribs, and Kate Perkins called to say the FBI wouldn't arrest him at the airport, Drake was in his office Friday morning organizing his trip to Mexico.

First item on his list was thinking of a way to get close to Xueping in La Paz, without being recognized.

Flying to Baja California in the PSS Gulfstream would allow him to avoid being spotted at the airport, but he'd still have to pass through security and immigration at the FBO terminal. Xueping might be paranoid enough to have spotters looking for him to arrive at the La Paz airport on a private jet, but it was a risk he'd have to take. Unless he flew to another airport close to La Paz, like the airport at Cabo San Lucas.

He checked the distance from Cabo to La Paz and saw that it was one hundred miles, a two-hour drive. If he flew to Cabo later this afternoon, he wouldn't get there until eight or nine tonight. He could rent a car and get to La Paz before midnight or stay overnight in Cabo and drive the hundred miles the next morning. He needed to get there sooner.

Staring at a map of Cabo San Lucas and the area north to La

Paz on his laptop, something was trying to get his attention in the back of his mind. He'd never been to Cabo San Lucas, but he'd always wanted to go deep sea fishing there. Then he remembered that he'd been invited to Cabo several times by an old Delta Force buddy, Pete Ramirez, who was now a sports fishing charter boat captain in Cabo San Lucas.

Ramirez's nickname was "Rammer". He'd been a fearless breacher in Afghanistan who never let a solid steel door, reinforced gate, or solid wall keep Drake and the team from getting through it to get to a target.

Drake searched for sports fishing charters in Cabo and found *Tier One Charters* and Captain Pete Ramirez, fishing out of the Marina Del Ray in Cabo San Lucas.

Drake called the number on the Tier One Charters' website and waited for someone to answer.

"Captain Ramirez," he heard over the sound of racing diesel engines.

"Rammer, is that you?" Drake asked.

"Who is this?"

"Someone who ordered you to break down doors."

"Major?"

"Are you out fishing?"

"Just heading back in. Where are you?"

"Five or six hours up north. I want to charter your boat for the next week or so. I need to do some fishing north of you. Are you available?"

"I am now. When will you be here?"

"I'll call from the airport, say five thirty or six today."

"Call me when you land. I'll come get you."

"See you then. Thanks Rammer."

At nine o'clock, Mike Casey was at the door of his office with a cup of coffee in hand.

"Dan Norris called," Casey said. "He asked if we want them to find out what UniMex is using the warehouse for."

"Does Morales have the Black Hornet nano drone?"

"No, I checked. Both of our nano drones are here."

"If I can get organized, I can be down there by dinner tonight with a Black Hornet. Morales can use it tomorrow. Tell them to wait until then."

"How are you going to keep Xueping from putting a target on your back when you get there?" Casey asked, and sat down in front of the desk.

"I'm flying to Cabo to go deep sea fishing. Remember Rammer Ramirez? He's a charter boat captain there. I'll have him take me up the coast to La Paz and find moorage for his boat, the *Tier One*, in the marina where Xueping has his yacht."

"That should work."

"Kate Perkins cleared me to leave Seattle. But you might have the FBI show up about the other night."

"No problem."

"Thanks Mike. Wish you were going with me?"

"Wish I had time to go fishing and guard your six? Yes, but I need to stick around and work on the New Zealand Defence Force contract with Liz. You don't need me, as long as you don't let it get too personal down there."

"I'll try to keep that in mind."

"Check with Steve Carson," Casey said. "He says the Gulfstream will be ready for takeoff by noon, maybe a little earlier."

Drake called Carson and confirmed a twelve o'clock takeoff.

The Kirkland Police Department hadn't returned his Kimber from the first triad shooting and he needed to replace it. He took the stairs down to the PSS armory to ask Master Sergeant Peters for a recommendation.

"Heard you're leaving. Where are you going?" Peters asked.

"Cabo San Lucas."

'You don't want to take a gun to Mexico."

"I know, Master Sergeant. I'll leave it on the plane. But I want something until I get there."

"How did you like the Sig Sauer P320 you borrowed from Sanchez last night?"

"I haven't spent much range time with the Sig, but it shoots okay."

Master Sergeant Peters left Drake at the supply room counter and returned with a pistol in a leather Falco OWB holster.

"This is the Sig P320 RXP XCOMPACT," the armorer said. "Fifteen rounds, two steel magazines, great trigger and red dot sights. It's as good a CCW weapon as there is, sir. Is there anything else you need?"

"A pair of the special Ray-Ban sunglasses we're trying out, a sat phone, and I'm good to go."

Master Sergeant Peters left again and came back, putting the sunglasses and an Iridium 9575 sat phone on the counter. He also handed Drake a new Benchmade Vector knife in a box. "They can arrest you in Mexico for carrying this, but I thought you might want one anyway."

"Thank you, Master Sergeant. Appreciate your help."

Drake left the supply room with his new weapons and continued down to the parking garage to his Porsche Cayman GTS. He had two hours to get home, pack, say goodbye to Liz and Lancer, and get to Boeing Field International Airport by noon.

Lancer greeted Drake when he walked up the stairs from the townhouse's garage and sniffed at the holstered pistol in his hand. "It's not what you're used to, is it, buddy?"

He petted Lancer's shoulders and looked around the second floor for Liz.

"Up here," Liz called out from the master bedroom on the third floor.

Drake took the stairs two at a time and saw Liz packing his rolling hardside luggage laying on the bed.

"How soon are you leaving?" she asked.

He crossed the room and wrapped his arms around her. "Wheels up at noon."

She looked up, and he saw the worry in her eyes.

"I'll be fine, Liz. Morales and Norris are there. I'm flying to Cabo San Lucas and meeting an old army buddy from Delta Force. He has a sports fishing charter boat and he'll take me to La

Paz. I'll stay on his boat to stay out of sight and be back before you know it. I'll be fine."

She wrapped her arms around his chest and squeezed. "You're not fine right now," she said when he winced. "That's why I'm worried, even if you have an entire company of younger guys around to protect you."

"Ouch, that hurts me more than my sore ribs."

"You know what I mean. You're going down there to find out what Xueping's up to, nothing more. We'll let Kate and the FBI take care of him, if this plot is real. You'll wind up in a Mexican jail if you start a fight with Xueping, his triad and this Chinese cartel."

"I won't start a fight, but I won't run from one, either."

Liz squeezed his chest harder.

"Okay, okay, I promise I'll try not to get in a fight in Mexico."

She shook her head and pressed her cheek against his chest. "Be safe and hurry back to me."

He lifted her chin and kissed her. "Yes, ma'am, I will."

She squeezed him harder. "And…?"

"Did I forget to say that I love you?"

"That's better. Don't forget to take your passport. It's in the safe."

Chapter Twenty-Nine

THE PSS GULFSTREAM G-650 landed at Cabo San Lucas International Airport (CSL), the smaller privately owned airport, at six o'clock Friday evening.

Drake called Pete Ramirez while they taxied to the Universal Aviation FBO terminal. When he cleared customs, his brother-in-arms was in the passenger lounge waiting for him.

"Rammer, it's been a while," Drake said as they shook hands and hugged, slapping each other on the back.

Ramirez was shorter, broader through the shoulders, and still felt as solid as Drake remembered him being.

"Too long," Ramirez said. "I thought you were going to come down and go fishing with me."

"I always wanted to, just never got around to it."

Steve Carson joined them, and Drake introduced him. "Pete, this is Steve Carson, our pilot. Steve, meet Peter Ramirez, the "Rammer". He was the best breacher I served with in Delta Force."

"Nice meeting you, Pete," Carson said.

"Same here, amigo. Are you fishing with us?"

"No, staying tonight and flying back tomorrow."

"Where are you staying?" Ramirez asked.

"Royal Solaris Los Cabos."

"Nice place. I'll drop you off there after we get something to eat. I made a dinner reservation for us at La Pampa. It's a steakhouse near the marina where I have my boat. I don't eat steak often, but Drake has me booked for a week and we're celebrating."

"Lead the way, Rammer," Drake said. "I'd like to get an early start tomorrow."

Ramirez's white Toyota FJ Cruiser was parked in front of the terminal, with a young boy leaning against the right front fender. Rammer handed him a ten-dollar bill and opened the rear door to load their luggage.

"Is this new?" Drake asked.

"2022 Toyota FJ Cruiser, five seats and all-wheel-drive," Ramirez said proudly. "I won two tournaments this year and my clients deserve a pleasant ride. That, plus I always wanted one of these. When Toyota started making them again, I had to have one."

La Pampa was an Argentina Steak House on Marina Boulevard offering grilled meat, Argentina wines and live music. When they entered, a young man was sitting on a stool by the window, playing a guitar and singing *The Girl from Ipanema*.

They allowed Ramirez to order sausage and cheese empanada appetizers, caprese salad, rib eye steaks for each of them, a bottle of Pantagonia pinot noir, and sat back to enjoy the music and the lively atmosphere.

After the server had taken their order and left, Ramirez leaned forward on his elbows across the table from Drake and asked, "If we're going to get an early start tomorrow, why don't you tell me what kind of fishing you're planning on doing in La Paz?"

Drake looked around the room and said, "I'll explain when we're on your boat?"

"I have a crew of two men I usually take with me," Ramirez said. "Do you want me to bring them with us?"

"Tell me about them."

"Like me, they became naturalized U.S. citizens after serving in the army. They've seen combat in Iraq and Afghanistan. I've known them all my life. I'm guessing that's what you wanted to know."

Drake smiled and nodded. "In case it's needed, what kind of equipment do you have on your boat?"

"For fishing?" Ramirez asked, and smiled.

"Of course," Drake said, "For fishing."

"The usual, rod and reels, some spear guns for clients who snorkel and fish that way. I'm also allowed to have guns on my boat because I live on board. As a citizen, I can have one handgun and nine rifles for self-protection and hunting, which I do."

"If we need to spend a night or two in La Paz, say moored at the Marina Palmira, could you arrange that?"

"If there's a slip available, I think so. I've used the marina for tournaments near there. There are no tournaments for the next couple of weeks."

"Then I think we're set. I don't think we need your crew for this one. I'll explain later," Drake said.

Ramirez sat with his fingers steepled in front of his face, looking at Drake. "I've always trusted you, Major. I'm willing to again, although I have a feeling that we're going to La Paz for more than just fishing. Is this something I need to discuss with my crew before I take you to La Paz?"

"Pete, all I'm asking you to do is take me from Cabo to La Paz and then let me stay on your boat in the marina for a couple of days. I have two men already there. Anything I do onshore, I'll do with them. I only ask about the things you have on the boat in case I screw up and you need to protect yourself."

"From a cartel?" Ramirez asked.

"Couple of Chinese guys who might be triad."

Ramirez got a wide grin on his face. "Hell yes! Now you're talking, sir. We have enough trouble with Mexican cartels, without the Chinese moving in. I have friends who will help us in La Paz if we need them. There aren't a lot of us, but we've pledged to do whatever we can to take our country back from the cartels."

"That's music to my ears, Rammer," Drake said. "I knew I could count on you."

Steve Carson had been quiet, listening to Drake and Ramirez. He took a business card out of his wallet and handed it across the table to Ramirez. "If you ever need a pilot and I can help, call me."

"I will, amigo. Thanks. Now get ready to enjoy the best Argentina food you'll ever eat," Ramirez said, nodding toward the server` walking to their table with a plate of empanadas and a bottle of wine.

Chapter Thirty

DRAKE WOKE up Saturday morning before sunrise. When he said goodbye to Steve Carson the night before, he'd been a little jealous. Carson was spending the night at a nice resort and he was leaving for a night on a boat.

He looked around the mahogany-paneled bow stateroom and grinned. Pete Ramirez was living on a Hatteras GT59 sports fishing yacht as luxurious as any hotel or resort in Cabo San Lucas.

The faint smell of frying bacon on the other end of the yacht got him out of bed and into a pair of cargo shorts and a white T-shirt. Drake walked barefooted down the hallway and up the stairs to the main salon.

Ramirez was busy cooking breakfast. "Good morning Major. Sleep well?"

"Like a baby, Rammer."

"Help yourself to some Mexican Chiapas coffee and juevos rancheros. The tortillas will be ready in a minute."

Drake poured a cup of coffee and looked out the side window at a larger yacht moored next to them. "Any of your neighbors live on their yachts?"

"That beauty next to us gets used once a month, if that. The owner lives in Dallas, Texas, and doesn't sleep on it even when he's here. The yacht on the side it goes out fishing on weekends, but no one lives on it."

"How often are you out fishing?"

"I'm booked for all the major marlin tournaments this year, but I don't take people out fishing as much as I used to. Tournaments are intense and held June through November. There's big prize money involved and you need to prepare for them."

"So, you work five or six months out of twelve? Not bad, Rammer."

"Oh, there are other things I do to keep busy."

"The friends you mentioned last night?"

"Si," Ramirez said and passed Drake a plate. "Enjoy."

The spicy salsa and fried eggs on top of refried beans with slices of avocado for breakfast, complimented the rich Chiapas coffee perfectly.

"How long will it take to get to La Paz?" Drake asked.

"How fast to do you want to go?"

"How fast can we go?"

"The GT59 is a tournament fishing yacht built for speed. It'll do forty knots, or forty-six miles per hour. La Paz is a hundred sixty kilometers away. We could be there in two hours, give or take a few minutes. The ride wouldn't be the smoothest."

"Do we have a slip at the Marina Palmira?" Drake asked.

"Si, I called before you got up."

"Then the sooner we can get there, the better. When we leave, I'll call my friends and let them know we're on our way."

Ramirez piloted his yacht out of Marina del Ray at eight o'clock and had the twin diesel CAT engines singing at two thousand RPMs as soon as they were clear of land and flying over the water of the Sea of Cortez.

Drake sat next to Ramirez on the open convertible bridge and marveled at the speed of the yacht and the beauty of the blue waters of the Sea of Cortez.

"It's beautiful, Rammer. How long have you lived here?" Drake asked over the roar of diesel engines.

"I was born in Cabo. My dad used to fish for tuna here. Mom and Dad moved to California when I was three and I moved back here when I left the army."

"What did you mean when you said you and a few friends were trying to take Mexico back from the cartels?"

Ramirez stood up and said, "Take the helm, I'll be right back."

Drake moved onto the pilot's seat and resisted the temptation to pull back on the throttle to slow the yacht down a little. Instead, he gripped the steering wheel firmly with both hands and powered on.

Ramirez returned to the open convertible bridge with a custom-built AR 15 CQBB rifle and a pair of Nikon 7x50 Ocean Pro binoculars. He handed them to Drake and took the helm back. "We keep an eye on the bad guys," he said. "You can't trust the police or the army to keep you and your family safe. When someone needs help, we take care of it ourselves."

"Are all your guys equipped like this?"

"We all do our own thing, but pretty much. After they let you buy an AR-15, they don't pay much attention to how you customize it. Not everyone has night vision goggles like these that I keep on the boat, but a few do who still have friends in the army."

"Are all of your rifles like this one?"

"Five of the nine are. I have a Remington 870 shotgun, two over and under shotguns, 12 and 20 gauge, a Benelli tactical pump-action for protection, and a Taurus Raging Hunter 44 mag on the yacht."

"That's quite an armory!"

"It's a violent place, gringo."

Two hours later, Ramirez slowed the Hatteras down when they were a quarter mile offshore from the Marina Palmira and let it settle in the water.

"I'll go to the marina office and check in," Ramirez said. "Where's the Chinese yacht moored?"

"There," Drake pointed at the largest yacht in the marina.

They watched the Benetti Oasis 40m superyacht draw closer as they motored slowly toward the entrance to the marina.

"Two crewmen are watching us with binoculars," Ramirez said.

"I see them."

"Do they know what you look like?"

"I suppose so. The ones who got a good look, up close and personal, are dead. But they tried to kill me twice and knew who they were hunting for. I'll stay out of sight as much as possible."

"Stay below when we get in the marina," Ramirez said. "They might not have been able to see there were two of us on this convertible bridge."

"That's wishful thinking. Loan me one of your weapons while you check in."

Chapter Thirty-One

DRAKE WATCHED Ramirez through a tinted galley window, walking toward the marina office. The Hatteras was in a slip on the far side of the marina, seventy-five yards and three docks away from the Xueping's superyacht.

He focused Ramirez's binoculars on Xueping's crewmen standing at the railing on the upper sundeck. At the moment, they were watching three nearly naked women with binoculars, who were sunbathing on the forward deck of the yacht next to them.

From their position on the top deck of the superyacht, they had a view of the whole marina, including the Hatteras he was on. Leaving the boat without being seen was going to be a problem.

It was time to contact Morales and Norris and put together a plan to find out what Xueping was doing in La Paz.

Drake used the sat phone he brought with him and called Morales.

"I'm at the marina, Marco," Drake said.

"I know. I watched Ramirez go to the marina office."

"Where are you?"

"Watching you from the balcony of our hotel room."

"Is Dan with you?"

"He's playing blackjack in the casino. Xueping and two of his friends are at the private gaming tables upstairs."

"We need to meet and plan our visit to that warehouse you found. Let's meet on Rammer's boat."

"Did you bring my toy?" Morales asked.

"It's in my duffel bag. When you and Dan get here, make it sound like you're talking about finding a charter boat to go fishing. No one will pay attention to two high rollers who want to go Marlin fishing with a tournament-winning skipper."

"When do you want us to come?"

"As soon as you can."

"Roger that," Morales said.

Drake used the time until Ramirez returned, studying the layout of the marina and the adjacent waterfront. He had a clear view of the hotel where he thought Morales was staying, the casino across the street from the marina, and the hills surrounding the town. He didn't see anyone who was looking back at him.

When Ramirez left the marina office and walked onto the dock, he swung his binoculars back to Xueping's superyacht and saw the men on the sundeck had their binoculars trained on Ramirez.

Ramirez came on board and joined Drake. "The marina manager says the big Benetti yacht is leaving Monday. He thinks it's heading north up the west coast."

"Then we'd better get busy. Marco Morales and Dan Norris are coming here to meet us," Drake said.

"I know Morales," Ramirez said. "I don't remember meeting Norris."

"You probably didn't. He was a commander of a Hostage Rescue Team at Quantico for the FBI."

"I noticed the guys on Xueping's yacht watching me."

"You should feel flattered. They were watching women sunbathing on the yacht next to them when you started back."

"Maybe they're expecting trouble. Any way they would think you were coming?"

"They came after me in Seattle. When they failed, I guess they could know I'd come after them."

Ramirez sat down on the surround leather sofa at the back of the salon and looked at Drake. "Is that why you're here, to kill these guys?"

Drake smiled and shook his head. "I'm here to find out if there really is a plot to hit America. If there is, I'll do what I can to stop him. That's all the payback I'm after."

He looked out the galley window and saw Morales and Norris walking down the dock toward them. "I told them to act like they're looking for a charter to take them fishing. Talk with them outside, then invite them in here so we can talk."

"Got it," Ramirez said and walked out to the stern cockpit.

Drake stood just inside the salon door and listened to Morales introduce Norris to Ramirez, asking how soon they could go fishing for blue marlins. and heard Ramirez inviting them inside to have a beer.

Morales and Norris had perfected the look of two rich guys in Mexico enjoying themselves. Morales was wearing shorts, a psychedelic-looking red, yellow, orange, and blue silk guayabera shirt, and sandals. Norris was more subdued, wearing a Panama hat, cream-colored linen pants, a lime green guayabera, and brandy-colored huarache loafers.

Morales pirouetted in front of Drake and said, "What do you think?"

"That shirt makes me dizzy."

"That's the point. People can't take their eyes off my shirt to look at my face. I have two more shirts like this at the hotel," Morales said.

Ramirez took four bottles of Modelo Negra beer out of the galley refrigerator and passed them around. "Happy hunting."

"Xueping was leaving the casino with his friends when I came here," Norris said. "They left in a black Mercedes and headed north. Ying's villa is on a hillside north of town. They could be going to his place."

"The marina manager says Xueping's yacht is leaving the

marina day after tomorrow," Drake said. "How soon can we have a look inside that warehouse?"

"The warehouse is north of here in Pichilingue. Our best chance will be at night to make use of the Black Hornet's thermal imaging capabilities," Morales said.

"Okay," Drake said. "What can we do before dark that will be productive?"

"We could go to Ying's villa and see if that's where they are," Norris said. "There's a spot on the hill behind the villa with line of sight to the parking area and the back terrace."

"Is this the Ramon Ying, the CEO of UniMex?" Ramirez asked.

"It is," Drake said.

"Mind if I tag along? We know he does business with the cartels. He's one of the men on our watch list who needs to be dealt with." Ramirez said.

"Fine," Drake said. "You can tell us what you know about the man on the way to his villa."

"I'll go get the jeep we rented," Norris said.

"How do we get Drake out of here without being spotted?" Ramirez asked. "Xueping's guys are keeping a close watch on the marina."

Drake looked at Morales and grinned. "That won't be a problem. I'll trade shirts with Marco and borrow Dan's hat. No one will look at my face, right Marco?"

Chapter Thirty-Two

WHEN DAN NORRIS called to say he was in the marina parking lot, three men left the Hatteras GT59 and walked down the dock. With his sunglasses, Norris's Panama hat, and wearing Morales's psychedelic shirt, Drake was confident his garish attire would prevent him from being recognized by Xueping's men.

Drake let Ramirez ride shotgun and sat back behind Norris under the Jeep's black sunshade as they drove north along Highway One.

"How far is the warehouse from here?" Drake asked Morales, sitting next to him.

"Forty kilometers, a fifty-minute drive. Sunset's at six thirty this evening. If they're working three shifts at the warehouse, we'll want to get there before the night shift comes on, at eleven or twelve o'clock. We should leave La Paz around eight o'clock."

"Let's accomplish as much as we can before Xueping leaves," Drake said. "Eight's fine."

"Are we also thinking about using the drone to find out what they're doing on the yacht?" Norris turned his head around and asked over his right shoulder.

"Why do you think they're doing anything on the yacht?" Drake asked.

"We've watched men coming and going from the yacht that don't look like guests or crew," Norris said. "They remind me of the guys Kevin has working for us at headquarters."

"IT guys?" Drake chuckled. "What does an IT guy look like?"

"Kind of geeky, like they never get out or exercise, pale, with glasses. You know, geeky looking," Norris shrugged and said.

"Don't let Kevin hear you describing IT guys like that," Morales warned. "He's training for a half marathon and working out with Sanchez. She's teaching him krav maga."

"How many people have you seen coming and going from the yacht?" Ramirez asked.

"Xueping and his two friends, four Chinese bodyguards and another twelve or thirteen. Four, who look like they might know how to sail a yacht. Eight or nine, who look like the geeky types Norris was talking about," Morales answered.

"That's too many for a Benetti Oasis," Ramirez said. "It's built to accommodate ten guests in five staterooms, and a crew of seven in four homes. You've counted nineteen or twenty. What about women?"

"The women don't stay overnight," Morales said. "The men go to the casino for dinner, then gamble or leave with the women somewhere, then return to the yacht after midnight."

"What could that many IT guys be doing on that yacht?" Drake asked. "Do they stay there at night?"

"The only time they leave is at noon, when they walk over to the casino and have lunch," Morales said.

"We need to know what they're doing," Drake said.

"How?" Morales asked.

"You can hack the yacht's IT network," Ramirez said. "Yachts like the Benetti Oasis will have audio-visual and satellite communication systems. A couple of those geeky guys will be ETOs, electro-technical officers, trained to make sure those IT systems work. The onboard security problem they have is that the guests and crew have devises that connect to the onboard network. Clone one of their iPhones and you have access to the yacht's IT network."

Drake leaned forward and said to Norris, "Dan, when we get back, download the BlueScanner app on your phone. When those geeky guys you love leave the yacht at noon, get close to one of them and clone his phone. Kevin will know what to do with the transferred data."

Ramirez turned around and looked back at Drake with a curious look on his face.

"IT security is our business, Rammer," Drake said. "Bluetooth hacking is one of the first things we teach employees of our clients."

Norris retraced the route he'd taken up Calle Ignacio Altamirano and turned the Jeep off Pedregal de Costes onto the dirt road that led to the hillside above Ramon Ying's villa.

Norris pointed to Ying's villa. "It looks like Xueping's there. That's the black Mercedes S-500 he left the casino in."

Drake tapped Norris on his shoulder and held his hand out for the compact binoculars on the center console. "Let me have a look."

Four men were sitting in a semi-circle under a covered veranda next to a large swimming pool. A young woman was serving them finger foods from a silver platter.

He recognized Xueping, but not the other three men. "Which one is Ying?"

Norris took back the binoculars. "He's the one on Xueping's left."

"Who is the one on his right?" Drake asked.

"We don't know his name," Norris said.

Ramirez reached over for the binoculars. "Let me look."

After a moment, he said, "I know Ying. I don't recognize the one on his right, but I know the young woman serving them. She's the sister of one of the men I told you about, Drake. Her name is Juanita Vasquez."

"Do you think she'd be willing to tell us what she hears them talking about?" Drake asked.

"I don't know her well enough to ask, but her brother could. I'll call him and find out," Ramirez said. "I also know the Mexican to the left of Ying. That's General Maxímo Martín."

"Let me have the binoculars," Morales said. "That's the guy who landed in the helicopter at the UniMex warehouse."

Chapter Thirty-Three

RAMON YING REFILLED General Martín's glass with his favorite Corazón tequila and proposed a toast. "Arriba, abajo, al centro, pá dentro General." My colleagues and I want to thank you for what you do for us. A bonus will be wired to your Cayman account this month."

"I appreciate your generosity," General Martín said. "If there is more I can do to assist you, just tell me."

"The protection you have provided in your military region is all we can ask for, General. Can we look forward to seeing you again next month?"

"Sí, as long as the gods continue to bless me at your tables, I will come. My wife looks forward to my weekends here, and the money I give her when I return. Her appreciation only lasts for a short time, so I must come as often as I can."

General Martín checked the time on his yellow gold Rolex and got up from his chair. "I have a massage in half an hour at the casino," he said. "Would your driver take me back?"

"Of course, General," Ying said. "Until next time, then."

Ying stood and nodded to his bodyguard, who opened the door into the villa for General Martín.

"How much do you let him win?" Francis Zheng asked.

"Twenty thousand a month," Xueping said.

"On top of the wire transfers? You pay him too much."

"He's worth it. "He made sure the other cartels knew to leave you alone when you started operating in Mexico."

Ying stood and stretched before pouring himself another glass of tequila. "The last batch of pills is ready for shipment. When will you need more?" he asked Xueping.

"It depends on how successful the first attack is. If the mortality rate is what we hope it will be, we'll wait a month. The DEA will try to shut down on our dark website.

"If they do, we move sales to another of the online platforms we've created and send another wave of pills. They can play "whack a mole" for as long as it takes until their men of fighting-age are dead."

"You're sounding like General Wang with his new opium war," Zheng said. "We're doing him a favor that happens to be very profitable, but I'm not doing this for him or the government. If they don't pull this off, that's their problem. I plan on still being in business."

Ying's servant, Juanita Vasquez, was standing at the edge of the veranda with a platter of ceviche and camerones. She was waiting for the bodyguard to allow her to approach and serve the men, when he signaled her to wait.

Xueping's sat phone was buzzing as he walked away from where the other two men were sitting, with it held to his ear.

Ying saw his servant standing at the door of the villa and waved her over.

"I know you like shasimi and kuai," Ying said to Zheng, "Try some ceviche and tell me what you think."

Zheng filled a small plate with a little ceviche and ringed the plate with camarones. "It looks like Hawaiian poke. If it tastes like poke, I won't like it."

Ying was loading a plate with ceviche when Xueping returned and sat down.

"We have a problem," he said. "General Wang says the American attorney is here in Mexico."

"How does he know that?" Ying asked.

Xueping waved off the servant girl when she held out the platter to him and waited until she walked away to answer.

"The state security found the flight plans for his company's Gulfstream at airports from New Zealand to Seattle, and then to Los Cabos," Xueping said. "If he's in Baja California, he's here because he knows we're in La Paz."

"How could he know that?" Zheng said. "You flew here in your own plane."

"I don't know. What I do know is General Wang wants me to call him and say we found him, interrogated and killed him, before I leave the day after tomorrow."

"How do you plan to do that?" Ying asked.

"How do we plan to do that," Xueping corrected. "Zheng, have your men at the airport in Cabo check with immigration and see if the travel information collected by the biometric kiosks confirms he's here."

"I can have that information within the hour," Zheng said.

"He could also have flown to the La Paz airport," Ying said. "Check with immigration there, as well."

"Zheng, how many men do you have here in La Paz?" Xueping asked.

Zheng thought for a moment and said, "Ten here in La Paz, twenty or so in Cabo and more spread throughout Baja California. In the mainland, there are hundreds in my cartel, but it will take a day or more to get them here."

"Ying?" Xueping asked. "The only men I have here are the workers at the warehouse. Four guards are there on each of three shifts, so twelve if they all show up for work."

"Keep your men at the warehouse for now. Tell them to report anything unusual. If he's here, he could know about the warehouse."

"What about your yacht?" Zheng asked. "He could have seen you on it, if he's here."

Xueping smiled. "I'm not worried about him getting to me. My yacht has the best security system money can buy. I didn't show you, but it has a safe room in case pirates start hitting superyachts instead of oil tankers. There are men on board and spread around the marina. If he comes for me, it's game over."

Chapter Thirty-Four

DRAKE WATCHED Xueping sit down after being on his phone and tapped Norris on the shoulder. "Let's head back to town."

"Do we have a plan?" Norris asked.

"Not much of one, but it's all I can think of at the moment," Drake said. "You and Marco go to the casino and clone the phone from one of the geeky guys from the yacht. Rammer and I will go back to the marina. I need to call Kate Perkins and see if she's identified the third Chinese guy. Rammer's going to reach out to the brother of Ms. Vasquez. She may have overheard something. We'll find out if her brother can get her to talk to us."

"What about tonight?" Morales asked.

"What time is sunset?" Drake asked Ramirez.

"It was seven twenty last night," Ramirez said. "Add a minute for tonight."

"We'll meet at Rammer's boat at seven thirty and leave for the warehouse when it's dark. You and Norris hang out around the casino. We'll be on Rammer's boat, unless we leave to meet with the girl's brother or the girl, if she'll talk to us."

Norris turned the jeep around and drove down the dirt road until he reached Pedregal de Cortes Avenue and stopped.

"Do you want to stop somewhere for lunch?" he asked.

"You guys eat at the casino and be there when the yacht guys come in," Drake said. "Drop us off at the marina. We can grab something around there to eat."

"Roger that," Norris said.

They drove south on Highway One with the blue shimmering waters of the Sea of Cortez on their right until they took the exit by the four-star Marine Water Front Hotel and drove toward the Marina Palmira.

Morales spotted it first. "Xueping's beefed up security. A Chinese guy sitting in that F-150 pickup at the exit. Another one standing in the shade at the hotel's spa. This doesn't feel right."

Ramirez said, "Drive on to the food truck in the back of the marina parking lot. You'll have a better view of the whole marina from there. I'll get out and buy something while you check it out."

Norris turned off and drove up to a smoked meat barbeque food truck offering smoked tri-tip wraps, pulled pork tacos and mixed combo platters.

When Ramirez left to study the menu board on the side of the food truck, Morales got out to stretch and recon the marina.

"There's one in front of the manager's office, one walking the main dock and one at the end of the dock Xueping's yacht is on," Morales reported.

"We saw two men on the yacht's upper deck with binoculars. Why does he have six men guarding his yacht?" Drake asked. "What's changed? He didn't have that many this morning when we got here."

"Maybe that's why," Norris said. "You're here."

"How could he know that?" Drake asked.

"You went through customs at the Cabo airport. If he has connections, he could have access to the traveler information Mexico collects when visitors arrive. He must know you're coming for him."

"If he knows I landed in Cabo, it doesn't mean he knows I'm here in La Paz," Drake said.

"We need to keep it that way," Morales said as he got back in the jeep. "If Xueping is working with one of the cartels, he has a small army at his disposal. We don't have the manpower or resources to deal with that."

Ramirez returned with a sack. "There are a couple of tri-tip wraps here, if anyone's hungry. Where to?"

"The casino," Drake said. "We'll drop Dan and Marco off, go see Ms. Vasquez's brother and figure things out after that."

"The casino it is," Ramirez said and started the engine.

"Two guys walking our way at six o'clock," Norris said. "Muy rapido would be good."

Ramirez gunned it and drove across the parking lot and back out to Highway 11.

Drake leaned forward and said to Ramirez, "Where do we find her brother?"

"Daniel Vasquez owns and operates Danny's Dive Shop down the road. It's not far."

"How do you know him?"

"He's one of my friends I told you about. He keeps an eye on things in La Paz for us."

"Training?" Drake asked.

"Navy SEAL."

"Hooyah! A frogman," Morales chuckled. "He'll fit right in with four army guys."

"You'll like Danny," Ramirez said. "He knows how to get things done."

"Such as?" Morales asked.

"He's been known to administer justice to cartel members who need to be taken out of the game."

"My kind of guy," Morales said.

Ramirez pulled to the curb two blocks away from the casino. "Might be better if you two walk the rest of the way. We can bring the jeep back after we meet with Danny."

"How are you going to get back to your boat without Drake being seen?" Norris asked Ramirez.

"Danny can help us with that."

Morales got out of the jeep and asked, "Are we still meeting on Rammer's boat at the marina tonight?"

"I'll let you know," Drake said. "Maybe on Rammer's boat, but not at the marina. We'll see."

"Roger that, boss. Stay out of trouble until then," Morales said.

"I will, unless trouble comes calling," Drake said.

Chapter Thirty-Five

DANNY'S DIVE Shop was a block away from the Marina Cortez next to a yacht brokers' office. Daniel Vasquez was alone in the shop, standing behind the counter and an open laptop.

He looked up when the bell above the door jingled and grinned. "Welcome amigo. Are you looking for customers in La Paz because they're not knocking on your door in Cabo?"

"I'm in La Paz because I heard they weren't knocking on your door, either. Come meet my friend, Adam Drake. He chartered my boat for the day to come here and see some friends of his."

Vasquez came around the counter to shake hands with Drake. "Buenos dias, señor Drake."

When they shook hands, Drake took stock of Daniel Vasquez: Five foot seven, one hundred sixty or seventy pounds, with broad shoulders, a strong right hand and biceps stretching the fabric of his dark blue T-shirt. With a tanned face, thick black hair and Crow's feet wrinkles bracketing his eyes, Drake couldn't guess his age.

"Call me Adam," Drake said. "Pete speaks highly of you."

"When a friend of his tells me that, it usually means he's here to ask me to do something for him."

Drake smiled. "You know him well, it seems."

Vasquez nodded his head. "Yes, I do."

"We saw your sister today, Danny. She's working for someone we both know, Ramon Ying," Ramirez said. "She was serving Ying and three men food on the veranda of his villa. One of them was General Martín. Drake is interested in knowing what she may have heard them talking about."

"Why are you interested in knowing that?" Vasquez asked Drake.

"I'm trying to find out if one of his guests, a Chinese triad leader by the name of Samuel Xueping, is involved in a plot to harm the U.S."

"What plot would that be?"

"That's what I'm trying to find out."

"Drake was on his honeymoon in Australia when he was kidnapped and tortured by Xueping," Ramirez said. "He was trying to find out what Drake knew about some plot to against America. Drake escaped and followed him here, after Xueping tried to kill him twice. I know Drake from the army. He was special ops in Afghanistan and Iraq. He asked me to help him."

"Is Xueping the Chinese guy with the superyacht moored in the Palmira Marina?" Vasquez asked.

"Yes," Drake said. "How do you know about him?"

"Word gets around. I've heard that he's been winning big at the casino with a couple of his Chinese friends and General Martín. We've been watching the general. He comes here once a month and wins big at the casino. We believe he's being paid off, but we don't know by whom."

"The general landed last night in an army helicopter at the UniMex warehouse in Pichilingue. He was met by Ramon Ying, who was entertaining him at his villa today when we saw your sister there," Drake said.

Vasquez stepped back and crossed his arms over his chest. "What do you know about the UniMex warehouse?"

"Only that Ying left Xueping's yacht to go there and meet the general," Drake said. "Two of my friends followed Ying and saw the helicopter land. I don't know what the warehouse is being used for. We're going there tonight to find out."

"It's rumored to be a fentanyl pill lab," Ramirez said. "Danny and some of our friends have been trying to prove it."

"You knew about Ying?" Drake asked Ramirez.

"It's one reason I agreed to take you here."

"If I agree to help you and get my sister involved, will you allow me to go with you tonight?" Vasquez asked.

"We have a rented jeep," Drake said. "It will be crowded, but I don't see why not."

"I have an idea that might make it easier for all of us to get to the warehouse," Ramirez said. "Why don't we take my boat up to the marina at Pichilingue. Your two guys can go in the jeep and the three of us can go in my boat and rendezvous with them there. That would get you out of La Paz for a while, so Xueping's guys don't see you."

"Are they looking for you?" Vasquez asked Drake.

"They might be. Xueping has beefed up security at Palmira Marina after we pulled in this morning and moored Rammer's boat there."

"If you need to get back to the marina without being seen, I can help with that," Vasquez said. "I have a Zodiac at Marina Cortez that can get you to Pete's boat without walking through the marina."

"That would work, thanks," Drake said. "What about your sister? Will she be willing to talk with us?"

"She might not want to talk with you, but she will talk with me. Let me call her and find out. Grab a beer. Pete knows where there are."

Drake walked over to a display of scuba diving gear hanging on the wall and picked out a pair of blue Mares Avanti fins. "I really enjoyed scuba diving in Australia. If I had time, I'd do it here before I leave."

Ramirez joined him and said, "If you want to make sure no one sees you at the marina, you could slip over the side of Danny's Zodiac and swim over to my boat. Kill two birds with one stone."

"I like the way you think," Drake said, and selected a Cressi dive mask and snorkel to go with the fins.

Vasquez walked out from the back room and looked at the gear on the counter. "Going scuba diving?"

"Rammer thought it would be a good way to get from your Zodiac to his boat without being seen," Drake said, and took out his wallet.

"Take them and leave them with Pete. You don't need to pay me."

"Yes, I do. I plan on using them when I get home. What did your sister say?"

"She will stop by on her way home. I didn't tell her why I wanted to talk in case they monitor calls at the villa. But don't worry, she'll tell me if she heard anything."

Chapter Thirty-Six

THE DIVE SHOP inflatable moored at the Marina la Paz was a Zodiac Pro 7 with a T-top, like the one Drake rented on Hamilton Island to take Liz scuba diving.

"Do you take people out scuba diving?" Drake asked Vasquez.

"Usually just friends. There's plenty of other places that do. It wasn't profitable and I'm not patient enough to teach beginners how to dive."

Vasquez eased the Zodiac out of its slip and motored slowly out of the marina until they were in the dark blue waters of the Sea of Cortez. He accelerated until the Zodiac inflatable was up on the plane and a hundred yards offshore, before turning to starboard toward the Marina Palmira.

Drake was standing to the left of Vasquez at the console, with Ramirez to his right. "Xueping's superyacht is moored on C dock at the far end of the marina," he said. "Rammer's boat is on A dock. When we enter the marina, I'll slip over the side and swim the rest of the way."

"Are you sure?" Vasquez asked. "If his yacht is that far away, he won't see you."

"The guy has men all over the marina," Ramirez said. "If the

Major wants to swim to my boat, it will minimize the chance of him being seen. Besides, I want to see if he can swim that far."

"How far will that be? A hundred yards?" Vasquez laughed. "I guess for a guy from the Unit, that is a long way."

"And here I thought I might grow to like you," Drake said, as he moved back to the aft bench seat and took off his sandals and T-shirt.

Ramirez looked around the Zodiac for something to carry Drake's sandals and T-shirt in, before asking Vasquez if he had a fish bag onboard.

"There's one in the storage bin under the rear bench seat," Vasquez said and began a sweeping turn to starboard toward Marina Palmira. Fifty yards before entering the channel entrance to the marina, he slowed the Zodiac and let it settle in the water.

Drake sitting on the leeward tube of the Zodiac, with his snorkel mask up on his forehead and his fins on, when Vasquez turned around and grinned. "You sure you want to swim that far?"

As soon as the Zodiac entered the channel, Drake leaned back and fell into the water without answering Vasquez.

Ramirez put his left hand on Vasquez's shoulder and said, "He's here with two of his friends to take on a Chinese triad and Ramon Ying's cartel, with no backup. Cut him some slack. We need to help him as much as possible. This is our fight, too."

"I know, I know," Vasquez said. "Old rivalries die hard."

When they entered the marina proper, Ramirez saw one of Xueping's men walking down the dock toward his boat. "Good thing Drake decided to swim. I'll get out first and find out what he's doing. Make sure Drake doesn't draw his attention when he gets here."

"Got it."

Vasquez guided the Zodiac slowly up to the stern ladder and nudged it there to let Ramirez off. As soon as he was up in the cockpit, Vasquez quickly tied the Zodiac off and muscled it around, so it was floating perpendicular to the dock. If Drake came up on the same side of the Zodiac he left it on, he would be out of sight from the dock.

Ramirez waited until he was sure Xueping's man was walking all the way down the dock to his boat before he greeted him. With the tattoos on his bulging neck visible above the shirt he was wearing, and the little fingers missing on each of his enormous hands, Ramirez knew exactly who he would be talking with.

"Hola amigo," he greeted the man when he stopped on the dock beside the boat.

"Is this your boat?"

"It is."

"Anyone else on it?"

"Who's asking?"

"Me."

"That means nothing to me, sorry."

"Where did you come from?"

"I don't think that's any of your business."

"I won't ask again."

"It's time you shove off, amigo. I don't care how many times you ask me."

Ramirez reached under the teak lid of the cockpit storage locker and took out the speargun he kept there.

The man smiled and said, "You gonna shoot me with that?"

"Maybe, if you don't leave."

"You'll answer me when I come back."

"Not likely."

The man smiled again. "We'll see," he said and walked away.

Ramirez walked back to the stern and looked down to see Drake in the water beside the Zodiac. "Come on up before he comes back."

Vasquez helped Drake over the side of the Zodiac's tube and said, "Did you hear all of that?"

"Every word. I guess they're expecting me."

"Maybe you should leave this marina?"

"If we leave now, they'll assume I was here and keep looking for me. I'll stay here for a while," Drake said, and headed up the ladder.

"Pete," Vasquez called out. "You need me to stay?"

"No," Ramirez called down. "Go meet your sister. I'll call you about meeting up with us later tonight."

Vasquez shoved off and Ramirez went inside. "Need a towel?" he called to Drake, who was down in the bow stateroom.

"Have one, thanks," Drake said, as he walked back up the companionway into the salon, drying his hair.

"What are you thinking?" Ramirez asked.

"I'm thinking I'd like to spend some time alone with that guy. He sounds like one of the men who tortured me."

"I mean about staying here. We could take the boat up to the port of Pichilingue and join the others there."

"And have Vasquez ride with Morales and Norris?" Drake asked. "That would work, but I don't want to leave here too soon. I might need to stay around for a couple more days. Your boat and this marina are the best places for me to keep an eye on Xueping. If they think I left on your boat and I'm running away, they will come after us."

"Here's an idea; let's invite Vasquez and some of our friends for a party here on the boat. If we have a dozen tough looking guys drinking beer, they won't want to come and mess with us."

"Do it," Drake said. "I'll buy the beer."

Chapter Thirty-Seven

AN HOUR BEFORE SUNSET, men started arriving for a party on *Tier One*, Ramirez's boat.

Morales and Norris were the first to arrive. Ten minutes later, Danny Vasquez led six men down the dock and was warmly and loudly greeted by their host.

Drake stood down in the companionway until everyone was on board before taking the steps up to the salon and joining the men.

After he introduced himself to the six men, he pulled Vasquez aside to hear if his sister had overheard anything.

"She's afraid, but she told me what she heard," Vasquez said. "Ramon Ying has General Martín on his payroll and pays him twenty thousand dollars a month. Ying said a shipment of pills was ready for shipment, and one man said something about a new opium war.

"The same man said they weren't doing this for General Wang and China. They were doing it for the triad."

"She said one man stepped away to take a call and came back saying they had a problem because the American attorney was in

Mexico. After hearing that, they dismissed her and that's all she heard. She doesn't know the names of Ying's two guests."

"Is she sure she heard the name General Wang and China mentioned?" Drake asked.

"That's what she said."

"It makes sense, China being mentioned. This all started in Australia when I saw Xueping leaving Hamilton Island on his superyacht. I thought it was just his triad when they came after me, but China has used the triads to do things they don't want to be blamed for."

"Learning you're in Mexico explains the extra security at the marina. He must be afraid of you."

"He's not afraid of me. He's afraid I'll find out what's he doing," Drake said. "Is your sister in danger, Danny?"

"I don't like her working for Ramon Ying, but she isn't in danger unless they find out she told us what she heard."

"Tell her to be careful. Xueping's dangerous."

Morales came over and clinked beer bottles together with Vasquez. "Your sister's okay?' he asked.

"She's fine, Marco. Thanks for asking."

"Drake, Rammer said you're taking his boat to Pinchinlingue tonight," Morales said. "As close as the marina there is to the UniMex warehouse, there's no need for us to drive the jeep there. I can fly the Black Hornet from the boat."

"Okay," Drake said. "But if we run in to trouble, it would be an advantage to have a vehicle there."

"If we run into trouble, we're safer leaving by boat than driving back to La Paz in the jeep."

"All right, it's your op. We'll go on Rammer's boat."

Norris motioned Drake over and told him he'd been able to clone the phone of one of the geeks from Xueping's yacht. "What should I do with it?"

"Can you get it to Kevin McRoberts in Seattle?"

"I can upload it to my laptop and get it to him," Norris said, "But my laptop's back at the hotel."

"Is that the only thing you brought with you that can be traced back to the company?'"

"That and my ID, if anyone takes the time to check me out. But Mexico already has all that information from the airport when I landed."

"Before we leave for Pinchinligue, use your laptop and transfer the data from the phone you cloned to Kevin. Then bring your laptop and Marco's here, just to be safe.'" Drake said.

"When are we leaving for Pinchinligue?" Norris asked.

"I'm not sure. Let's ask Rammer." Drake waved Ramirez over.

"Qué pasa?" Ramirez asked.

"When do you think we should leave for Pinchinlingue?" Drake asked.

"It's roughly twenty-five miles to the port, so not more than forty minutes to get there," Ramirez said. "If we leave by nine o'clock, it will be plenty dark when we get there."

"Let's plan on leaving at nine, Dan," Drake said. "That will give you plenty of time to get to the hotel, get the data to Kevin. Maybe he can look at it and get back to us tonight."

"Who's going with us?" Ramirez asked.

"You, me, Dan, Marco, and Danny," Drake said.

"If we're leaving that late, do you want me to order dinner for these guys and make it look like an actual party?"

"What kind of dinner?" Drake asked.

"The food truck in the parking lot does catering. Say, food for ten men and more beer."

"Great," Drake said, and handed Ramirez a credit card. "Get a receipt, in case I ask the company to pay for it."

Vasquez stepped away and came back with a beer for each of them. "What are you planning on doing about Ramon Ying and General Martín?" he asked Drake.

"What would you like us to do?"

"Let us take care of them."

"You mean you and the men Ramirez told me about?"

"We've been taking out the little guys when we get a chance," Vasquez said. "Exposing Ying and General Martín will let the cartels know there's someone else they should worry about, other than the government, which they don't worry about at all."

"They'll come after you"

"They will. They have before. No one knows who we are, because we fly under the radar and never meet as a group."

"Would it make a difference if I said no?" Drake asked.

"Not really. This is our fight."

"If there's anything I can do to help with that, just ask."

"Thanks."

Drake left the salon and went down to his stateroom to check in with Liz and then Kate Perkins. Hearing that China was involved was information that was too important to keep to himself. Letting Perkins know about Xueping and General Wang wouldn't stop what he was there to do, but he promised Perkins he would keep her informed in exchange for her getting the FBI off his back in Seattle.

Chapter Thirty-Eight

DRAKE SAT on the edge of the bed and thought about what he should tell Liz. They had vowed to always be open and honest about everything, and Liz knew what he was doing in Mexico. She knew there were risks involved, just as there had been when they exposed the Chinese spy operation.

This time, with a Chinese triad, a Mexican drug cartel, and a Chinese general involved, the risk was significantly greater.

"Hi Liz, still at the office?" he asked.

"Hello handsome. Yes, I'm still at the office. No reason to leave, except to feed Lancer and sleep a couple hours. How's Mexico?"

"I've only been here twenty-four hours, but it's nice and warm and not nearly as beautiful as Hamilton Island."

"How about your friend on the big yacht?"

"He's here in La Paz, on the other side of the marina. I'm staying on the boat an old friend of mine owns."

"Do I know this old friend?"

"His name is Pete Ramirez. I served with him in Iraq and Afghanistan. He has a sport fishing charter service I booked for a couple of days."

"Have you learned anything?"

"A little," Drake said. "Xueping met with the Chinese CEO of UniMex, a big pharma company in Mexico. He's connected with a Mexican drug cartel and has a Mexican army general on his payroll."

"So, you're down there poking around in something that involves a Chinese triad, a Mexican drug cartel, and a dirty Mexican army general? I don't like the sound of this, Adam."

"I'm staying out of sight, Liz. I'm okay. I should be home in a couple of days. Where is Mike keeping you?"

"I'm staying at his house with Lancer. His kids love Lancer. We're going to have a tough time taking him away from them."

"Tell Mike to get his own dog."

"He's thinking about it, believe me."

"I have to go. I love you, Liz."

"I love you too. Stay out of trouble."

"I promise. I'll call you tomorrow."

That went as well as it could have, he thought. I was honest. I told her what I was doing and didn't really lie by omission, really. The problem will be if I tell Kate Perkins more than I told Liz and they talk she'll know I didn't tell her everything. I think I'll wait until tomorrow to call Kate Perkins and have another chance to talk with Liz.

He returned to the salon and found the party in full swing. Ramirez had music playing on the boat and the men were enjoying themselves, laughing and telling war stories. It reminded him of after mission gatherings in Afghanistan.

Ramirez came over and told him Morales had gone with Norris to their hotel. "They promised to be back by the time the food arrived."

"Any activity on Xueping's yacht?"

"Not on his yacht, but there are men walking around all over the marina. Having this party was a good idea. They haven't come down our dock to check on us."

"Danny asked me what I was planning on doing with Ying and General Martín. He said that you and your friends would like to deal with them. Is that right?"

"We're talking about it. Why? What were you going to do about a Mexican national who's well-connected and a dirty Mexican army general? The FBI can't operate here without being arrested as spies."

"I understand that, Rammer, but your government hasn't been able to deal with the cartels."

"That's why it's up to us. We can fight from the shadows. There are enough of us with military training to make a difference. All we lack is the firepower to match the cartels."

"I might be able to help with that," Drake said.

Ramirez looked past and saw the food truck caterers coming down the dock. He patted Drake on the shoulder and said, "If you can, that would be great."

Drake watched Ramirez wave at the caterers and jumped onto the dock to greet them. Morales and Norris were walking behind the caterers.

When they got on the boat, they walked directly to Drake and pointed to the companionway.

"You should stay below until we leave," Norris said. "Soldiers are going around asking if anyone has seen this gringo and showing them a picture of you. It looks like it was taken at the airport."

"They're using General Martín to look for me."

"We should leave the marina," Morales said. "We would look like just another booz cruise going out to watch the sunset."

"Go talk to Vasquez," Drake said. "See if his friends can stay onboard a while longer. We could put them ashore somewhere away from town, if we have to."

"Roger that," Morales said, and left.

"Having the Mexican army looking for you is going to be a problem," Norris said. "Maybe you should leave with Ramirez and let us stay here to finish this."

"What's left to finish after tonight?" Drake asked.

"I mean leave before we go to the warehouse. Marco and I can go to Pinchinlingue with the drone, go back to our hotel, and no one will ever know we were at the warehouse."

"Did you get the data from the guy's phone to Kevin?"

"Before I returned here."

"Tell Ramirez what we're thinking. I don't want to get him in trouble if he takes me back to Cabo tonight and they find out."

"Maybe you shouldn't return to Cabo," Norris said. "They know you landed in Cabo. They'll be looking for you there, as well as here."

"Damn it! This isn't what I planned."

"Does any mission ever go as planned?"

"Not many of them. Okay, let's improvise. We'll leave with the men Vasquez invited, make it look like a booz cruise, then land somewhere and drop the men off. Rammer will know where to take me after that."

Chapter Thirty-Nine

SAMUEL XUEPING and Francis Zheng lit two Cohiba cigars, a gift General Martín had presented them with when he welcomed them to Mexico, on the upper sun deck of Xueping's superyacht.

Xueping poured a glass of cognac for each of them and sat back to enjoy smoking his cigar.

The night was still, except for noise coming from a boat across the marina, and pleasantly warm.

"How long will it take you to get this last shipment to Vancouver?" Xueping asked Zheng.

"It will cross over to Culiacán tonight and take our usual route north. Three days, at most."

"And how many days for distribution in America?"

"Two more days," Zheng said. "Everything will be in place by next Friday."

"Excellent! General Wang wants an update tonight. I wish I could tell him we found the attorney."

"Why is finding this attorney so important? There's nothing he can do now to stop us."

"Tell that to General Wang," Xueping said.

"With General Martín using his soldiers to search La Paz, we should have him by morning. Tell Wang that."

Xueping's personal bodyguard came up the stairs to the sun deck and waited to be summoned before approaching.

"We have searched all the boats in the marina, except for the boat having the party," the man reported. "We didn't find anyone matching the description you gave us."

"Has the Mexican captain finished searching the city?"

"He hasn't called me yet."

"Let me know as soon as he does," Xueping said, and dismissed the man.

"If the army can't find him, I'll have my men look, if you want," Zheng offered.

"I'm leaving early Monday. If they don't find him today, I might ask for your help tomorrow. I don't want him returning to America."

"How long will you stay in San Diego?"

"I'll keep the Benetti there until the first wave of pills is distributed," Xueping said. "For the second wave, I'm moving my other Benetti to Miami. We'll operate the dark web platform from there. When it's in place and the second wave is on its way, I'll return to Hong Kong."

Zheng lifted his glass of cognac and said, "Here's to our success then, and your safe return. I'll come visit you when this is over."

―――

DRAKE STAYED in his stateroom until the *Tier One* was clear of the marina before he joined the others in the salon.

"How soon will you head in to let the others off?" he asked Ramirez.

"I thought I'd head out into the Sea of Cortez for an hour to make it look like a real booz cruise before going back to Marina la Paz, where Vasquez keeps his Zodiac. Is that okay?"

Drake looked at his watch. "That's fine. It will give Morales and Norris plenty of time to get to the warehouse and back before midnight."

"Would you like Vasquez to go with them?"

"Why?"

"He's local. If they get stopped, he could act as their guide and make it easier to get past soldiers or the police."

"Sure, if he's willing to go. Where do you think I should go from here?"

Ramirez handed him a beer and pointed to the spread of barbequed ribs, burritos and tacos. "You need to eat before the food's gone. What's left for you to do here?"

Drake grabbed a paper plate and loaded it with some ribs and potato salad and leaned against the counter in the galley. "It depends on what we find out about the warehouse and if the data from the phone Norris cloned gains us access to the IT network on Xueping's yacht. With that, I don't know what else I can accomplish here."

"Xueping is leaving Monday, according to the marina manager. Do you want to follow him and see where's he's going?"

Drake finished eating a mouthful of baby back rib. "With the phone Norris cloned, we can track its GPS if it stays on board, even if we don't have access to the yacht's IT network. We may not need to follow Xueping."

"If they're looking for you here, they'll be looking for you in Cabo. We could go fishing tomorrow, stay offshore, and then decide what you want to do."

"Sounds like a plan. I might even get lucky and catch something."

"Major, when you catch something on my boat, luck has nothing to do with it."

Drake listened to Vasquez's friends for the next hour talking about the success they were having interfering with the cartels, and the plans they were making for future operations. By the time Ramirez turned toward the marina where Vasquez kept his Zodiac, he had a good idea of the ways he and Sound Security and Information Services could help them.

At Marina la Paz, he said goodbye to his new friends and sat down with Morales and Norris to go over the plan for the evening. By nine o'clock, Ramirez was backing *Tier One* away from the dock and heading out into the Sea of Cortez.

Drake watched the lights of La Paz get smaller in the distance and the night growing darker from the stern cockpit, before joining Ramirez.

Chapter Forty

DAN NORRIS SLOWED DOWN to exit Highway 11 onto Avenue Pichilingue and saw two Mexican army Humvees pulled across the road fifty yards ahead, with their hazard lights blinking.
"Looks like we're not driving any closer to the UniMex plant," Norris said.
"Let me handle it," Vasquez said.
Two soldiers approached carrying assault rifles and walked to each side of the jeep.
"What is your business?" the soldier asked Norris.
"We're taking the ferry tomorrow to Mazatlan," answered Vasquez from the seat behind Norris. "Is there a problem?"
"Where are you going?"
"To the hotel over there," Vasquez said, hooking his thumb to the right.
"Do you have reservations?"
"We're meeting a friend who made the reservations. He's arriving in his sailboat. Can we go to the marina and meet him?" Vasquez asked.
"No, the marina is closed to the public tonight."
"For all night?"

"Sí, all night."

"May we go to the hotel, then?"

"Sí."

The soldiers walked backwards, facing the jeep until they were past the turnoff to the hotel.

"Any idea what's going on?" Norris asked Vasquez.

"Something down at the marina they don't want anyone to know about, "Vasquez said.

"Marco, is this close enough for you to use your little drone?"

"The Black Hornet has a range of two thousand meters. We're close enough."

"All right," Norris said. "Let's see if they have room in the inn for us tonight."

He turned off Avenue Pichilingue and drove the short distance to the Club Hotel Cantamar.

Vasquez jumped out and said, "I'll go see."

Norris and Morales sat and listened to the jeep's engine clicking as it cooled while they waited for Vasquez to return.

"Are you thinking what I'm thinking?" Morales asked.

"If you're thinking General Martín has something to do with this, the answer is yes."

"It has to involve the warehouse."

"Maybe they're moving something to the mainland, using the ferry."

"Like drugs?" Morales asked.

"Like drugs."

Vasquez came out of the hotel and walked back to the jeep.

"We have two rooms," Vasquez said. "It's not that I didn't want to bunk with you two, but I told the soldiers we're meeting a friend."

"We don't have luggage, Danny." Norris pointed out.

"Don't worry, I took care of it," he said, rubbing his thumb and first finger together.

Morales, carrying a small duffel bag with the Black Hornet drone inside, and Norris followed Vasquez inside, nodding to the hotel clerk as they walked by, and took the elevator to the top floor.

Their rooms were okay, standard issue inexpensive hotel rooms, except the windows didn't open.

"No problem," Morales assured Norris, as they checked out their quarters for the night. "I'll slip outside and launch from there."

"This is when I wish I had more than a Benchmade in my pocket with soldiers out there. Did you recognize those assault rifles?"

"FX-05s, they call them "Fire Snakes". Made in Mexico copying the H&K G36, it's designed for urban fighting to use against the cartels. Yes, I recognized them."

Vasquez came into their room and asked, "How soon are you going to use the drone?"

"I'll slip out in a couple of minutes."

"The stairs are at the other end of the hall," Vasquez said.

"Thanks," Morales said.

"You think we should stay overnight?" Norris asked Vasquez.

"It depends on what these soldiers are doing here. If it involves drugs, they'll be very suspicious of anyone near the marina. If it doesn't, they won't give a damn if we leave the hotel and go back to La Paz."

"We'll know soon enough," Morales said. "I'll hit the head and take off."

He returned in a minute, slipped the straps of the Black Hornet PRS base control station over his head, and adjusted the length so it was centered in the middle of his chest.

"If I'm not back in thirty minutes, get out of here before they come looking for you," Morales said.

"Make sure you're back in thirty," Norris warned. "I have no interest in spending time in a Mexican jail."

"Roger that, jefe!" Morales saluted and left.

There was no one in the hallway and no noise coming from any of the rooms on the top floor. In fact, it sounded like they had the entire floor to themselves.

There was no lighting in the stairway and his eyes adjusted to the dark by the time he paused at the stairwell door.

It was quiet outside when he opened the door an inch and listened. The only sounds were from the rigging of a sailboat slapping against a mast in the marina next to the hotel, and the hum of the Humvees' diesel engines at the roadblock.

He moved to the far end of the north wall of the small hotel and opened the base control unit and turned it on. When the screen lit up, he lifted the little drone out of its slot and held it between his thumb and first finger.

The Black Hornet PRS nano drone weighed just 1.16 ounces and was a feather in his hand, as he started its rotors whirling and gave it a gentle toss in the air to begin its flight.

Morales flew the Black Hornet up to an altitude of three hundred feet and turned it south toward the UniMex warehouse. The army Humvees were still parked across Pichilingue Avenue, with the soldiers leaning against them and smoking.

Following the road straight south, he had the drone hovering over the warehouse in less than ten seconds. With a maximum flight time of twenty-five minutes, there was plenty of time to find a way into the warehouse and record the activity inside.

Dropping to a height two feet below the roofline, Morales flew the Black Hornet laterally along the side of the naturally ventilated warehouse and then around the end of the building.

He found a row of windows high on the walls that were open and canted outward for airflow. The drone had a rotor diameter of four inches, and he flew it along the row of windows, looking for one with an opening wide enough to allow entry.

When he found one, he carefully inched the drone through the narrow opening and hovered it inside to survey the scene below. The warehouse floor was stacked high with boxes labeled pharmaceutical supplies.

When he flew the drone to the far end, he saw a long metal table with a row of pill presses on one side and on the other side, bins and a row of pill molds. No workers were operating the presses and molds, but at the end of the metal table, a dozen workers were loading cellophane-wrapped bags of blue pills in boxes.

He flew the drone closer and hovered silently near the ceiling, recording what he was seeing down below. The cardboard boxes had a logo and lettering that read "Bumble Bee Tiny Shrimp" and the workers were layering two rows of canned shrimp on top of the bags of blue pills before they closed each box and sealed it with packing tape.

Morales turned the drone in a full circle and flew it back to the window it had entered.

The real Bumble Bee company would not be happy that someone was shipping illegal fake pills in boxes with its famous logo and product name on the sides," Morales thought.

Chapter Forty-One

DANNY VASQUEZ KNOCKED on the door of Morales and Norris's hotel room after an early morning walk around the area and reported when he stepped inside, "There's a great restaurant nearby that serves breakfast, if you're hungry?"

"What time does it open?" Norris asked.

"Eight," Vasquez said.

Morales was sitting on his bed, studying the images on the screen of the Black Hornet's base control unit. "I need to get this to Drake. The warehouse is a fentanyl pill lab."

"How can you tell it's fentanyl?" Vasquez asked.

"Look," Morales said and patted the bed next to where he was sitting.

When Vasquez sat down next to him, Morales turned the screen toward him and pointed to a discarded bag on the floor. "See the letters ANPP? That's a fentanyl precursor."

He moved the cursor and focused it on the boxes at the end of the metal table. "They're shipping those blue pills in cellophane-wrapped bags in boxes, under cans of Bumble Bee Tiny Shrimp."

"How are they moving the pills?" Vasquez asked.

"Marco said he saw an old shrimp boat at the end of the pier at the warehouse," Norris said. "They're probably crossing the Sea of Cortez in the shrimp boat to the Mexican mainland. Culiacán is the home of the Sinaloa cartel, and it's straight across the Sea of Cortez from here."

"We know most of the Sinaloa guys around here, but we didn't know about this pill lab," Vasquez said. "Do you want me to let the local DEA guy know about it?"

"I thought DEA agents were *persona non grata* in Mexico?" Morales said.

"They are," Vasquez smiled. "We help them stay under the radar."

"What now?" Norris asked.

Vasquez looked at his watch and said, "The restaurant's open. I say we go have breakfast and figure it out."

"I'm not comfortable leaving the drone here," Morales said. "I need to take it with me."

"The case looks a lot like a case for binoculars. No one will notice," Norris said. "Let's go."

They followed Vasquez across the hotel's parking lot and north to the tip of the Pichilingue peninsula and the Marisco El Molinto Pichilingue seafood restaurant.

When they entered, their hostess led them through the restaurant to a covered deck overlooking the Sea of Cortez and handed them menus.

"The breakfast special today," she told them, "is our Omelette del Mar, with four cheeses bathed in a gremolata sauce of lemon zest. It's very good. Would you like coffee or something from the bar while you look at your menus?"

They ordered coffee and took a quick look at their menus."

"Seafood omelette," Norris said. "What's the seafood?"

"Shrimp," Morales said.

"Bumble Bee Tiny Shrimp, no doubt," Norris chuckled. "I'm having pancakes and eggs."

When a server came and took their orders and left after

pouring three cups of coffee for them, Norris's phone buzzed in his pocket.

"It's Drake," he mouthed and walked to the far end of the deck.

"What did he say?" Morales asked when he returned.

"He said to look out five hundred yards at eleven o'clock," Norris said. "He's out there on *Tier One* with Ramirez."

"Is he coming in?"

"I told him why we had to stay the night. He said to check and see if the soldiers are still there. If they are, he'll meet us somewhere else. If they aren't, he'll come to the dock here."

"I'll go check," Vasquez said.

In the distance, they saw a flash of a reflection from the lens of a binocular on Ramirez's tournament fishing yacht.

"Did he say anything about the data you sent Kevin from the phone you cloned?" Morales asked.

"That's what he wants to talk about."

Norris raised his hand to ask for another cup of coffee and, before their server came with the coffeepot, Vasquez returned.

"The soldiers are gone and so is the old shrimp boat," he reported.

Norris walked to the railing of the deck and waved Drake in.

They watched the yacht move toward them and ate quickly when their breakfast orders finally arrived.

Vasquez finished first and got up to leave. "I'll meet them at the dock and pay the docking fee before they get here," he said.

"Thanks, Danny," Norris said. "We'll be right behind you."

He finished the last bite of his pancake and handed Morales a fifty-dollar bill out of his wallet. "You get to pay, slow eater. See you at the dock."

Morales smiled with a mouth full of food and made a rude gesture, when he saw the hostess out of the corner of his eye walking over with their check.

After waiting for ten minutes for the hostess to return with his change, and assuming there wasn't any, Morales left and joined the others at the dock behind the hotel.

As soon as *Tier One* nudged against the dock and a line was thrown to Vasquez, Norris and Morales got on board, followed by Vasquez, who jumped on as the yacht starting moving away.

Ramirez backed his boat away from the dock and turned it around to leave Pichilingue for open water.

Chapter Forty-Two

RAMIREZ RETURNED *Tier One* to a position five hundred yards offshore and turned off its diesel engines.

The sun was still warming the morning chill, so they moved inside to the stern cockpit to talk.

Drake listened to Morales describe what he saw in the warehouse and studied the images on the drone's base control unit.

"Other than the empty precursor bag on the floor, was there anything you saw that links the pill lab to Xueping?" he asked.

"Nothing that's out in the open," Morales said.

"Do you think there's something that's not out in the open?"

"The cartels keep a close watch over their inventory. The temptations are always there for a worker to skim a couple of pills to sell later, so they'll keep records. Those could be there. They were boxing the pills for shipment. There might be a copy of the manifest somewhere in the warehouse for what they loaded onto the shrimp boat. No one's going to trust a shrimp boat captain to deliver everything."

"Can we get into the warehouse?"

"Not without being seen," Morales said.

"It's Sunday," Vasquez said. "There may be no one working today."

"Marco?' Drake asked.

"I didn't look for a way in. I can take another look."

"Go ahead," Drake said.

"Why risk going in the warehouse?" Norris asked.

"Because we need to know what Xueping's up to," Drake said. "Kevin accessed the superyacht's IT network. Xueping's operating a DarkNet site from his yacht to sell counterfeit prescription drugs, like oxycodone, Xanax and Adderall.

"This all started in Australia about a rumored plot to cripple America. Then Danny's sister heard about a new Opium War. If Xueping's involved in this with China, we need evidence to prove it."

"How would China be involved?" Norris asked. "They manufacture fentanyl precursors the pill labs use, but we've known that."

"I don't know," Drake said. "But if China is involved, the president will want proof that they are."

"I'll find a way into the warehouse if you'll take me there," Morales said.

Drake looked to Ramirez and asked, "Can you get us close enough to the warehouse to send Marco in from your boat?"

"There's a dock at the warehouse where the shrimp boat was last night," Vasquez said.

"Let's go look," Ramirez said.

"Rammer, when we're close enough, let Marco use the drone to see if anyone's working today," Drake said.

Ramirez nodded and climbed up to the ladder to the open convertible bridge to get underway.

"Marco, I'm going in with you," Drake said. "I want to see this for myself."

"Hang on," Ramirez called down and pushed the throttle forward. The *Tier One* shot forward and raced south until it was parallel to the warehouse on the Pichilingue peninsula, when he slowed and let the yacht settle in the water.

Morales held the Black Hornet up, blew it a kiss and let it fly up out of his fingers. When it was over land and hovering above the warehouse parking lot on the other side, he reported there were no cars there.

Looking down at the screen of the base control unit, he said, "I'm back over the warehouse and the area between the warehouse and the dock. I don't see anyone."

"Is there a way in?" Drake asked.

Morales maneuvered the drone closer to the back of the warehouse. "There's a metal service door at the back of the warehouse."

"Anything else?"

"The ventilation windows, but we'd need a ladder to get up to them. Then we'd have a twenty-foot drop to the floor once we're inside."

"What about at the other end of the warehouse?"

"Let me see?" Morales said and flew the Black Hornet to the other end of the warehouse.

"There's another door there, but anyone in the office building next to the warehouse could see us."

"If no one is working today, who would be there to see us?"

"It's worth a try, if we can't get in through the service door at the other end," Drake said.

"I have a few tools onboard," Ramirez said. "That might help; a crowbar, some screwdrivers, and a bolt cutter I keep here for missions with Danny and our friends."

"That will have to do," Drake said. "Take us in to the dock, Rammer, and let's try it."

Ramirez took his boat back onto plane and swung around the southern tip of the Pichilingue peninsula into Puerto Pichilingue, where the ferry to Mazatlán was located.

He continued past the UniMex warehouse and turned around to idle up to the UniMex dock, with the bow of *Tier One* pointed south in case they needed to leave quickly.

Morales sent the Black Hornet up again and flew in the open window he used before to gain entry to have a look around. After a careful sweep of the interior of the warehouse, he reported it was empty.

Ramirez came down from the yacht's open convertible bridge and ducked into the salon. When he returned, he held out a Taurus Raging Bull 44 magnum revolver to him.

"In case there are any surprises in there," Ramirez said. "If you need to use it, get back here as quickly as you can. On my boat it's legal. Off the boat in your hand, it's not."

Drake took the revolver, spun the chamber to make sure it was loaded, and handed it back to Ramirez.

"If there's someone in there, we'll find another way to get what we need," Drake said.

"Take it anyway," Ramirez insisted, "Just in case."

Chapter Forty-Three

DRAKE LED the way and jogged from the dock up the walkway to the rear metal door of the warehouse. He studied the metal door, looking for the location of its hinges, before he tried to pry it open.

When he raised the crowbar and looked for a spot to force it into a gap between the door and the door's frame, Morales reached over and pulled on the door's handle.

"Should've tried that," Drake said humbly when the door opened, Morales stepped aside and let Drake enter the quiet warehouse.

Dust particles floated in the light streaming in from the windows and the warehouse smelled stale and unused.

The pill lab Morales saw was on the right side of the door, near the wall.

Drake walked over to the end of the metal table and looked along the rows of pill presses and pill molds. From the simplicity of the setup, it amazed him that what it produced could be so profitable and so deadly.

On the floor at the far end of the table were empty bags, like those he'd seen plant fertilizer or potting soil packaged and sold in. None of them had markings on them, except the letters that showed what they contained and identified the company that manufactured them.

There were open boxes of N95 masks, latex gloves, and a stack of bottled water cases, but nothing that was helpful.

"If we hadn't seen Ramon Ying here, there's nothing that would directly link him to this pill lab," Morales said. "It could just as well be someone within his company operating a pill lab he doesn't know about, or someone letting a cartel use the warehouse off the books."

"Clean and professional," Drake agreed. "It's big business. They're not amateurs. I thought they might be a little careless and leave something behind that would be helpful. I was wrong."

The metal door flew open and Norris shouted, "We've got company headed our way."

Drake and Morales sprinted to the door and ran with Norris back to *Tier One*, idling at

the dock. As soon as they jumped on board, Ramirez gunned the engines and raced away.

Two white Ram ProMaster cargo vans turned off Pichilingue Avenue and drove onto the

UniMex site, headed toward the end of the warehouse Drake and Morales had just run out of.

Vasquez watched the two vans with the binoculars Ramirez had given him. "They aren't

looking our way," he said. "They might not have seen the boat at the dock."

"Can you tell who they are?" Drake asked.

"The lettering on the side of the first van says it's from the Casino Cortéz."

"Rammer let's stick around and see what they're bringing to the warehouse," Drake called up to Ramirez.

Ramirez pulled back on the throttle lever and shifted into neutral.

They were a hundred yards south of the warehouse dock and

watched two men get out of the first van and open its rear cargo doors. The second van pulled beside the first van and two men got out of it and did the same thing.

With the rear doors opened, they had a direct line of sight and saw each van was carrying cardboard boxes.

"Can you see anything on the boxes?" Drake asked.

"Yeah, but I don't get it. They're labeled "casino chips", Vasquez said.

"We saw boxes at a warehouse in Australia with those same labels, Danny. That's how Xueping is shipping fentanyl precursors to Mexico," Drake explained. "He sends them to his casino and then brings them here to Ramon Ying's pill lab."

"What will you do with this information?" Vasquez asked.

"I'm in touch with the FBI," Drake said. "I'll make sure they pass the information along to the DEA."

"Or we could handle it for the DEA," Vasquez said.

"That's a big undertaking, Danny," Drake said. "Let's talk about it later."

"Are we finished here?" Morales asked. "We need to check out of the hotel."

"Yeah, we're finished here," Drake acknowledged. "When you three have checked out, head back to La Paz. We have the rest of the day before Xueping leaves tomorrow to decide if there's anything else we can think of to do."

Ramirez shifted out of neutral and pushed the throttle lever forward to return to the hotel dock, where they dropped off Morales, Norris and Vasquez.

When Norris came back and waved after checking out of the hotel, Ramirez backed *Tier One* away from the dock and asked Drake, "Where to?"

"Not La Paz or Cabo. Some quiet place to think and make a couple of phone calls."

"No place better than on a boat to do those things," Ramirez said. "Are you thinking of leaving from Cabo, or do you want me to take you to another airport?"

"What are my choices?" Drake asked.

"Are you flying commercial or on the Gulfstream?"
"Not commercial, with Xueping looking for me."
"We can find an airport up north or cross over to Mazatlán."
"Let's wait until I make some phone calls and we have something to eat."
There are leftover ribs and pulled pork in the galley," Ramirez said. "Go get something to
eat. I'll find a quiet place."
"On my way. You need anything?"
"Toss me up a beer and I'm fine."

Chapter Forty-Four

RAMIREZ FOUND a cove on the southern end of Isla Espirito Santo, a small island north of Pichilingue, and turned off the yacht's engines. When he came down from the bridge, Drake was sitting in one of the fighting chairs in the cockpit, looking across the water with a bottle of Modelo beer in his hand.

"Are you and your friends willing to scale this up to stop the cartels?" he asked Ramirez.

"If we aren't, who will? Our government is corrupt and ineffective. Your DEA can't stop them and your open borders make it easy for them to get their product into the biggest market for drugs in the world. If the cartels can operate with impunity in Mexico, they will never stop killing people with their poison, like they did with my younger brother."

"I didn't know you lost a brother."

"He overdosed after we knew each other in Afghanistan."

Drake took a long pull on his beer and turned to look at Ramirez. "Is it revenge or patriotism?"

"Does it matter?"

"It might. I'm trying to decide the same thing," Drake said.

"If you find out there's nothing to this rumor, will you forget about Xueping?"

Drake took a deep breath and exhaled through his lips. "I don't know."

"Then I say carry on until you figure it out," Ramirez said, and left Drake looking across the water toward Pichilingue.

By the time he finished his beer and hadn't figured it out, Drake retrieved his sat phone from the salon and returned to the cockpit to call Liz.

"Miss me?" he asked.

"Let me think. It's Sunday. I'm not in the office. I'm watching a movie with someone who loves me right next to me on the sofa. What did you say your name is?"

"I knew it was a mistake to leave you with him."

"Of course, I miss you! Are you okay?"

"I'm sitting on the back of a fishing yacht with a clear blue sky overhead, talking to a beautiful woman. Why wouldn't I be okay?"

"Two broken ribs might be one reason."

"They're sore, but nothing I can't live with."

"When are you coming home?" Liz asked.

"That's what I'm trying to figure out."

"Mike told me Kevin gained access to Xueping's superyacht IT network. Is there anything there about a plot?"

"I don't know. I haven't talked to Kevin."

"He's probably in his office."

"I'll call him. Are you okay?"

"Abandoned and lonely, but okay, for now."

"I'll be home as soon as I can."

"I know. Be careful."

"I will," Drake said, and ended the call.

Drake glanced down to the Omega Seamaster on his left wrist she'd given him for Christmas and saw it was one o'clock in the afternoon, Pacific Standard Time. As much as he wanted Kevin McRoberts to be out of the office on a Sunday, he knew Liz was right. Kevin was probably at headquarters.

"Mr. Drake, how's Mexico?" Kevin asked.

"Sunny and warm. I understand you accessed the superyacht's IT network."

"It was easy, with the data from the cloned phone Mr. Norris sent me."

"Is there anything you found on the yacht's network that mentions this rumored plot?"

"Not that I've seen."

"What have you seen?" Drake asked.

"I've seen four different individuals involved with a DarkNet platform they're using to sell drugs. I've seen emails from laptops and PCs onboard. Navigational data, purchase orders for supplies, what I expected to see."

"Did any of the emails involve a Chinese general?"

"I haven't seen a Chinese general being mentioned."

"What about communications from a sat phone, like the one I'm using now? Do you have access to those?"

"Satellite transmissions, both uplink and downlink transmissions, are easy to intercept, Mr. Drake. Do you want me to work on that and see what I can find?" Kevin asked.

"Yes, especially from Xueping. His yacht is leaving La Paz tomorrow. Can you monitor where he's going?"

"Sure thing, Mr. Drake."

"Call me if you find anything, anything at all. Don't worry what time it is."

"Will do, Mr. Drake."

"Thanks, Kevin."

There was one more call he knew he needed to make, but he wasn't sure what to tell Deputy Director of the FBI, Kate Perkins.

"Where are you?" Kate Perkins asked when she answered.

"Mexico, why?"

"I told the Seattle office I'd keep an eye on you and they're asking."

"At the moment, I'm in a boat on the Sea of Cortez."

"Have you found out anything?"

"No," Drake said. "I know Xueping is operating a website on the DarkNet to sell illicit fentanyl pills from his superyacht. I know

Ramon Ying is involved, along with a General Martín in the Mexican army. But I haven't found anything that confirms the rumor about a plot to cripple America."

"Who needs a plot to cripple America, when fentanyl is doing a pretty good job of it already," Perkins said. "In the first year of the pandemic, over one hundred thousand Americans died from overdosing on illicit drugs. Fentanyl-laced fake prescription pills were a major cause of that, with fentanyl being a hundred times more potent than morphine and fifty times more potent than heroin. It's never been this bad."

"Overdosing on drugs isn't new. Why is it so bad now?"

"Because fentanyl is cheap and unbelievably profitable. The cartels lace pills with it and the user has no way of knowing how much fentanyl is in the pill. Thirty milligrams of heroin are lethal. Three milligrams of fentanyl will kill you. Did you know the number one cause of death in America of males between the ages of eighteen and forty-five is drug overdose?"

"I didn't," Drake admitted.

"I apologize for preaching to the choir, but this a crisis no one wants to talk about. It's a war and we're losing badly. If you find anything about a plot, call me."

"I promise, Kate. I'll let you know when I'm coming back, in case my FBI friends in Seattle still want to mess with me."

"If they cause any trouble, let me know. I'll take care of it."

"Thanks."

Drake sat back in the fighting chair and thought, *maybe there is no plot to cripple America. If fentanyl is already killing Americans, and Xueping's triad is already selling fentanyl-laced pills online to Americans, what more could China do that isn't already being done?*

Chapter Forty-Five

DRAKE FOUND Ramirez going over his scheduled charters for the rest of the month in the galley when he came in from the aft cockpit.

Ramirez looked up and asked," Have you decided which airport you want to fly out of?"

"How long will it take us to get to Mazatlán?"

"I can get you there in six, seven hours, if I push it."

"I'd like to wait to see Xueping leave La Paz tomorrow before I fly home," Drake said. "That leaves us the rest of the day

"What would you like to do between now and then?"

"Other than sink Xueping's yacht? I don't have any idea. What about you?"

"If we're going to Mazatlán tomorrow, I need to gas up and reload the galley. Are Morales and Norris going with you?"

"If no one knows they're here with me, it's better if they fly home the way they arrived."

"All right, have you ever caught a Marlin?"

"Never even tried."

"Then today's the day you do," Ramirez said. "I'll get you set up."

Drake went back out to the cockpit, faced the sun, and stretched. Being on the water brought back memories of his honeymoon and how relaxed he'd been. It was something he promised himself he would to do more often, now that he knew the rest of his wife's bucket list included seeing Paris in the spring, staying in a villa in Tuscany, and a bareboat sailing vacation in the Caribbean.

He flinched when his sat phone chirped and startled him.

"Boss, I just got a call from Danny," Morales said. "His sister says Ying is hosting a going away dinner tonight for Xueping. She's offered to help us in any way she can."

"By doing what?" Drake asked.

"She said she's willing to wear a wire?"

"Too dangerous. If she gets caught, they'll kill her."

"What if there's a way to make sure she doesn't get caught?"

"Like what?"

"Like remotely activating the microphone on her iPhone and recording conversations in Ying's villa?"

"Could we do that?" Drake asked.

"Sure, by downloading an app that will make it possible. They're available on the internet. My sister uses one to make sure she knows what my nephew's doing."

"Explain."

"You download the app to your laptop and get the number of the phone you're targeting. When you want to record conversations in the phone's vicinity, you use the app to activate the microphone. It records the conversations on your laptop, and you can listen to them whenever you want."

"She would have to be in the room when the conversations are happening," Drake said. "If they're talking about some plot, the one they didn't want me to hear about, how likely is it they'll talk about it when she's in the room?"

"She doesn't have to be in the room, her phone does. She could hide it somewhere. They might not talk about it in detail, but they might say enough to let us figure it out."

"I don't know, Marco. We're talking about asking a young girl to do something that might get her killed."

"Boss, she volunteered. They hate the cartels. She's had friends killed for no reason and she wants it to stop, as much as her brother does."

"Let me think about it and I'll call you back."

"It will have to be soon. She has to be at the villa by six o'clock."

"I'll call you in ten minutes," Drake promised.

Ramirez was changing the lure on a deep sea trolling rod in the companionway when Drake came in from the cockpit.

"Rammer, we might have a change of plan," he said. "Danny's sister wants to help us eavesdrop at Ying's villa tonight. He's hosting a going away dinner for Xueping."

Ramirez came up the steps from the companionway to the salon and asked, "How is she planning on doing that?"

"Morales says we can use an app to activate the microphone on her iPhone and record conversations."

"Is Danny okay with that?"

"Danny is the one who told Marco she was offering to do it."

"Man, I don't know. She's an innocent. She shouldn't get involved in what her brother and our friends are doing. We've all seen combat duty. She's still in school."

"I know. It's putting her in harm's way. But it might be the only way we find out what Xueping is up to."

"If she does this, we need to have a way to get her out of there if she's in trouble."

"That might be difficult," Drake said. "There were bodyguards at the villa when we were up on the hillside. Xueping added up his security when he found I was in Mexico. He'll have more security this time."

"Let me work on that. Who's going to coach Juanita if she's going in?"

"I'll meet her and go over the plan with her and Danny."

"I don't like this, Major."

"I don't either, Rammer, but it's an opportunity we won't have again to get someone close to Xueping."

Chapter Forty-Six

RAMIREZ EASED *Tier One* into the slip Danny Vasquez was standing next to at the Marina La Paz and shut off the engines.

"I paid for one night," Vasquez said. "I figured you wouldn't be here longer than that."

"Thanks, Danny," Drake said as he got off the yacht. "Is Juanita here?"

"She's at the dive shop with Morales and Norris," Vasquez told Drake as he helped Ramirez tie up. "Are you coming with us?"

"I want to meet your sister," Drake said. "She's doing this to help me."

"Juanita's doing this to help all of us, Major. She's been asking for a chance for years."

"She's a brave woman."

"You have no idea. She wants to join the army as soon as she turns eighteen."

Ramirez joined them and handed Drake his hat and sunglasses. "No need to end this party before it gets started. The cartel has eyes everywhere."

"Thanks for reminding me," Drake said, and fell in behind Ramirez and Vasquez. "Lead the way."

They didn't pass anyone who gave them a second look on the short walk to Danny's Dive Shop in the hot afternoon sun.

"Siesta time?" Drake asked.

"A lot of the shops close between one and four o'clock," Vasquez said, "But I stay open. When customers come to return the gear they rented, they expect the shop to be open."

"Keep your head down, Major," Ramirez said. "Soldiers across the street, nine o'clock on the next block."

Drake looked without turning his head and saw two Mexican army soldiers walking side by side with assault rifles slung across their chests.

"Are they looking for me?"

"They walk along the waterfront twice a day to remind the tourists this isn't the U.S.," Vasquez said. "Assault rifles on the streets of La Paz aren't necessary, but they keep things quiet around here."

Danny's Dive Shop didn't have customers when they got there, and Danny led them back to the storeroom where Juanita, Morales, and Norris were waiting for them.

Juanita Vasquez lit up when she saw Drake was there. "Senor Drake, my brother has told me much about you. I am honored to meet you."

"The honor is mine, Juanita," Drake said, and went to shake the pretty young woman's hand.

She had another idea and gave him a big hug. "Thank you for allowing me to help."

When she stepped back, Drake asked her if she understood what they were asking her to do.

"Si, senor. They ignore me. It will be easy to hide my phone so you can hear what they are saying."

"Where do you think you'll be able to hide your phone?"

"Senor Ying likes to be outside on the veranda. There are big planters where I could hide it."

"What if he stays inside with his guests?"

"That would be when he invites his guests to come inside for dinner," she said. "That will be harder, but I'll find a place."

"Juanita, if you feel you're in trouble and need to get out of there, we'll be close by," Drake told her. "Think of something you could say to tell us to come get you."

She closed her eyes for a moment and smiled. "If they find the phone and ask me if it's mine, I could say, No way! My brother bought me a new iPhone. That's an old one."

"Is your phone an old iPhone?"

"Si senor. It is now, but it won't be for long, right brother?" Juanita asked.

The men laughed and looked at Danny.

"Looks like you're buying your sister a new phone, amigo," Morales said. "She has to believe it to be convincing."

"I just bought her a new Moped scooter so she could get to work," Vasquez protested. "A new iPhone will cost me more than the Moped did!"

"War is expensive. We knew taking on the cartels was going to cost us," Ramirez reminded him and grinned.

"Not in this way," Vasquez said.

"Danny, do you have friends who can help us pull her out if she asks for help?" Drake asked.

"Yes."

"Juanita, what time are Ying's guests arriving?" Vasquez asked.

"I have to be there by six o'clock, an hour before they get there."

"Sunset is a little after seven o'clock," Vasquez said. "When it's dark, we can get down to the back wall of the gated community. Ying's villa backs up to the wall."

"Sounds like you've already thought about this," Drake said.

"As soon as she started working there."

"Ying and his friends will have armed bodyguards. Will we have the firepower to deal with them if we have to?"

"We all belong to the same hunting club and have weapons,

Major," Vasquez said. "We know how to use them. I know Pete has weapons on the boat you can use."

"One last thing before we get out of here," Drake said. "How will we get Juanita away from the villa and where will you take her? Ying will know where the two of you live."

"But he doesn't know where our friends live. We'll have our cars and trucks nearby. Getting away won't be a problem. Who will listen to what Juanita's phone is picking up?"

"Rammer will listen with a laptop," Drake said. 'I'm not sure where he plans on being."

"Marina Palmira is the closest to Ying's villa, but he'll have men guarding his yacht," Ramirez said. "I'd suggest staying out on the water, somewhere close to Marina Palmira. As a last resort, I can be there to get everyone away by boat."

"That's it then," Drake said, and put his hand on Juanita's shoulder. "You are more important than anything we might learn tonight, so be careful. I know you're brave, but these are dangerous men. If you feel you're in any danger, remember the signal No way, all right?"

"I won't forget, senor Drake. My new iPhone will help me remember."

Chapter Forty-Seven

RAMON YING STOOD in front of his villa's massive carved mahogany front door to welcome his guests.

Sam Xueping's four bodyguards got out first and stood at the four corners of a white stretch limousine rented for the occasion. Then Xueping got out, followed by Francis Zheng and two beautiful women wearing matching silver lame mini dresses and red stiletto heels.

"Welcome, my friends," Ying said as he greeted each man and shook their hands. The women followed the men inside, without making eye contact with Ying as they passed by.

His young maid was standing in the foyer with champagne flutes held out on a platter for each of the guests.

Ying waited for the bodyguards to enter the villa before he closed the door and joined his guests in the great room, where plates of tapas and fresh fruit were set out for them on the bar.

"Please, help yourselves to some fruit and tapas," he said to the two women as he waved toward the bar, "While I take the men to my study for a moment."

Ying walked to the door of his study on the other side of the great room and held it open for Xueping and Zheng to enter.

"I can see by the look on your face that you're about to rob me of my appetite for the evening," Xueping said.

"Forgive me for choosing to deal with this first," Ying said. "I thought you would want to know that two men were snooping around in my warehouse this morning."

"Do you know who they were?" Xueping asked.

"I have the feed from the warehouse on my laptop, but you will know who it was. It's the attorney you've been looking for."

"How could he know about your warehouse?" Zheng asked.

"I don't know."

Xeuping looked around the study and asked, "Is it safe to talk in your villa, Ramon?"

"Probably safer than on your yacht, I think. I have it swept for bugs once a week and they swept it today for our dinner tonight. I built the villa with six-inch thick cement walls, with plaster on the interior walls and stucco on the exterior walls. All the doors are solid wood and the roof tiles are made of cement. No Wi-Fi or cell phone signals will escape or penetrate this villa."

"What about your staff?" Zheng asked. "Do you let them in the villa with devices that can record things?"

"I collect their cell phones when they enter the villa and return them when they leave. I don't talk business when any of them are around."

"You did yesterday when we were here," Xueping said. "That young maid was on the veranda when we were talking."

"I don't think she overheard anything you should be concerned about, Sam," Ying said. "She's young and wouldn't understand, even if she heard something."

"Yes, she is young and also exquisite, just as I like them," Zheng said. "Perhaps I can borrow her for a while before I leave tonight."

"Take her with you," Ying said. "Just bring her back before you sail away with Sam."

"Do we know where this attorney is now?" Xueping asked.

"General Martín hasn't found him," Ying said.

"My men haven't seen him, either," Zheng said. "Until you told me he was in your warehouse, I thought he was still in Cabo."

"Will we know if he comes here?" Xueping asked.

"Why would he come here?" Ying asked. "He's after you, Sam, not me."

"He came to your warehouse, Ramon. Looks like he has an interest in you as well," Zheng pointed out.

"If he comes here, we'll know about it. Motion detectors cover every inch of the backyard, with buried intrusion sensors to warn my armed guards if anyone tries to get in here."

"If you're wrong and he comes for you, don't kill him," Xueping said. "I want that pleasure."

"Is there anything else?" Zheng said. "The smells from your kitchen are making me hungry, Ramon."

"I hope you'll enjoy a special dinner I had my cook prepare. Shrimp tamales roasted in garlic sauce. Paella with calamari, mussels and chorizo. An avocado, orange and jicama salad and tres leches cake for dessert. We'll finish with Don Julio 1942 tequila and Cohiba Siglo Vll cigars on the veranda."

"Lead the way, Ramon. Let's see if it tastes as good as it smells," Zheng said and opened the door of the study for Ying.

The dining room was separated from the kitchen by three floor-to-ceiling panels of glass etched with images of Aztec warriors. A long black ebony table adorned with a red, orange and green tropical floral centerpiece was set with pewter plates, silverware and crystal wine glasses.

Ying took his seat at the head of the table and nodded to the young maid, who Francis Zheng was admiring, standing at the end of the etched glass panels, to pour wine for his guests.

When their glasses were full, Ying raised his and said, "Here's to success and the sweet taste of victory."

"To victory," Xueping and Zheng repeated.

Ying nodded again to the young maid to bring out the first course. She returned moments later with an older woman, each carrying plates of steaming tamales. They showed his guests how to peel back one end of the banana leaf wrapper to eat the tamale.

"It's like undressing a beautiful woman to savor her sweetness," Ying grinned, as he noticed his young maid blushing as she returned to the kitchen.

When she couldn't hear him, he pointed his fork at Zheng and said, "She blushes like a virgin, Francis."

"Then this will be a special night, Ramon."

Chapter Forty-Eight

WHEN THE SPOTTER on the hillside above the villa reported Ying's guests arriving in a limousine, Drake called Ramirez a second time. His first call had been after Juanita entered the villa at six o'clock to see if her iPhone was activated.

It wasn't.

An anxious hour later, Ramirez still wasn't receiving anything from the villa.

"What do you think, Rammer?" Drake asked.

"I've been going over all the reasons I could think of to explain why I'm not getting anything. They could have taken her phone when she got there. She didn't say it was something they'd done before, but they could have this time."

"It's possible that Ying made sure the villa was built with materials that block the emission of cell phone and Wi-Fi signals," Drake said.

"It's also possible, Major, that she messed up and got caught," Ramirez said.

"If she did, we need to get her out of there."

"But if she didn't mess up and we go in, she'll be in the middle of it," Ramirez said. "Those bodyguards won't let us walk in and walk her out without putting up a fight."

"I know. Let me talk with Danny and see what he thinks we should do."

Drake walked back to the group of men standing behind a stand of Chain Link Cholla and brush and called Danny aside.

"Ying's guests have been in his villa for over an hour and Rammer's not receiving anything," Drake said. "It's possible they took her phone, or the villa itself blocks cell phone signals, or she hasn't been able to hide her phone. It's also possible, Danny, they discovered what she was trying to do."

"But it's also possible her phone didn't work as a microphone, for some reason," Vasquez argued.

"Are you okay with waiting to see what happens?"

Vasquez closed his eyes and rubbed them with his hand before saying, "No, but I don't think we have a choice. If Ying was careful enough to build his villa to block cell phone signals, he'll have motion sensors installed. Some villas in this neighborhood do. A friend of mine installed a lot of them. If we go in, people will die. I don't want her to be one of them."

"It's your call, Danny."

Drake walked away when his phone vibrated in his pocket.

"Senor Drake, the men are moving out to the veranda," the spotter on the hillside reported. "Juanita is bringing a bottle of tequila out to them."

"Is she staying out on the veranda?"

"She's not staying to pour their tequila. She's going back inside."

"Thanks Mateo. We can't see over the wall in back. Does Ying still have anyone back there?"

"The two men who were there before are standing at the back of the veranda behind Ying and the other two."

"If you get a good look at their faces, use the telephoto lens on the camera you brought and take some photos of the third man. We still need to know who he is."

"Roger that."

Drake turned around and studied the men standing around Danny Vasquez. For volunteers willing to take on the cartels and a corrupt Mexican army, they were well-organized and well-equipped. They were fighting men with combat experience, committed to a secret war they were willing to fight.

He didn't know how they trained or where they got their equipment, but he was confident they were prepared for whatever happened that night.

Each man wore body armor over a long sleeve black tactical shirt, jeans, black caps and hunting boots. They carried Sig Sauer P320 pistols with threaded barrels and suppressors, with sheathed long blade knives on their belts. They even brought two Armadillo collapsible tactical ladders to scale the back wall of the villa.

Drake, Morales and Norris stood out, wearing jeans, borrowed black T-shirts and trainers, but they'd been given body armor and P320 pistols.

He wasn't as concerned about getting into the villa with the men Vasquez had organized, as he was concerned about getting out of the villa with Juanita, and out of La Paz and Mexico without being caught.

Vasquez saw him looking his way and walked up the hillside.

"Mateo saw Juanita come out onto the veranda a few minutes ago and go back inside," Drake said. "It looks like Juanita's okay."

"Gracias, Major. What do we do now?"

"We wait to see if she leaves on her Moped and then we call it a night," Drake said. "It was worth a try. This is quite a band of brothers you've put together, Danny. I'm impressed."

"We've been lucky so far, and yes, we are a band of brothers. The cartels have made our lives miserable, but one day that will change with God's blessing and help from friends like you."

"What kind of help do you need most from friends like me?"

"Mostly equipment, like the little drone Ramirez told me Morales used at the warehouse. With one of those, we could really hurt the cartels."

"I imagine you could, Danny. They're expensive, but I'll see what I can do."

Drake's phone vibrated again.

"Major, the bodyguards are in the villa's carport standing in front of a black Mercedes S500," Mateo said. "It looks like someone's getting ready to leave."

Chapter Forty-Nine

THEY WAITED another twenty minutes after two older women left the villa for Juanita to leave, but they didn't see her leave on her Moped. Drake knew that Danny Vasquez was probably right when he said his sister was in trouble.

The back wall of the villa was the same wall that surrounded the gated community. It was made of stone, adobe, and concrete, with security defense spikes on top.

Drake watched as Vasquez and his men erected a collapsible ladder on both ends of the wall at the edge of the villa's back yard. The first man in line at each ladder held a heavy blue moving pad to throw over the spikes on top of the all.

Juanita had given her brother a sketch of the interior of the villa that included two entrances to the villa that she knew about. One was through the sliding doors at the back of the veranda. The other was an exterior door into a storage room and cooler at the back of the carport, where perishable meats and vegetables were kept.

Vasquez and the seven men he recruited for the night were standing at the bottom of the ladders, four men at each ladder.

Drake was standing in line behind Vasquez, and Morales and Norris were in line at the other ladder.

When Vasquez gave the signal, the first man at each ladder climbed to the top and spread the moving pad over the spikes. As soon as the pad was in place, he climbed over the wall, dropped to the ground and stood aside with his back to the wall. In less than a minute, the men at each ladder were over the wall. The last man had pulled the ladder up and dropped it over the other side for exfil back over the wall.

Drake dropped to the ground beside Vasquez and looked to his right at Morales and Norris and waved them over. They'd climbed separate ladders to shorten the time to get over the wall, but Drake wanted Morales and Norris at his side when they engaged Ying's bodyguards.

Vasquez moved to the front of the line of his three men and sprinted across the yard to the corner of the wall. When they were stacked up behind him, he took a quick look across the veranda.

The familiar sound of 5.56mm rounds being fired shattered the stillness of the night, as stucco exploded on the wall where Vasquez's head had poked around.

"They won't make it across the veranda from where they are," Drake whispered to Morales. "Cover me when I run to that half wall that borders the swimming pool."

Morales tapped Drake's shoulder and moved out to give him cover, firing four silenced rounds across the veranda at the open sliding door.

Drake ran across the black cinder rock border of the landscaped yard and crouched behind the stone half-wall bordering the swimming pool. As he ran, he saw two bodyguards stepping to the side of the open sliding door in the middle of a floor-to-ceiling expanse of glass at the back of the veranda. Given their choice of cover, he knew the glass had to be bulletproof.

He signaled there were two tangos and hold position. There hadn't been gunfire coming from the other side of the villa, giving the men from the other ladder time to get inside from the carport and flank the two bodyguards.

Drake fired two rounds at the open sliding door and ducked back down. Morales understood what he was doing and fired again from his position to keep the bodyguards focused on their position.

Shots were fired from inside the villa and moments later, someone called out, "Tangos down!"

Drake followed Vasquez and his men across the veranda and stepped inside the sliding door. Two men were on the floor with their assault rifles kicked away from their bodies.

Vasquez moved on to search the villa for Juanita and shouting soon erupted from the second floor.

"Where's Juanita, Ying?!" Vasquez shouted.

"You're a dead man! Get out of my house!"

"Is she in there with you?"

"Is who in here with me?"

"My sister, Ying!"

"No one is here with me."

"Then you're going to die alone, Ying. There's no way for you to escape."

"If I tell you where she is, will you leave?"

Drake ran up the stairs and saw Vasquez motion for two of his men to move to the other side of the door. He raised his hand and help up one finger, then two fingers. When he raised the third finger, the larger of the two men kicked the door in and stepped aside to let Vasquez enter the room.

Two shots rang out from inside the room and Drake moved to the door. Ying was on his back on the floor and Vasquez was pummeling his face.

"Tell me where she is, dammit!"

Drake saw one man was down on one knee.

"You okay?" he asked the man.

"One shot hit me, one missed," the man said. "Just had the wind knocked out of me. Glad I had the vest on."

Vasquez had stopped beating Ying and had the barrel of his pistol jammed in Ying's mouth. "I will not ask again."

"Danny, there are other ways to get him to talk," Drake said. "Get him up on his bed and lend me your knife."

Vasquez and the man with his pistol pointed at Ying's head, grabbed Ying's arms and stood him up.

Ying looked at the long blade of the Ka-Bar knife in Drake's hand and said, "That won't make me talk."

"Maybe it will, maybe it won't. Either way, I'll know the truth when I'm finished. Take off his clothes," Drake directed.

Ying struggled while he was being stripped and hissed between his teeth, "What is it you expect me to say? I don't know where she is."

"You mean the young woman you don't know?" Drake asked. "Hold him down. This won't take long."

"What do you think you're going to do, castrate me?"

"That depends on what you tell me," Drake said. "If you tell me where his sister is, I won't. If you don't, I'll let him do it."

Ying shook his head. "You're too late. They took her and I don't know where she is."

"Who took her?" Drake asked. "Xueping?"

Ying glared at Drake. "You don't know who you're dealing with, do you? It's not Xueping. She might be on his yacht, but Zheng took her. Even if you find her, you won't want her back."

"Who's Zheng?" Drake asked Vasquez.

"Francis Zheng is the head of the Los Zheng cartel," Vasquez said softly. "He deals in sex trafficking, narcotics, prostitution, gambling and anything else he can make money doing."

Chapter Fifty

DRAKE PULLED Vasquez aside and walked with him to a corner of Ying's bedroom.

"What will you do with Ying?" Drake asked.

"We'll clean up here and take the trash out. That will include Ying."

"Danny, I'll get your sister back. I have resources and I'll find Xueping and Zheng. But I need you to get Ying to tell us what Xueping is planning. I don't care what you decide to do with him after that."

"I can't stay here and do nothing! She's my sister!"

"You have people here to protect, Danny. When they find out Ying is missing, all hell will break loose. If Juanita is on Xueping's yacht, he's not going to hang around La Paz for long. We can follow him on Rammer's boat. We've hacked into his navigation system. We'll know where he's going."

"What will you do when you catch up with him? You'll be a sitting duck in the water. He'll start shooting as soon as you get close to him."

"We'll think of something. Dan Norris is a former FBI Hostage Rescue Team commander, and he's done this before.

Morales and I have experience as well. If he's headed to America, I'll have the FBI waiting for him when he gets there."

"What if he's not headed north?"

"I have friends south of here as well. We'll get Juanita back, Danny. Trust me. You need to get things cleaned up here and we need to go after Xueping."

Drake held out his hand and waited for Vasquez to shake it.

Vasquez locked eyes with Drake and finally shook his hand. "I'm trusting you, Major. Don't let me down."

"I won't Danny."

Vasquez nodded and told his men to take Ying downstairs. They needed to clean up and leave.

Drake followed the men down the stairs, with Ramirez, Morales and Norris behind him, and walked on through the villa to the veranda.

"We're going after Juanita," Drake said. "Rammer, can I charter your boat for another week? We're going to chase down Xueping and get her back."

"The *Top Tier* and her captain are yours for as long as you need us," Ramirez said. "I can always reschedule charters."

"Do we have wheels to get us out of here?" Drake asked.

"The jeep's up on the hillside," Norris said. "There's another Mercedes in the carport, but Vasquez might want it to get Ying out of here."

"The jeep's fine and the ladders are still on the wall. Make sure there's no sign of us being here. Police your brass and wipe clean anything you touched on the way in. Meet at the wall when you're ready to leave. I'll let Danny know we're leaving."

Drake was the last one to get back to the wall, after talking with Danny and picking up his brass, and the last one to climb the ladder and drop the other side.

Morales saw him flinch when he landed and asked, "How are the ribs?"

"Better, but I'd be lying if I said that didn't hurt a little."

"Need a hand to get up the hill?" Morales asked with a teasing grin.

Drake answered by running up the hillside after Norris and Ramirez.

When they reached the marina twenty minutes later, Xueping's superyacht was gone.

"I didn't think he'd hang around," Drake said. "Do we need to gas up, Rammer?"

"I took care of that when we got back from Pichilingue and let the manager know we were leaving. We can shove off whenever you're ready."

"Go check out of the hotel and leave the jeep at the rental agency," Drake told Morales and Norris. "I'll check with Kevin and find out which way Xueping's headed."

Ramirez started the boat's twin diesel engines and kept the lights off in the salon until Morales and Norris returned, while Drake called Kevin McRoberts in Seattle.

"Are you in your office, Kevin?"

"Hi, Mr. Drake. I'm at my condo. Do you need me to go to headquarters?"

"I need you to check on the location of Xueping's yacht."

"I can do that from here. I brought my office laptop home with me. Give me just a minute to check and I'll tell you."

While he waited. Ramirez handed him a beer. "I'm always hungry after a little action. You want anything?"

"Sure, as soon as I find out where we're going."

"Mr. Drake, he's headed south towards Cabo San Lucas," Kevin said.

"I'll be following him on my friend's fishing yacht. When Xueping is down near the tip of Baja California, I need to know if he's headed south to Central America or north up the Baja coast. Watch him for me, Kevin."

"Sure thing, Mr. Drake."

Ramirez had a plate of pulled pork from last night out on the galley counter with bread, condiments, and jalapenos for sandwiches.

"Which way is he headed?" Ramirez asked.

"South toward Cabo."

"I thought he might head for the mainland and drop her off to Zheng's cartel over there," Ramirez said. "She's better off on Xueping's yacht."

"Why?"

"The cartels are rough on their women and the Chinese cartel has a reputation for being even worse," Ramirez said. "Zheng is a sex trafficker. If he's planning on selling Juanita, he'll keep her looking as good as possible. If they handed her over to Zheng's cartel, they won't care what she looks like."

"I'm not sure Vasquez will be comforted knowing that."

"He knows. That's the world we live in."

Drake heard Morales and Norris running down the dock before he saw them.

Morales was the first to reach the yacht. "Time to leave," he said, out of breath. "Soldiers in Humvees are in the marina parking lot."

Chapter Fifty-One

DRAKE SAT beside Ramirez in the flybridge of the convertible Hatteras GT59 the next morning, enjoying the sunrise and a calm, flat sea. He took another sip of coffee from the steaming mug in his hand and smiled.

"I'm jealous of the life you've made for yourself, Rammer."

"Dreaming about mornings like this got me through my last tour. I used to go fishing with my dad every summer when I was in school. I knew this was what I wanted to do some day."

"Why did you join the army?"

"Probably the same reason you did, to fight an enemy."

"Do you want to get some sleep? You've been at the helm since we left La Paz."

"Maybe later. Are Morales and Norris still sleeping?"

"Morales is making breakfast and Norris is showering."

"We should see Xueping's yacht soon," Ramirez said. "What's the plan when we do?"

"I'm working on that," Drake said. "Kate Perkins, the Deputy Director of the FBI, was in a meeting when I called. She's a friend and knows why I've been to Mexico. If Xueping stops in San Diego or Los Angeles, she can coordinate Immigration and

Customs Enforcement to search his yacht for Juanita. If he doesn't stop in either of those ports, the U.S. Coast Guard can board the yacht offshore and search for her."

"What if he stops in Ensenada? That's what I would do if I thought someone was following me?"

"That's the part I haven't worked out. Can we keep him from stopping in Ensenada?"

"There might be a way, but it would be difficult and dangerous. Let me think about it."

Drake got up and crossed the flybridge to the ladder. "I'll see how soon breakfast is ready."

Morales was mashing an avocado when Drake came into the salon.

"It's not fancy, but you'll like it," Morales said. "Scrambled eggs and chorizo, mashed avocado, and tortillas in the warmer."

"Smells great, Marco. I'll take a plate up and spell Rammer for a while. He says we should see Xueping's yacht on the horizon soon."

Drake put two warm tortillas on a plate, filled them with the egg and chorizo scramble, put a scoop of mashed avocado on top, and returned to the flybridge.

"Let me take over for a while," Drake said.

Ramirez stood with one hand on the helm and said, "Hold her at 28 knots to make sure we have gas to reach Turtle Bay."

"Aye, aye Captain. Get some sleep. I have the helm."

Ramirez watched him for a moment, to make sure that he did, and climbed down the ladder.

Drake settled back in the captain's chair, set his plate on the flat space to the right of the helm, and took a bite of the tortilla he'd rolled into a burrito. Morales was right, it was delicious.

He scanned the expanse of blue water ahead and saw there wasn't another vessel insight. But it wouldn't be long, he knew, until he saw Xueping's superyacht. Kevin McRoberts had access to the yacht's navigation system and given them its current heading and location.

The Benetti Oasis 40m was cruising at twelve knots an hour

and had a range of four thousand nautical miles. That was the crux of the matter and the problem they faced. The *Tier One* could cruise at thirty-eight knots, three times as fast as the Benetti, but it could only go halfway up the coast of Baja California without stopping for gas. The Benetti could go to Canada and back without stopping.

There was nothing in the superyacht's navigation system or IT network that identified its destination, however. The best they could do was follow Xueping's yacht closely enough to act, if an opportunity presented itself, and hope for the best.

Thinking about Juanita being on the superyacht with Xueping and Zheng was infuriating. He was the one responsible for letting her be captured by a triad leader and the head of a vicious Chinese cartel.

Dan Norris came up the ladder to the flybridge and held out his sat phone. "You have a call from Kate Perkins."

"Take the helm, Dan, while I talk with her," Drake said, and climbed down the ladder to take the call below.

"Good morning, Kate. Thanks for returning my call."

"Where are you?"

"On a fishing yacht chasing after Sam Xueping's superyacht, in the Pacific Ocean off the coast of Baja California."

"What have you found out?"

"I hope to have something soon."

"But you can't confirm anything?"

"Not right now."

"We're hearing the Mexican army is looking for you. Care to explain why?"

"I can explain part of it," Drake said. "You're better off not knowing all of it. Xueping's looking for me because he doesn't want anyone to know what he's mixed up in."

"That you think he's mixed up in?"

"That I think he's mixed up in. A corrupt army general is providing him protection in Mexico. I think that's how he knew I was in Mexico. I went through customs when I landed in Cabo San Lucas."

"That explains why you're leaving Cabo, but why are you chasing Xueping's yacht?"

"Because a young Mexican woman is missing, a sister of one of the men helping me. I believe she's on the yacht with Xueping and Francis Zheng. Zheng and his cartel are known human traffickers."

"I know about Zheng. His cartel's responsible for most of the illicit fentanyl coming from Mexico. What's the rest of the story you don't want me to know about?"

"Trust me, Kate. I'll tell you everything as soon as I can."

"You called me. I assume there's something you wanted."

"I want you to get ICE and the Coast Guard to intercept Xueping's yacht and rescue the young woman."

Chapter Fifty-Two

BEFORE HE HAD time to replace Norris at the helm, Dan Vasquez called.

"Have you caught up with Xueping's yacht?" Vasquez asked.

"Not yet. Rammer says we should see it soon."

"What will you do when it's in view?"

"There's not much we can do."

"Then think of something! Ying says Xueping gave Zheng my sister to do whatever he wanted with her. You know what that means."

"Calm down Danny. I've asked ICE and the Coast Guard to be prepared to intercept the yacht and rescue her."

"Major, that won't happen until his yacht's in U.S. territorial waters. That won't be for another day or so."

"We'll think of something. What else did Ying tell you?"

"Everything. Xueping supplies the fentanyl precursors for Ying's labs and Zheng distributes the fake pills. Xueping is working with Wang, a Chinese general, to kill as many American men as possible in some "opium war". They're ready to flood America with free illicit pills containing lethal amounts of fentanyl."

"Did Ying say how they're going to flood America with these pills?"

"Xueping has an online marketplace on the DarkNet," Vasquez said. "When a buyer places an order, Zheng's cartel uses the postal service to deliver the pills. They're planning a big promotion where the pills will be free in what they're calling their "first wave"."

"Do you believe Ying when he says China's behind this?"

"Ying says General Wang uses Xueping when he doesn't want something traced back to China. That's all Ying knew. He wasn't holding anything back."

"Anything else I should know?" Drake asked.

"We know about Ying's pill labs and his involvement with the Los Zheng cartel. We're going after the Los Zheng cartel, but we can't do it alone."

"When we get your sister back and stop Xueping, I'll see if we can help with that."

"Just get my sister back, Major. That's all the help I need right now."

"Understood, Danny, and thanks for dealing with Ramon Ying."

Drake sat down to think in one of the fighting chairs in the cockpit.

He was pulled in two directions: If what Ying told Vasquez was reliable, millions of American would suffer from a flood of free and illicit deadly pills; men, their families and friends. If he rescued Juanita Vasquez, as he promised he would, and didn't foil China's opium war, he might save one life at the expense of many other lives that could have been saved.

There had to be a way to do both.

Drake found Ramirez in his stateroom coming out of the shower.

"If Xueping's yacht loses power and is adrift at sea, you're obligated to render assistance, aren't you?" Drake said.

Ramirez wrapped a towel around his waist and frowned. "You are. Why?"

"How would the captain of his superyacht react if we approached and offered assistance?"

"A captain of an expensive yacht like that will be a professional with experience. He'd welcome help unless he thought there was a threat to his ship and crew. Superyachts are becoming targets for pirates these days."

"How would you convince him you weren't a threat?"

"If there was a reason for you being in the area, I'd want a third party I trusted to tell me you aren't a boatload of pirates. Where are you going with this?" Ramirez asked.

"We have access to Xueping's navigational system and onboard networks," Drake said. "If we cause the yacht to lose power and happen to be in the area, say fishing for Marlin, we could offer to help and find a reason to board the ship and rescue Danny's sister."

"That's a dangerous plan, Major. Xueping's bodyguards would keep us at gunpoint the whole time we're onboard, if they let us board at all."

"But it could work. What third party would you trust to make sure another vessel wasn't a threat?"

"I would call the U.S. Coast Guard," Ramirez said. "The Coast Guard's eleventh district covers the waters two hundred miles offshore from the Oregon-California border to the border between Mexico and Guatemala."

Drake smiled and said, "Rammer, we can make this work. I'll find out if the access we have to the yacht's onboard networks will let us shut down the yacht's engines and cause it to drift at sea. I was going to ask the Coast Guard to intercept Xueping's yacht, but we'll do it instead."

"We'll still have to neutralize the bodyguards."

"We'll think of something," Drake said. "I need to make sure the Coast Guard will play along. You think of a way to deal with the bodyguards."

Drake left Ramirez and went to the flybridge to relieve Norris and call Kate Perkins.

Chapter Fifty-Three

PERKINS ANSWERED SO QUICKLY she must have her phone in her hand when he called.

"I hope you have more information than you did last time because the Coast Guard isn't cooperating," Pekins said.

"The information I have comes from a source I trust, but who has to remain anonymous. You'll have to trust me that what I'm telling you is reliable and actionable. Can you do that?"

"Drake, you're asking the Coast Guard to intercept a yacht owned by a Chinese national on the grounds that a victim of human trafficking might be onboard. I have to give them more than you've given me."

"Here's what I've learned," Drake said. "Francis Xueping is working with a Chinese general named Wang to unleash an opium war against America. China supplies the fentanyl precursors to pill labs in Mexico. The Los Zheng cartel will use the postal service to deliver illicit pills containing a lethal amount of fentanyl from a store on the dark web. The first wave of the pills will be offered for free. The plan is to poison and kill as many Americans as possible to demoralize the country, like the British did to China."

Drake waited for Perkins to say something.

"Can we prove any of this?" she asked quietly.

"I'm working on that. There might be evidence on Xueping's yacht. My goal is to save this girl and get the evidence you and the president will need later."

"Can we stop these pills from being delivered?"

"I don't know when they plan to start this, Kate. The only thing I can think of is to take the DarkNet site down as quickly as possible to stop deliveries."

"Who will do it?" she asked.

"You could do it, but I think I can do it faster."

"Why?"

"I have access to the IT networks on Xueping's yacht. We might find the address of the DarkNet site there."

"Have you told the president any of this?"

"Not yet."

"But you told him you were looking into a plot against America?"

"Yes."

He heard her take a deep breath and exhale.

"All right, what do you want the Coast Guard to do?"

"We're going to shut down the yacht's engines and approach to offer assistance," Drake said. "We think the yacht's captain will contact the Coast Guard to make sure we're not pirates. All we need the Coast Guard to do is say we've already contacted them and offered our assistance until they get there. After we've rescued the girl, they can move in and take control of the yacht and its crew."

"Drake, that's the Coast Guard's job! You don't have authority to do that."

"Kate, they'll kill the girl if they think the Coast Guard is on the way. We have a best chance to keep that from happening."

"How soon are you planning to do this?"

"As soon as you talk the Coast Guard into helping us."

"I'll see what I can do. Will you have the yacht's exact location for the Coast Guard?"

"The exact location the yacht's GPS will give us."

"I can't count the ways this can go wrong, Drake."

"I know. I'll take full responsibility if it does."

"That won't save my job, but thanks."

"You're welcome. Call me as soon as the Coast Guard agrees to help."

Drake stood at the helm and scanned the horizon for Xueping's yacht. They had to be getting close and the plan to board the yacht he made sound so simple to Kate Perkins wasn't even on the drawing board yet.

He called PSS headquarters to see what Kevin McRoberts could do to disable the yacht.

"Good morning, Kevin. I have a project for you."

"Fire away, Mr. Drake."

"Can you shut the engines down on Xueping's yacht?"

"I don't know much about yachts, but I'll find someone who does. When do you want me to do it?"

"We have to stop at Turtle Bay for fuel this morning, so sometime this afternoon. Call me when you're ready to do it."

"How long do the engines need to be shut down?"

"Until I tell you to start them up again. I don't need the yacht to be disabled permanently."

"Is there anything else you need me to do?"

"Look for anything on a computer, laptop or phone you can access on the yacht that establishes a connection between Xueping and a Chinese general named Wang. Also, find the DarkNet site Xueping will be using to sell illegitimate synthetic opioids in America. We need to shut it down."

"Right away, Mr. Drake."

"One more thing, Kevin. When we shut down the yacht's engines, I'll need the yacht's exact location."

"No problem. I have access to the yacht's navigation system."

"Thanks, Kevin. I'll let Mike Casey know what you're doing for me."

Ramirez came up the ladder to the flybridge and sat in the helm chair next to Drake.

"I'll take it from here when you're ready, Major. Have you figured out how we're going to get Danny's sister off the yacht?"

Drake told him what he was planning on doing. "Will it work, Rammer?"

Ramirez stroked his beard and smoothed his mustache while he considered the plan.

"If the yacht is drifting without power, having a reason to approach it isn't a problem. The law of the sea requires a master of a vessel to render assistance to a vessel in danger or needing help. The problem is being invited to board it."

"What assistance can we offer the captain or crew they might need that would get us onboard?"

"How will you shut down the engines?" Ramirez asked.

"We have access to the yacht's electrical and IT networks. Kevin is reaching out to someone who can tell us how to do it."

"The Benetti Oasis 40m has two MAN V12 1400 diesel engines," Ramirez said. "I upgraded the engines on this yacht and had two MAN V12 2000 engines installed. I know enough about MAN diesels to fake it and tell the captain I'm a factory-trained MAN engine specialist who could get his engines running again. I'll know what his problem is. It shouldn't be hard to convince him I can help and get invited onboard."

"That gets you on the yacht. What then?"

"That's what you officers are supposed to figure out."

Chapter Fifty-Four

DRAKE LEFT Ramirez at the helm and returned to the galley for another cup of coffee, while he waited for Kevin McRoberts or Kate Perkins to call him back.

Marco Morales set his empty plate on the galley island and reached for the coffeepot behind him. "More coffee?'

Drake held out his cup and asked, "Ready for some action?"

"Where and when?"

"Here at sea and soon. I'm waiting for a couple of calls to give us the go ahead. We're going to pay Xueping a visit on his yacht and rescue Juanita."

"How are we going to that?" Norris asked as he came up the stairs from the companionway below.

"Kevin is going to shut down the engines on Xueping's yacht and, being the good guys that we are, we're going to pull alongside and offer to help."

"How does that get us onboard to search for Danny's sister?" Morales asked.

"This boat has the same engines as Xueping's yacht," Drake said. "Rammer's going to say he's factory-trained to work on these engines and offer to see if he can get them going again. When he takes one of you with him on the yacht, you take over the yacht and we find Juanita."

"Sounds like we might have a way to get on his yacht," Norris said. "But what then? His bodyguards aren't going to roll out a red carpet for us."

Drake shrugged and smiled. "We'll have the element of surprise on our side."

"I'd like to have a little more than an element of surprise going for us," Norris said.

"How about six AR-15's, a Benelli tactical shotgun, an over/under 12 gauge, and a .44 revolver?"

"I'm feeling a little better knowing that, but we're still a little thin on a plan."

"Dan, you're a former FBI HRT commander," Drake said. "You've done this before. I'll leave it to you to come up with a plan?"

His Iridium sat phone buzzed inside its carry bag on his belt, and Drake went out to *Tier One's* cockpit to answer it.

"I know how to turn off the engines on the yacht, Mr. Drake," Kevin McRoberts said.

"That was quick."

"Mr. Casey gave me the name of the salesman trying to sell him a boat. I got the name of a marine service technician from him and he told me, hypothetically, how it could be done. I'm ready to try it whenever you say."

"Do we know this will work?"

"He promised me it will. He's a gamer. I told him I'd show him how to be a winner in the video game tournaments he enters."

"Do you have the location of Xueping's yacht?"

"It's on my screen. Do you need it?"

"Not right now. How far ahead of us is it?"

"It's just passing Turtle Bay."

"We're stopping at Turtle Bay for fuel. Be ready to turn off the yacht's engines between Turtle Bay and Ensenada. I'll call for the yacht's location when we have it dead in the water."

"I'll be ready whenever you call me," McRoberts said.

With that part of his plan ready to implement, Drake called the Deputy Director of the FBI, Kate Perkins.

"Is the Coast Guard willing to help us?" he asked.

"The officers of the Coast Guard's Eleventh District aren't happy about it, but the Coast Guard Cutter Haddock is underway from San Diego. I had to go to the Commandant of the Coast Guard to make this happen."

"I owe you, Kate."

"If this threat proves to be real, the entire country will owe you for following up on this."

"When Xueping's yacht is between Turtle Bay in Baja California and Ensenada, its engines are going to shut down," Drake said. "The fishing yacht I'm on, *Tier One*, is a Hatteras GT59 owned by Pete Ramirez out of Cabo San Lucas. We'll be close to Xueping's yacht when it loses power.

"If the Coast Guard is called to make sure we're not pirates, tell the Coast Guard to clear us. We'll approach, offer assistance, and then rescue the young woman. We'd welcome the Coast Guard to be close enough to back us up if we need help."

"Are you prepared for what's likely to happen?" Perkins asked.

"I have Marco Morales and Dan Norris with me. Pete Ramirez is former Special Forces. We have the best shot at getting Juanita Vasquez, that's the young woman's name, off that yacht alive. We have to try, Kate."

"What will you do with Xueping and Zheng?"

"Turn them over to the Coast Guard and let you handle it from there."

"I'd like them alive when you do."

"We'll do our best."

"Call me when you shut down the yacht's engines and I'll tell the Coast Guard."

"I will."

"Good luck and say hello to Dan for me."

"Sure thing," Drake said.

Dan Norris and Kate Perkins were lovers once, and Drake

wished they still were. Maybe seeing each other when this was over would give them a second chance.

Drake felt *Tier One* change course and head to Turtle Bay to refuel. It was time to check in with Liz and let her know what they were doing.

"Hello, Liz."

"Where are you?"

"Heading into Turtle Bay to refuel," Drake said. "Where are you?"

"I'm in Mike's office. He told me what you're doing."

"I didn't have time to call Liz. I'm sorry you didn't hear it from me."

"Are Xueping and his friend on this yacht?"

"They are, as far as we know. They left La Paz in the middle of the night. Zheng was with him earlier."

"Adam, they've tried to kill you twice. Why can't you let the Coast Guard and the FBI handle this?"

"You talked with Kate Perkins."

"She called me this morning."

"I'm responsible for a young woman being on the yacht with a known human trafficker and the head of a Chinese triad, Liz. If the Coast Guard intercepts that yacht, they'll kill her. I have to try to save her."

"I know, and I love you for it. Please be careful and come home."

"I will, I promise."

Chapter Fifty-Five

RAMIREZ PULLED BACK on the throttle and let the GT59 settle in the water as they made an approach from the west with the sun at their back. Xueping's superyacht was adrift ten miles offshore from San Carlos, Baja California.

Drake stood beside Ramirez on the flybridge, with his binoculars searching for Xueping or Zheng. The only person he saw was a man standing at the rail on the upper deck with binoculars, looking back at him.

"I don't see anyone pointing guns at us," Drake said. "There's one man at the rear of the upper deck watching us."

"The Benetti Oasis 40m accommodates nineteen, including guests and crew," Ramirez said. "We should see Xueping's bodyguards visible somewhere. Security can't be this lax."

"Unless they're luring us in to get us closer."

"We'll know soon enough. I'll use a bullhorn when we're fifty yards away."

Morales and Norris were below, hidden behind the tinted windows in the salon, holding AR-15s. When Ramirez offered to help get the yacht's engines running and was invited onboard, the plan was to take whatever opportunity presented itself to take control of the superyacht.

Drake was staying on the flybridge to call the play and locate the bodyguards or crew resisting the takeover. Ramirez's tactical shotgun gave him the firepower to control the initial encounter until Morales and Norris were in position out in the cockpit. It wasn't much of a plan, but their combined skills and experience, plus the element of surprise, gave them confidence they would succeed.

That, and a shared understanding that failing to rescue Danny's sister was unacceptable.

Ramirez shifted into neutral and let his fishing yacht drift closer to the superyacht. When he was close enough to it to be heard, he stood and raised the bullhorn to his mouth.

"Ahoy, Benetti Oasis. Do you need assistance?" Ramirez called out. "I didn't hear a distress call, but I see you are adrift."

A tall man wearing a white short-sleeve shirt with four gold bars on its shoulder epaulets came out onto the rear of the upper deck with a bullhorn. "We lost power and we're working on the engines, but we're not in distress. Thank you for stopping by."

"Are your engines MAN V12 diesels?" Ramirez asked.

"They are," the captain responded.

"My engines are MAN V12s and I'm factory-trained to work on them. I can look at yours, if you'd like."

"I'm sure we'll get them running soon, but thanks for offering help."

"How long have you been without power?" Ramirez asked as they drifted closer to the superyacht.

"Two hours," the captain said.

Drake saw a member of the crew wearing a white T-shirt with a logo on it and shorts walk out and say something to the captain.

After a brief exchange between the two men, the captain raised his bullhorn and said, "*Tier One*, if you have time, you are welcome to come aboard and render assistance."

Ramirez waved to the captain and shifted out of neutral to move alongside the super yacht. "He called the Coast Guard to check us out. He can't see the name *Tier One*. It's only on the stern."

Two men dressed like the man who spoke to the captain walked out onto the open-air stern of the superyacht and dropped black fenders over the stern to let *Tier One* come alongside.

"Take Morales with you," Drake told Ramirez. "He has a friendlier face than Norris. When he locates the bodyguards, send him back to get your tools while you're looking at the engines. We'll follow Morales and round up the bodyguards and crew."

"I hope it's that easy," Ramirez said.

"It might be, Rammer. I don't see any of his bodyguards."

"His crew might be just as dangerous. Be careful. I don't want to be stranded down below if you don't pull this off."

"If they don't find that revolver under your guayabera, you'll be fine."

Ramirez gently pulled up to the stern of the superyacht and saw a Chinese symbol above the words "*Hong Kong*" where you would expect the name of a yacht to be displayed. As he caught the line a crewman tossed him to tie off to the superyacht, he asked what the Chinese symbol meant.

"It's the name of the yacht, *Black Dragon*," the man said.

After *Tier One* was tied off, Ramirez hopped aboard and walked behind the crewman on the open-air stern to the main deck where the captain was waiting for him.

Ramirez held out his hand and said, "Peter Ramirez out of Cabo San Lucas, captain."

"Captain McNally, Mr. Ramirez. You're a long way from Cabo San Lucas."

"I have an old client in San Diego who wants to make the run down the coast for a tournament next week. He pays well. I couldn't turn him down."

"What engines did you say you have on your boat?"

"MAN v12 2000's."

"I thought the Hatteras ran Cat diesels."

"I had mine fitted with the V12 2000s. I like to get out ahead of the tournament competition. The MAN V12s let me do that."

"Then come along and have a look at my engines." The captain said as he walked away.

"Do you mind if my first mate comes along, in case I need any of my tools?" Ramirez asked.

The captain stopped and turned back to Ramirez. "Can't you bring what you'll need with you?"

"There are too many, and I won't know what I'll need until I have a look at your engines."

"Call your man and hurry along," Captain McNally said. "I need to be in San Diego by first light tomorrow."

Drake watched Ramirez walk back to the stern of the superyacht and call for Morales. While he waited for his first mate to join him, he gave Drake a thumbs up.

When Ramirez and Morales disappeared inside the main deck of Xueping's superyacht, Drake climbed down to join Norris in *Tier One's* salon.

"Did you see anyone else, other than the two who dropped the lines to Rammer?" Norris asked.

"From the flybridge, I have a better view of the upper deck than you do, but all I saw was the Captain and the two guys at the stern."

"This doesn't feel right," Norris said.

"We'll wait until Morales comes back before we go with Plan B."

"If Marco comes back. And what's Plan B?"

"That's what you were supposed to figure out."

Chapter Fifty-Six

MARCO MORALES WALKED QUICKLY across the open air-lounge at the stern of Xuiping's superyacht and jumped down into the cockpit of *Tier One*. As he opened the door into the salon, he saw out of the corner of his eye that one crewman had followed him. The man stood just inside the main lounge in the shadows.

"There are two crewmen down in the engine room with the captain and Rammer. Two women were in the galley just beyond the main lounge. The captain said the owner and a friend left the yacht to go fishing. One man is in the main lounge and followed me back here. He's standing at the top of the stairs to the open-air lounge."

"That leaves four I can't account for, if Rammer's right, that there's a crew of nine. I didn't see any bodyguards, but the tender's missing from its garage just forward of the engine room,"

"Do you think the rest of the crew and any of Xueping's bodyguards are down below?" Drake asked.

"I didn't have time to the check the owner's home on the main deck or the VIP homes on the lower deck. I don't know if anyone's up on the sun deck," Morales said.

"I didn't see anyone on the sundeck," Drake said. "Can you get us past the guy watching you?"

"No problem," Morales said. "What's the plan?"

"Dan likes Plan B. You take out the guy watching you, then you and Rammer take control of the engine room. Dan and I will make sure there's no one in the owner's home on the main deck, then we find our way down to the VIP homes and crew quarters on the lower deck and look for Juanita."

"Use of force?" Morales asked.

"Nonlethal, unless you have to defend yourself," Drake said.

"Marco, do you think the crew is triad, like the bodyguards?" Norris asked.

"The ones I've seen aren't Chinese and covered in tattoos," Morales said. "I don't have much to go on, but my sense is they're just crew Xueping hired for his yacht."

"You'd better get back," Drake said. "What tools did Rammer say he needed?"

"A multimeter and an adjustable inspection mirror, things I'd recognize."

Morales went below to get the tools for Ramirez and Drake exchanged the tactical shotgun for the AR-15 short barrel rifle like Norris was holding.

"I wonder how Ramirez got the Mexican government let him keep these close-quarter battle weapons," Norris said.

"He didn't ask permission, is my guess," Drake said.

Morales came back with the tools and asked, "You ready?"

"How will we know when you've taken out the watcher?" Norris asked Morales.

"Give me two minutes before you come on board. If you don't see that he's down in the main salon, you'll know I screwed up and we're not surprising them."

"Good luck, Marco," Drake said, patting his back and sending him on his way.

Drake and Norris waited two minutes before they slipped out of *Tier One's* salon and jumped onto the swim platform of the superyacht. They sprinted across the open-air lounge to the rear of the main deck.

The crewman who'd been watching Morales was facedown at the top of the stairs up to the main deck.

The main lounge was empty when Drake and Norris ran past the main dining area and stopped to check the galley. Both women were busy with their backs turned, talking and preparing the evening meal.

Drake motioned Norris forward to check the owner's suite and stood at the top of the main stairwell to make sure no one was coming up from the lower deck.

"Clear," Norris said when he returned.

The diagram they found online for the Benetti Oasis 40m showed a lobby at the bottom of the stairwell and four VIP staterooms, two port side and two starboard side. Beyond the VIP staterooms were four Bunk-bed crew homes, a crew mess, two bathrooms and a laundry.

Drake led the way down the stairs and moved to the left side of the corridor that divided the four homes. Norris followed and moved to the right side of the corridor.

With a nod from Drake, both men moved to the doors of the first two VIP staterooms with their short-barreled AR-15s held muzzle up.

Drake opened the door of the first stateroom and stepped inside. It was empty, and the double bed was made. He stepped back out in the corridor and mouthed "Clear".

Norris opened the door of the stateroom on his side of the corridor, looked inside, and closed the door. It was also empty.

Drake moved down the corridor to the next stateroom on his side and held his right fist up. Laughter was coming from inside. He cupped left hand and held it up beside his left ear. Then he held up two fingers for two voices.

Norris moved to the next door on his side and signaled that he was ready.

Drake pointed to himself and his door, then to Norris and his door, and raised three fingers. When Norris nodded, he signaled two, then one, and both men opened their stateroom doors.

Two large bodyguards were sitting in the stateroom Drake entered, sitting at the foot of a double bed watching TV and laughing. The man closest to the door turned when the door opened. When he saw Drake, he lunged toward a Glock 17 on a mahogany nightstand at the head of the bed.

"Don't," Drake said.

The bodyguard shouted something in Chinese and slid across the bed onto the floor.

The other bodyguard stood and glared at Drake as he reached a hand back toward a wooden-handled meat cleaver on a dresser beside the bed.

Norris ran into the room with his rifle pointed at the man's head. "Stop," he shouted.

Chapter Fifty-Seven

"GET ON THE FLOOR, both of you," Drake ordered, keeping his rifle trained on the bodyguard closest to him.

When both men were on the floor lying face down, Norris collected the Glock and cleaver and moved back to stand beside Drake.

"Shoot them if they move," he told Norris loudly enough for both men to hear him. "I'll go get some duct tape from the engine room and send Ramirez back to help you make sure these two will not be a problem."

Norris smiled and said, "Shooting them would be easier."

Drake winked and said, "That's up to you and Rammer when he gets here. I don't care either way."

"Roger that."

Drake left the VIP home and took the stairs up to the main floor, checked to make sure the women were still busy in the galley, and walked across the open-air lounge to the port side stairs down to the engine room.

The captain and two of his crew were sitting on the floor on the far side of the engine room when Drake got there. Ramirez was holding his Raging Hunter revolver loosely in his hand, talking with Morales.

"What have you told the captain?" Drake asked Ramirez.

"I told him we're not pirates, and no one would get hurt if he cooperated."

"Find some duct tape and go help Norris. He has two bodyguards on the floor in the first VIP home at the bottom of the main stairwell. When the bodyguards won't be a problem, start looking for Juanita."

"Roger that," Ramirez said.

"The duct tape is in that cabinet," the captain pointed and said.

When Ramirez found the duct tape and left, Drake walked over to the captain and reached down to shake his hand.

"Captain, my name is Adam Drake. You may or may not know why we're here. I'll explain. Mr. Xueping and his friend, Mr. Zheng, are human traffickers, among other criminal endeavors. They have a young woman onboard they intend to sell as a sex slave. Do you know where the young woman is?"

"I know nothing about that."

"You might not, but you're complicit in the crime, nevertheless. The Coast Guard will be here soon, and your cooperation will make things easier for you."

"The owner brings many women onboard. I don't keep track of all of them."

"If the young woman is here, where would he hide her?"

"I don't enter the owner's stateroom or the VIP staterooms. It could be any of them."

"Do you know who the owner of this yacht is?" Drake asked.

"Of course, he's a real estate billionaire from Hong Kong. He owns hotels and casinos."

"He's also a Chinese triad boss involved in a terrorist plot against America. That makes him and anyone helping him subject to the United States Patriot Act of 2001. If you know anything about what he's planning, now would be the time to tell me before the Coast Guard gets here."

A worried look on the captain's face told Drake he knew more about Xueping than he was admitting.

"Mr. Xueping charters this yacht to the rich and famous who can afford it," the captain said. "If any of them are involved in terrorism, I wouldn't know about it. I only see Mr. Xueping when he's on his yacht. I know nothing about what he does when he's not onboard."

"Other than human trafficking, you mean? Is there anything else he does when he's here you want to tell me about?"

The captain shook his head. "The only thing I'm not sure about is the two young men he insisted I add to my crew when we left San Diego. They stay in their rooms. The only time I see them is when they're eating in the crew mess."

"What do you think they're here for?"

"They're a couple of computer geeks. I do not know."

Drake was thinking about what else he should ask the captain about when Ramirez ran into the engine room.

"We found her! They locked her in one of the VIP staterooms. She's traumatized by what she thought was going to happen to her, but other than that, she's okay. Norris is with her up on the main deck."

"Thank God she's okay," Drake said. "How close is the Coast Guard?"

"I'll go call them," Ramirez said and left.

"Marco, why don't you go get the duct tape Rammer borrowed and let's make sure these three aren't going anywhere. I want to call Kate Perkins as soon as possible. She needs to know we have Juanita and that Xueping and Zheng aren't here."

"Be right back," Morales said.

"Captain, when did Xueping and Zheng leave?" Drake asked.

"Several hours ago. They left in the Zodiac tender with two of their bodyguards. Said they were going fishing"

"Do you know where they would have gone ashore?"

"Mr. Xueping said they were going to Don Eddie's fishing village."

Chapter Fifty-Eight

WHILE THEY WAITED for the Coast Guard to arrive, Drake met with Juanita and learned she was unharmed and handling her abduction better than expected, given her young age. When she told Zheng she was a virgin, they had left her alone to preserve her value in the sex slave market.

Drake left the superyacht's crew and the two bodyguards under the watch of Morales and Norris and returned to the *Tier One* to call Kevin McRoberts at PSS headquarters.

"Great job shutting down the engines, Kevin. We have Juanita, but Xueping and Zheng left the yacht in a tender before we got here. Can you track Xueping or Zheng with the phones they're using?"

"I should be able to, if they're using any of the phones that accessed the yacht's IT network. Are Xueping and Zheng the only ones who aren't on the yacht?"

"They left with two of the bodyguards."

"If the crew and the other bodyguards stay on Xueping's yacht, I'll track the phones that are left," McRoberts said. "Did you secure the laptops or computers they were using for the dark web?"

"We have the crew and two bodyguards sequestered in the crew mess, but we didn't take the laptops they were using in their home."

"I found their DarkNet site. It would help me if you could take those laptops with you."

"I'll get them before the Coast Guard arrives," Drake said. "Did you find out if Xueping was in contact with a Chinese general?"

"He uses an encrypted sat phone, but I was able to ID the communication satellite he used. The Union of Concerned Scientists' database says it's owned by a private Chinese company, but that's all I could find out."

"Maybe Kate Perkins can find out for us," Drake said. "The best thing we can do is to shut down the DarkNet site and keep it from selling deadly counterfeit pills."

"I'm on it, Mr. Drake."

"Let me know where Xueping and Zheng are headed. They must have left the yacht when they found Ramon Ying was missing. They'll probably use one of Zheng's smuggling routes, so tracking their phones is the only way we have to find them."

"Understood, Mr. Drake."

"Thanks Kevin. I'll get the laptops to you as soon as I can."

Drake found Morales in the crew mess and sent him to take the laptops to *Tier One* before returning to the main salon to call Kate Perkins.

"Do you have the girl?" she asked.

"Yes, she's okay. When she told Zheng she was a virgin, they left her alone."

"Smart girl. Any casualties?"

"Not one," Drake said. "The captain and crew didn't put up a fight, and we surprised the two bodyguards in their stateroom but Xueping and Zheng got away. They left the yacht in a tender two hours before we shut down the engines."

"Are they in Mexico?"

"Unknown. They put ashore in Baja California. We're trying to track them with the phones we hope they're using."

"I'll have arrest warrants issued," Perkins said. "Maybe we'll get lucky."

"If they're moving on one of the smuggling routes Zheng uses, it won't be luck that helps us find them. Do we know where Zheng's base of operations is located?"

"It has been Vancouver, B.C. I'll see if the DEA or Canada have anything more current. Where will you be?"

"As soon as we finish with the Coast Guard, we'll see if we can pick up their trail. They told the captain about a fishing center on the coast. We'll start there."

"Let me know if you find out where they're headed," Perkins said.

"I will."

Drake walked out to the open-air lounge at the stern and saw the Coast Guard cutter Kate Perkins had enlisted to help them approaching from the northwest.

He knew someone had briefed the commander for the intercept of a vessel believed to be involved in human trafficking, but he had no way of knowing what the Coast Guard had been told about the men who had commandeered it.

Drake faced the speeding vessel and waved his hands back and forth over his head to welcome the Coast Guard's arrival. As the cutter slowed and got closer, he recognized it as a Marine Protector-class patrol boat.

"Permission to come aboard, Mr. Drake," he heard from a loudspeaker on the cutter.

"Permission granted," Drake said loudly.

He watched the cutter launch an inflatable with a boarding party of six Coast Guardsmen on board. The two men in front of the inflatable held rifles at port arms with three Coast Guardsmen standing behind them, including an officer wearing a white short-sleeve shirt and a white officer's hat. One Coast Guardsman stood at the rear console steering the boat.

Drake walked to the rear swimming platform and waited for the inflatable to come alongside Tier One tied there.

The officer moved forward in the inflatable and stepped onto the swim platform. "Mr. Drake, I'm Lieutenant William James, commander of the UCS Haddock. Are your men armed?"

"Lieutenant James, three of my men below are armed. My rifle is laying on the deck at the top of the stairs to the main salon."

"My orders are to intercept this vessel and assist you in rescuing a human trafficking victim. Is the young woman here?" Lt. James asked.

"She's in a home on the lower deck with one of my men. Her name is Juanita Vasquez," Drake said.

"Does she require medical attention?"

"She says she's fine, but a doctor should examine her to make sure."

"What about the two Chinese men responsible for her abduction I was told about? Are they here?"

"They left in a Zodiac tender about two hours ago with two of their bodyguards. Two other bodyguards are being guarded in a home below."

"And the crew of this yacht? Are they involved?" Lt. James asked.

"The captain says he doesn't know anything. I'm not sure that's true."

"Is there anything else I should know about before we search and seize this yacht?"

"The FBI will want to inspect it when it arrives in San Diego," Drake said. "Other than that, she's all yours."

Drake stood aside as Lt. James and four of his men began their search of the *Black Dragon* to take control of the vessel and transfer Juanita Vasquez to the UCS Haddock.

Chapter Fifty-Nine

THE SUN DISAPPEARED on the horizon behind them as Ramirez entered the Bay of San Quentin and headed toward Don Eddie's Landing, the "fishing village" where Xueping and Zheng said they were going when they left the *Black Dragon* with their bodyguards.

"Don Eddie's has a great new restaurant, overnight lodging and RV parking," Ramirez told Drake on the flybridge of his sports fishing yacht. "The old restaurant burned, and they built a new one in 2010. If you ever get back here, try the smoked fish tacos."

"Do you know someone here?" Drake asked.

"I stop in for lunch whenever I'm headed back to Cabo from San Diego. The owner's a friend. He has a fishing tournament here every Fourth of July I enter whenever I can."

Ramirez anchored *Tier One* offshore in the shallow bay and called for a dingy to take them ashore.

The owner was waiting for them at the restaurant bar. "Bienvenido Peter. Can I get you anything?"

"Maybe later, Tony. This is my friend, Adam Drake. We're looking for a couple of Chinese men you may have seen today."

"They didn't stay long," Tony said with a frown. "They beached a Zodiac down by the parking lot and left it there. My groundskeeper said they met men in two white SUVs and left. He thought they looked like some of the local narcotrafficantes we see from time to time."

"Is it possible they stayed around here somewhere?"

"Si, it's possible. My groundskeeper said they were in a hurry to get out of here, but they could be anywhere. Who are they?"

"Men you hope don't return," Ramirez said.

"Do you need rooms for the night?"

"*Tier One's* out in the bay. If we stay, we'll sleep there tonight. I would like to buy dinner for my friends and take it back to my boat."

"Claro que sí," Tony said. "I'll bring you menus."

Ramirez raised his hand to get the attention of the bartender.

"I'm buying," Drake said. "Order me a good tequila while I go outside and see if Kevin is tracking the phones Xueping and Zheng were using."

Drake left the restaurant bar and walked outside and saw a spectacular red and purple sunset reflecting off the calm waters of the bay. Laughter and cigar smoke drifted down from an upper patio, where patrons were enjoying the warm night and watching the sunset.

"Are you still at headquarters?" Drake asked Kevin McRoberts when the head of their IT division answered the call.

"I have a cot in my office," Kevin said. "I'll be here until you get back from Mexico."

That wasn't necessary, but Drake knew how the young man maintained a laser focus on any task they gave him until it was completed, to his satisfaction.

"Are you tracking Xueping?"

"I'm tracking the Iridium 9575 Extreme satellite phone Xueping used in the past. There were four phones that left his yacht. I lost the GPS signals from three of them before they reached the coast. If Xueping is using the sat phone, he's traveling on Highway One approaching Ensenada."

"Good work. Stay with him. The FBI will arrest him if he crosses the border," Drake said. "If he stays on the Mexican side, we'll catch up with him and bring him across."

"I'm monitoring their dark web drug site, but there's nothing new on it. Do you still want me to shut it down?"

Drake thought about what the FBI would need to prosecute Xueping and Zheng, if they didn't have hard evidence of a terrorist plot and had to prosecute the drug trafficking criminally.

"Capture and store the web content for now," Drake said. "When the site offers pills for free or at deeply discounted prices, let me know and we'll shut it down. That's the way they'll try to flood the market and kill as many people as possible."

"That's evil to the extreme, Mr. Drake."

"It is Kevin, and we're not letting them get away with it."

Drake encouraged Kevin to get some sleep and called the Deputy Director of the FBI, Kate Perkins.

"We believe Xueping is traveling on Baja Highway One just south of Ensenada," Drake told her, "Assuming it's him with the sat phone he's used before. We don't know who's traveling with him."

"I alerted customs and Border Patrol," Perkins said.

"He won't use a southern border point of entry. Can you have the Border Patrol waiting for him in California and Arizona if we provide his GPS tracking information?"

"That's a lot of border to patrol, but I'll arrange it."

"What's the Coast Guard saying?" Drake asked.

"They said to say thank you for helping them intercept and seize a vessel engaged in human trafficking."

"How's Juanita?"

"Doctors say she's fine. She's being interviewed in San Diego."

"What about the two Chinese and the yacht's crew?"

"The two bodyguards are in custody. The crew's being questioned."

"Pay special attention to the two computer geeks. They're operating a dark web drug site for Xueping and Zheng. Kevin McRoberts is capturing the site's web content for you."

"Where will you be tomorrow?" Perkins asked.

"We'll spend the night on Pete Ramirez's fishing yacht and head to San Diego tomorrow. Pete would like to take Juanita back to La Paz as soon as possible."

"Will she need protection?"

"Good question. I'll ask Ramirez to talk with her brother and find out what he thinks."

"I'll be in the San Diego field office all day tomorrow. Come see me," Perkins said.

"On my way."

Drake looked out to where Tier One was anchored and saw Morales and Norris standing in the aft cockpit, smoking cigars. If their takeout order was ready, it was time to buy a couple of bottles of tequila and take the dingy back out to join them for dinner.

Chapter Sixty

SAMUEL XUEPING LOOKED out the window of a Cessna Citation CJ2 at the lights of San Diego below, as the jet gained altitude, taking off from the Montgomery-Gibbs Executive Airport north of the city.

He was tired after driving from the fishing village to Tijuana and using one of Zheng's tunnels to slip under the U.S. border in San Diego. From there, it had been an uncomfortable ride in the back of a catering van to the airport to board the jet chartered in the name of his Panama offshore corporation, *Casino World, LLC.*, for the flight to Vancouver, BC.

He was also angry and vowed retribution on America for seizing his twenty-three-million-dollar superyacht. Leaving the yacht was necessary, as a precaution, when he learned that Ramon Ying had disappeared. But he now realized Ying must have told someone the young woman Zheng had taken was on his yacht. It was too much of a coincidence to believe the U.S. Coast Guard had randomly stopped the *Black Dragon* to search for human trafficking victims. Someone had told the Coast Guard she was onboard and arranged for her to be rescued.

As soon as they completed the mission for General Wang,

there would be a day of reckoning between himself and Frank Zheng for the loss of his yacht. Zheng considered his organization to be independent and was working with him on an equal basis. He would learn. He tolerated Zheng because the triad found the relationship to be profitable, but he was expendable. There were more loyal members of his organization available to take his place when he was eliminated.

Xueping filled his glass for a second time with the best whisky the charter service had available, Johnnie Walker Blue Label, and looked with disgust at Zheng sitting across the aisle. The man was watching pornography on a smartphone he borrowed from one of his men. Vice was a business a wise triad leader didn't become addicted to, as Zheng clearly was.

He looked at his favorite watch, a gold Rolex Cosmograph Daytona with a green dial, and saw that it was ten o'clock in the evening. They wouldn't touch down in Vancouver until after midnight, and he was hungry. He raised his hand to get the attention of the flight attendant and before she looked up, his sat phone chirped in the cup holder beside him.

"I see they seized your yacht," General Wang said. "What's going on?"

"It has nothing to do with our mission."

"Are you sure of that?"

Why, do you know something?"

"I know the American Coast Guard was told by the Deputy Director of the FBI you were involved in human trafficking and your yacht would be adrift off the coast of Baja California," General Wang said. "I also know the Deputy Director is a friend of the American lawyer I told you to kill."

"How do you know she's a friend of his, General?"

"Because she arrested one of our agents at his request, to keep the agent from getting to our embassy in Washington and escaping to China. That's why the Ministry of State Security has a file on him."

"That doesn't mean the lawyer is the one who tipped off the FBI," Xueping argued.

"Do you know where the lawyer is?"

"We haven't been able to find him."

"But you knew he was in La Paz when you were there."

Xueping knew it was pointless to pretend he didn't know where the lawyer was. The Mexican government knew he was looking for the lawyer and General Wang would know it as well.

"I was told he was in Cabo San Lucas. I didn't know he was in La Paz."

"Do you know where your friend Ramon Ying is?" General Wang asked.

Xueping blinked twice and tried to swallow but found that his mouth was as parsed as the dry creek beds he'd seen in Mexico. There was no way General Wang could already know that Ying was missing.

"I haven't spoken to Ying since we left La Paz."

"No one else has either. His office in Mexico City asked our embassy to notify them if we hear anything, because they haven't been able to reach him. I am concerned that you and your associates are failing to accomplish the mission we gave you."

"Everything is proceeding as planned, General Wang," Xueping said. "I will distribute an ample supply of pills from Canada across America this week in the first wave of our attack. The second wave will follow one week later. Nothing can stop us now."

"Make sure nothing does. When will you return to Hong Kong?"

"I will remain in Vancouver to oversee the first two waves and then I'll fly home, if everything goes smoothly."

"I look forward to seeing you when you come home," General Wang said. "Your country wants to thank you for helping us weaken our enemy."

Xueping ended the call without responding. He had no intention of returning to China until he knew General Wang realized that any attempt to conceal his involvement in this act of war and offering up the triad as a scapegoat would sign his own death warrant.

An offshore corporation he's set up in Belize no one knew purchased a small island estate in British Columbia, Canada, for him. He intended to hideout there until he knew it was safe to return to Hong Kong.

China was increasingly aggressive in the world because it believed America was weak and tired of war. He wasn't so sure. If the lawyer who followed him to Mexico from Austria represented the will of America to defend itself, he was going to stay out of the line of fire if America decided to act.

If the enemy ever found out that China intentionally flooded America with deadly fake prescription pills to kill as many of its citizens as possible, war was inevitable.

Chapter Sixty-One

DRAKE LEFT the Harbor Island West Marina Tuesday to meet Deputy Director Kate Perkins at the FBI's San Diego field office. Ramirez had kept *Tier One* at full throttle all the way from Don Eddie's Landing anchorage to San Diego Bay so he could keep his noon appointment and brief her on what he'd learned and what he was planning on doing to find Xueping and Zheng.

Marco Morales and Dan Norris had taken a taxi earlier that morning to the airport to fly to Seattle, while Pete Ramirez was staying on *Tier One* to arrange for Juanita Vasquez's return home.

Deputy Director Perkins was waiting for him in a small conference room on the top floor of the fortress with its tinted-window façade the FBI called a field office.

Kate Perkins left her legal pad on the boat-shaped conference room table and stood to greet him with a handshake. She was alone in the room.

"I thought we should talk privately," she said. "I'm going to call down for a roast beef sandwich. Are you hungry?"

"I am, thanks. Roast beef sounds good. We ran out of food on Pete's yacht."

"Have I met Pete?"

"I don't believe you have. I served with him in Afghanistan. He has a sport fishing charter out of Cabo San Lucas."

Perkins walked to the conference room door and stepped outside. When she returned, she said that lunch was on its way.

"When you have time, I want you to meet Pete Ramirez. He has a small band of men with military backgrounds who are committed to taking their country back from the cartels. He would be an excellent source of intel for you."

"I'd like to meet him. Tell me what you can about Mexico."

Drake nodded, appreciating the opportunity she'd given him to leave out some details she didn't need to or want to know about.

"Samuel Xueping is smuggling Chinese fentanyl precursors into Mexico disguised as casino chip cleaning detergents. He shipped them from a warehouse in Brisbane, Australia, to his casino in La Paz, Mexico.

"The precursors are handed off to Ramon Ying, the CEO of Mexico's largest pharmaceutical company, who has a pill lab in his warehouse in Pichilingue, Mexico. Francis Zheng then smuggles the counterfeit pills to the U.S. for distribution from a DarkNet market website."

"Ramon Ying says the plan is to flood the U.S. market with free or discounted counterfeit pills laced with a lethal amount of fentanyl to kill as many Americans as possible. Ying says they're working with a Chinese general by the name of Wang."

"Do you know this or is this supposition?" she asked.

"Most of it I know firsthand."

"What part don't you know firsthand?"

"I wasn't there when Ramon Ying was questioned."

"Why was that?"

"Because I was chasing after Xueping's yacht," Drake said truthfully. "We believed Juanita Vasquez had been abducted by Xueping and Zheng."

"Where is Ying now?"

"I don't know."

"Can we get our hands on him and bring him in?"

Drake looked straight into Perkin's eyes and said, "That won't be possible."

Perkins blinked once and slowly nodded. "But you believe what he said is true?"

"I do."

An agent knocked on the conference room door and pushed in a cart with a tray of roast beef sandwiches with pickles, two servings of coleslaw, and a carafe of coffee, and two cups.

"Have you told the president about this?"

"I thought you might want to brief him?" Drake said.

"Can we stop this?"

"Some of it."

"Explain."

"We're ready to take down the DarkNet website," Drake said. "But the first wave of deadly pills is probably already in the U.S. or Canada, ready for distribution. They won't have a way to take orders on the website, but that won't stop Zheng's organization from getting the pills to customers. What we do won't stop China from supplying the cartels with fentanyl precursors."

While Perkins took time to make a few notes on her legal pad, Drake picked up half of a roast beef sandwich and took a bite of a dill pickle.

When she stopped writing and looked up, she said, "If you take down this DarkNet site, and I don't need to know how you're going to do that, getting our hands on this supply of pills before they're distributed should be our priority."

Drake finished chewing the first bite of his sandwich and said, "Agreed, but how do we do that? We don't know where they're keeping the supply of pills. It could be anywhere in America or Canada."

"If Xueping and Zheng are carrying out this plot on behalf of China, they will want to make sure the pills get distributed. If we find them, we have a chance of finding where the pills are."

"Kate, we might not find them in time to stop this."

"Do we know if this DarkNet website has offered the free or

discounted pills yet? If it hasn't, we might have time to find Xueping and Zheng. Do you have any idea where they are?"

"I might," Drake said. "We've been tracking a sat phone Xueping used in the past. Let me call Kevin at headquarters and ask if he knows where his sat phone is now. He'll also know what the DarkNet website is offering."

"While you do that, I'm going to find the agent I asked to find out if the DEA knows where Francis Zheng hangs out."

Chapter Sixty-Two

DRAKE WAS STILL TALKING with Kevin McRoberts when Kate Perkins returned.

"Kevin, I need to go. Call me as soon as the site offers free or discounted prices for any of its counterfeit pills."

Perkins sat down at the head of the conference room table with her legal pad. "The DEA says Zheng's headquarters are in Vancouver, BC. They're coordinating law enforcement efforts with the Royal Canadian Mounted Police to shut down his criminal enterprise. They haven't been very successful."

"That's where Kevin says the sat phone Xueping's using is now," Drake said. "Kevin also says he recorded a conversation from the sat phone last night between Xueping and General Wang. Their conversation confirms everything I told you about their plan to kill Americans, starting this week with the first wave of an attack."

The Deputy Director of the FBI repeated a four-letter word through her clenched teeth. "If China is involved in this, we'll need the president to give us a green light before we do anything. Tell Kevin to send me a copy of that recording."

"Kate, let me call the president," Drake said. "When he asked me to develop an intelligence contractor division of Puget Sound Security, Sound Security Information Solutions, he said he wanted an intelligence contractor available for what he called his special projects. I think I can get him to give me a green light to go to Vancouver sooner than you can get the FBI to work with Canada to stop these guys."

"You know I can't agree to let you do that?" she said.

"Kate, if the president tells me to do it, you won't have to agree to let me do anything. You need to put together a case that will support the president when he decides how to deal with China about this."

"I have to tell the Director about this."

"Wait until after I talk with the president," Drake said. "He might not agree with what I'm proposing."

"All right, I'll wait. Do you want to use a secure phone to call him?"

"I have his number for a secure encrypted line he told me to use. I can call him from here, but you might want to leave so you can deny being a party to this."

]"Come find me after you do what I didn't know you were going to do," Perkins said, and left the conference room.

Drake took a moment to organize his thoughts before calling President Benjamin Ballard.

"Good afternoon, Mr. President. Do you have time to talk?"

"I have fifteen minutes before a meeting with our U.N. ambassador. Adam. What have you learned?"

"China, or at least a Chinese general, is working with a Chinese triad and a Chinese cartel in Mexico to flood America with deadly counterfeit pills sometime this week."

"Can we prove that?"

"I wouldn't have told you if we couldn't, Mr. President."

"Of course. You say this is going to happen this week. Can we stop this from happening?"

"That's why I called, sir. I'm in the FBI's San Diego field office and discussed this with Deputy Director Kate Perkins. We believe the two men responsible for the plan to flood the U.S. with deadly fentanyl pills are in Vancouver, BC. I believe the intelligence division of Puget Sound Security you told me to develop can respond to this faster than the FBI can organize a task force to do it."

"Did Kate agree?"

"She let me take the initiative on this and call you before she runs it up the FBI flagpole."

"Smart girl," President Ballard said. "She going to make a great Director someday. What are you proposing, exactly?"

"I'm asking you to authorize me to put together a team to go to Vancouver, BC, and stop these two men before it's too late."

"There's not a lot of detail in that proposal, son."

"I'm working on that, Mr. President. I'm asking you to trust me. Kate will be working on putting together the information you'll need before you decide what to do about China."

"Do you want me to let Canada know what you're doing?"

"From what I read, sir, Canada's still trying to deal with the influence the Chinese gangs have in their private sector, according to the Project Sidewinder reports I've seen. It might be better if we let them know after the fact."

"All right, Adam. Do what you can to stop this and keep any more Americans from dying than already have. I'll deal with China when the time comes."

"Thank you, Mr. President. I'll report in as often as I can."

"Good luck son."

Drake found Kate Perkins by herself in an office with a phone held to her ear. When he knocked on the window, she waved him in.

"Send me the names of men you suspect handle Zheng's U.S. mail deliveries, Roger. I'll coordinate their arrests from headquarters," he heard Perkins say.

"I have a green light to go after Xueping and Zheng in Vancouver," Drake said. "I need to get to Seattle and put a team together."

"Do you have a PSS jet here?" she asked.

"No, I'll charter one."

"Use one of ours," Perkins said. "How soon will you need it?"

"I want to see Juanita before I leave and say goodbye to Pete Ramirez. Give me an hour."

"Come back and I'll have someone drive you to our hangar."

Drake walked across the office with his hand held out. "Smart thinking, rounding up the delivery men."

"I hope we're not too late."

"So do I."

Chapter Sixty-Three

ELIZABETH STROBEL DRAKE parked outside the Signature Flight Support terminal at Boeing Field in her company-owned white Porsche Cayenne, waiting for her husband to arrive from San Diego.

When he walked out with his brown canvas duffel bag hanging from his left shoulder with a tight smile on his face, she popped open the liftgate and jumped out to greet him.

"Welcome home, stranger," she said and kissed him.

Drake put his right arm around her shoulders and walked with her to the rear of the Cayenne. "Did you miss me?"

"A little. Lancer missed you more."

"Ouch!"

Drake tossed his duffel bag in the back of the Cayenne and hit the button to close the liftgate. "Has Mike put a team together?"

"The team is in the conference room waiting for you. He had lunch catered for them. There might be something left if you're hungry."

"I am, but knowing Mike and the guys, there won't be any leftovers."

Drake opened her door for her and asked, "When do I get to drive this?"

"When she's broken in," Liz said as she was getting in. "Maybe after we get back from Vancouver."

Drake closed her door and walked around the SUV knowing that challenging her place on the team would also challenge their relationship to the max. Liz had proven her ability on more than one occasion.

But having her beside him when they hit Zheng's warehouse would put her at risk and he hadn't worried about that before. He'd been in love with her, sure, but he'd known with her FBI training she could take care of herself.

She still could. But he knew she would resent him for trying to protect her now.

He got in beside her and said, "What do you think about taking Lancer with us to Vancouver?"

"Why?"

"He's not a drug dog, but if we're going into a dark warehouse, Lancer would be a plus on point."

"It's okay with me, if you think Lancer's up to it."

"I don't have time to take him out for a run before we go, but I think he is."

"Even if you had the time, you're not going for a run!" Liz protested. "Your broken ribs haven't healed. Maybe we should take Lancer with us and leave you at home."

Drake had to smile. A moment ago, he was thinking about trying to protect her.

"Point taken."

Over the next thirty minutes, on their way to the Puget Sound Security headquarters on the east side of Lake Washington, Drake gave Liz a detailed account of his time in Cabo and La Paz.

"Does Kate know about Ramon Ying?" she asked.

"She knows what Ying told us."

"But she doesn't know how you got him to talk."

"She didn't ask. If she had, I would have told her I didn't know, because I don't. She knew she was better off not knowing."

"Will that be a problem if we bring Xueping and Zheng back to the U.S. to stand trial?"

"It could, but China won't let them live long enough to be tried in an American court," Drake said. "Remember what happened to Tony Lee, the Chinese assassin, after they arrested him in San Francisco? They killed him in jail. If we don't kill Xueping and Zheng when we find them, China will."

Minutes later, Liz drove through the PSS headquarters security gate and down the underground parking ramp to park her new car next to Drake's older Porsche Cayman GTS.

"How soon do you want to leave for Vancouver?" Liz asked as they walked toward the stairs.

"As soon as we're ready. They know we're coming for them. Tonight might be the only chance we have to shut this down."

"Okay, I'll go pick up Lancer," Liz said as she turned around. "Do you want me to repack your duffel bag?"

"Just throw in a change of clothes and my black bomber jacket. I don't think we'll be gone that long."

Drake started running up the stairs and slowed to taking just two stairs when the chest pain from breathing hit him.

I'll have to make sure Liz doesn't see this, he thought, *or she'll insist I sit this one out.*

Mike Casey and the men he put together for Vancouver were waiting for him in the conference room on the top floor. Casey was sitting at one end of the long table. Mark Holland, the former chief of the NYPD Counterterrorism Bureau, was sitting next to him. The eight-man SSIS tactical team was across the table on Holland's left, with Marco Morales, Dan Norris and Kevin McRoberts sitting with their backs to him when he entered the room.

The chair next to Casey on his right was empty.

"Grab something to eat and join us," Casey said.

Drake detoured around the table and loaded a paper plate with a roast beef deli sandwich, a banana, and filled a cup from an air pot coffee carafe.

"Kevin found the plans for the warehouse where Xueping's

sat phone is presently," Casey said. "Mark called in a few favors the Mounties owed him and has a copy of the file they have on Zheng and his organization. We can expect they'll be heavily armed, although not well-trained. Canada doesn't know why we wanted the information on Zheng, but they will figure it out soon enough."

Drake nodded and sat down with his cup of coffee. "President Ballard said he'd take the heat. He's looking forward to reminding Canada they're responsible for letting the Chinese gangs set up shop and send drugs across our border."

"Rules of engagement?" Mark Holland asked.

"The president sanctioned us to do what's necessary to stop this Chinese assault on America any way we can," Drake said. "He's leaving it up to us to figure out how to do that. That means we defend ourselves, avoid collateral damage, and get in and out without Canada knowing we were there."

"We don't have time to plan and train for this like we're used to doing. But no one else knows what we know. No one else can react as quickly as we can to do what we're going to do tonight. We're winging it, but I know we can get the job done."

Chapter Sixty-Four

THE PSS GULFSTREAM G650 took off from Boeing Field at 5:00 PM PDT Tuesday with fourteen men, one woman, and a German Shepherd on board. Its flight plan listed Vancouver International Airport (YVR) in Vancouver, British Columbia, as its destination.

Based on information in the RCMP file, Mark Holland's plan targeted two locations for that evening. The first location was an industrial warehouse in Vancouver where Xueping's sat phone was located when the SSIS team left Seattle.

The RCMP file confirmed the warehouse was home to an Asian food importer and wholesaler. It was owned and operated by a Chinese immigrant who started the business with money traced to Hong Kong investors with ties to the Chinese Communist Party (CCP).

The second location was a mansion in one of Vancouver's exclusive neighborhoods, purchased for twenty-three million dollars by another Chinese immigrant. He had declared his world income for tax purposes to be forty-six thousand dollars when he became a Canadian citizen, three years before he bought the mansion. The RCMP believed the owner of the mansion was a member of Zheng's organization and that Zheng lived there with the man and several others.

If Xueping and Zheng weren't in the warehouse, the plan was to search for them at the mansion.

After circling over Vancouver for twenty minutes before landing, the G650 touched down at the Vancouver International Airport at 6:30 PM PDT. Steve Carson, PSS pilot, had called the Canadian Border Services Agency (CBSA) before departing Seattle. PSS was a member of the CANPASS program for private aircraft. Travel documentation and customs declaration for each passenger had to be provided to the CBSA before a private aircraft left an airport for Canada.

Carson called CBSA again to report landing and was told PSS G650 and its passengers had customs clearance and could proceed to the Signature Flight Support YVR terminal.

Fourteen passengers passed through the Signature Flight Support terminal, casually dressed and carrying travel duffle bags, accompanied by one German Shepherd on a leash, and loaded themselves and their luggage into two black GMC Yukon XLs. Carson stayed at the terminal to file a flight plan and prepare for a return trip to Seattle later that night.

Before the two Yukon SUVs crossed over the Fraser River after leaving Sea Island where the airport was located, each member of the SSIS team had changed into tactical clothing that closely resembled the uniform of the RCMP Emergency Response Team; black tactical pants and shirts, black boots and a black cap. They also wore body armor and carried a Motorola APX3000 Covert Surveillance P25 radio on their belt and a two-wire surveillance earpiece for communication.

Halfway to the warehouse, Kevin McRoberts reported the GPS signal from Xueping's sat phone wasn't sending a GPS signal. "It didn't move," McRoberts said, "it just stopped transmitting. Xueping has turned it off or removed its battery."

Drake was riding shotgun in the lead Yukon and asked McRoberts sitting behind him how long it would be before they reached the warehouse.

"Without a traffic slowdown, I estimate ten minutes."

Drake turned to Mark Holland, who was driving the lead Yukon, and said, "They might still be there, Mark."

"Or just leaving," Holland added. "Either way, we still need to see if the counterfeit pills are there. I say we proceed to the warehouse."

"I agree," Drake said.

The next ten minutes passed by in silence, as each of the seven passengers in the lead Yukon thought about the possibility of a firefight with members of a Chinese criminal organization known to be brutally violent. The only thing Drake heard above the sound of traffic outside was the sound of weapons being checked and Lancer panting behind him.

Without turning around, he knew Liz was petting Lancer sitting next to her with his ears raised and his head held high. Lancer was sensing the tension in the others and knowing there was danger ahead.

The Asian Food Supplier, LLC, warehouse was at the end of a row of twelve identical units in a modern industrial complex. The front windows on each side of the front door were tinted darkly with red lettering and an image of a red Chinese Dragon.

The commercial real estate advertisement still online showed a loading dock and ramp at the rear of the unit and one rear door. The interior of the warehouse had ambient light from a line of skylights that ended with an office loft above the small showroom and reception counter below.

Drake waited for the second Yukon to drive around to the loading dock in the rear and see if anyone was there.

"No vehicles or tangos back here," Dan Norris reported.

"Maintain position," Drake ordered.

"Shall we go look inside?" Holland asked.

"Let's make it look like a routine security check," Drake said. "I'll take Lancer with me. If no one's home, we'll all go in and take a quick look around."

Drake left his short-barreled H&K 416 A5 and suppressor in the front of the Yukon and opened the rear door to let Lancer out.

Liz handed Lancer's leash to him and whispered, "Be Careful."

Drake winked and said, "Come on, Lancer. Let's have a look."

Mark Holland was waiting for him in front of the Yukon, and together they walked to the front door of the warehouse.

"You sure you can get us in?" Drake asked. "I didn't think you could pick the lock on a commercial-grade keypad-operated door lock."

"Watch and learn. A fellow named Dominic taught me how to do this."

Chapter Sixty-Five

DRAKE WATCHED Holland take a zip-tie with a notch cut in one end out of his wallet and lean down to study the bottom of the housing of the 12-button keypad door lock.

"If you insert a zip-tie up into the bottom of these locks, find the lever and pull down… *voilá*, you can pick a Grade 1 security-rated lock like this one."

"Who taught you to do that?" Drake asked, stepping back to let Holland see if the door would open.

"An ethical lock picker," Holland smiled, and pushed the button on the cell phone jammer in his left hand to silence the warehouse's alarm system. Pulling down on the lock's handle, he opened the door an inch.

Drake pulled his pistol from the leg holster on his war belt and moved to the lead position as Holland stepped back. He listened for voices and let Lancer enter first.

The small customer reception area was dark, with the lights turned off, not much light coming in through the tinted windows. Two sales catalogs were on the left end of the counter and a potted plant with deep red lance-shaped leaves set on the other end.

Lancer quietly moved around the counter and stood with his nose raised in front of the single door into the back of the warehouse.

"We have the place to ourselves," Drake said. "The hair on his neck would stand up if he thought there was a threat inside."

He followed Lancer around the counter and opened the door. "Such!" he said, the command to search.

The warehouse was well-lit with overhead fluorescent lighting above the rows of tall metal shelving filled with boxes that had Chinese writing on them.

"I don't expect booby traps," he told Holland, "But why take a chance?"

Lancer ran back in a minute with his tail wagging and sat in front of Drake.

"Good boy, Lancer," Drake said, and patted Lancer's back before hitting the PTT button on his radio.

"There's no one here," Drake said. "Give us a minute to look around and we'll come back out the front."

"Roger that," Norris said from the second Yukon idling by the loading ramp at the rear of the warehouse.

Drake walked down the aisle on the far left to the back of the warehouse and continued across the loading area to return down the aisle along the wall on the other side. Mark Holland was standing next to a long worktable with four large boxes sitting on top.

"This warehouse doesn't look big enough to have Asian food customers all over the U.S.," Holland said. "I wonder why the boxes have the names of four U.S. cities and Number two written on them. Coeur d'Alene, Idaho. Minot, North Dakota. Cleveland, Ohio. Niagara Falls, New York."

"All just across the northern border," Drake said.

Holland took a folding knife out of his pants pocket and cut down the center of the packing tape on the closest box. When he lifted the top and reached inside, he whistled and held up a clear plastic bag filled with blue pills. "Look what we have here."

Drake joined him and took out a second plastic bag. One blue pill had the letter M inside a square box pressed on the side of it. Another pill had the number 30 pressed on one side. The front and back sides of Oxycodone pills.

"Counterfeit Oxycodone," Drake said. "Made in Mexico."

"The Number two could mean these are a second wave to be distributed from these four cities using the United States Postal Service," Holland offered. "They like to mail product from cities inside America to avoid detection."

Drake slapped the side of the box. "It also means we're too late. The first wave is already across the border to these or other cities."

"You said the FBI had a list of Zheng's suspected dealers," Holland said. "Perkins could round up the ones in these cities. It might not be too late, to stop the first wave."

"I'll call her right now."

"What do we do with these four boxes?"

"I'll ask Kate. In the meantime, get some help. See if there are any more of these counterfeit pills in here."

Drake found Kate Perkins' personal number and called her.

"Are you in Vancouver?" she asked.

"I'm in the warehouse where Xueping's sat phone was not long ago. Place is empty, except for four boxes of counterfeit Oxycodone pills. The boxes have the names of four cities written on top and the number two."

"The second wave?"

"That's my guess. If you have the names of Zheng's dealers and they're in these cities, round them up. It might not be too late to stop the first wave from being delivered."

"We're organizing the arrests of every Zheng dealer we know about. What are the four cities?"

"Coeur d' Alene, Minot, Cleveland and Niagara Falls. What do you want us to do with these pills?"

"I don't want to call the Mounties while you're still in Vancouver," Perkins said. "Take the boxes with you and make sure Zheng or Xueping get caught with them."

"You're devious."

"So are you. What are you going to do to find X and Z?"

"Clear out of here and see if they're at the mansion where the Mounties think Zheng lives."

"Zheng's gang will protect him."

"We're prepared for that."

"Call me if you find them."

"You'll be the first to know."

Drake slipped the phone back into the holster on his belt and watched Holland and three of the SSIS tactical team carry boxes out of the warehouse.

Chapter Sixty-Six

THE MANSION where they hoped to find Xueping and Zheng was in the heart of Vancouver's West Side in the Oakridge Neighborhood. It was a fifteen thousand square foot single-family residence with eight bedrooms, ten bathrooms, and a full-size indoor pool. The one-acre lot also had a tennis court, a putting green and a garage large enough to park nine cars.

"It's typical of the mansions the Chinese triads use to launder drug money," Mark Holland told Drake and the others in the lead Yukon. "Canada estimates the triads have laundered somewhere between eighteen to twenty billion dollars using the scheme. The money comes from triad-funded offshore accounts to buy expensive real estate at inflated values. When the property sells, the money is cleaned, or laundered, and sent back to secret private banks in Guangdong, China. The money is then recycled again and again in the same way."

"Can't Canada stop it?" Kevin McRoberts asked from the seat behind Drake.

"They're trying," Holland said, "But there are a lot of wealthy Chinese who moved to Vancouver from Hong Kong when China took over. Not all the wealthy Chinese are triad."

Holland pulled into the parking lot of a retirement community half a mile away from the mansion, to wait until they heard the second Yukon was in place. The southern side of the one-acre lot was heavily wooded and provided cover for Morales, Norris and half of the eight-man tactical team to infiltrate the property.

The lead Yukon with Holland, Mr. and Mrs. Drake, Lancer and the other half of the tactical team would park on the single-lane road to the north of the property and enter over a short stone wall with a row of tall Arborvitae planted behind it. A street-view of the property online when it was listed for sale a year ago showed there was enough space between the Arborvitae for a person to squeeze through.

Drake's phone vibrated in its belt holster.

"In place a block away," Morales said. "Call when you arrive."

"Roger that," Drake replied.

Holland put the idling Yukon in gear and started the drive west toward the mansion.

The gray light at dusk was growing darker when the black Yukon turned onto the one lane road east of the mansion.

"We're here," Drake reported.

Holland drove past the closed electronic security gate and pulled off the road beside the low stone wall in front of the mansion.

Drake pressed the PTT button clipped to his body armor vest. "Comm check One?"

The other six members of Unit One reported in.

"Comm check Two?"

Unit Two's six members also reported in.

Drake opened his door and waited for the others and Lancer to scramble out of the Yukon before ordering, "Execute! Execute! Execute!"

He ran to the end of the low stone wall, signaled for Lancer to jump over it, and hopped on the wall. Liz was up on the wall, six feet away to his left, with Holland and four of the tactical team already over the wall and standing down between the Arborvitae.

Drake jumped down from the wall and saw that Lancer's head

was up, his hackles were raised, and he was snarling quietly. He was locked on a target.

Thirty yards away across a grassy area, a man was smoking a cigarette. He was leaning against a retaining wall on the edge of a sloping driveway down to the mansion's nine-car garage. An AK-47 was on top of the retaining wall next to him.

There was no way any of them could cross the grassy area without the guard seeing them.

Drake leaned down and gave Lancer the command to attack. "Fahs!"

Lancer shot across the grass and launched a hundred and ten pounds of snarling fury in the air from the top of the driveway, striking the man in the chest and knocking him down.

Drake ran forward to keep Lancer from tearing the man's throat open when he saw the guard reaching to pull his gun from a shoulder holster. He kicked the man's hand away from the holster and shouted, "Aus!" for Lancer to let go.

When the man grabbed for his gun again, Drake pointed his H&K416 A5 assault rifle at the man's forehead. "Don't."

The muffled sound of two quick shots from his left turned his head enough to see a second guard on his back at the opposite end of the mansion. Turning back, the man on the ground had grabbed his gun out and was turning it toward him. Drake shot once, putting a black hole between his eyes.

The tactical team members were stacking up at the front door. Drake ran to join them, raising a fist to hold their position. He pressed his PTT button and asked for a sitrep from the rear of the mansion.

"Report Two," he said.

"One tango down, second tango on the patio ran inside," Norris said.

"One and Two, execute breach now," Drake ordered.

The first man in line moved to the door and reached out to see if the door was locked. It wasn't.

The front tactical team rushed inside, followed by Lancer, Drake, Liz, and Holland. The wide expanse of pink marble floor inside was empty, save for a black grand piano sitting silently to the left. A staircase with gold handrails curved up to the right to a second floor.

Drake motioned two men down the hallway to clear the rooms and signaled the other two men to go upstairs and to clear the floor.

Seconds after the men left, gunfire erupted from the rear of the mansion. Zheng's men were defending their position with AK-47s.

Chapter Sixty-Seven

TWO MUFFLED shots close ahead down the hallway moved Drake to the wall, waving Liz and Holland behind him. Lancer barked once from point, as the first tac-team member came into view and flashed Drake a thumbs up.

Following Lancer, they moved down the hallway to a large room on the left with an entertainment center with a tall black marble fireplace, a pool table, and a poker table. Across the hall to the right was a dining area with a master chef's commercial grade kitchen wrapped around behind it. Drake saw the reason for the OK sign.

A Chinese bodyguard was on the floor at the base of a black marble kitchen island. His white tank top was covered in blood flowing from two bullet holes center mass. Tattoos ran up his arms from the back of his hands to a tattooed black dragon skullcap on his shaved head. An AK-47 was on the island next to a bucket of Kentucky Fried Chicken and a tub of mac and cheese.

Gunfire erupted upstairs, jerking Drake's head around. He turned to Dan Holland and pointed upstairs, signaling that he and Liz would keep moving to the back of the house.

Lancer moved forward across the room when the door on the

other side crashed open. Another bodyguard stumbled out and froze when he saw a snarling German Shepherd twenty feet in front of him.

Drake stepped to the right, and Liz stepped to the left. Both had their HK416-A5 short-barreled assault rifles pointed at his head.

"Drop your weapon," Drake commanded.

The bodyguard's eyes flashed toward the kitchen on his left and the dead bodyguard there. He flinched when he heard the door behind him open and squeezed his eyes shut while he made up his mind.

When he opened his eyes, he smiled and raised his AK-47.

Drake and Liz both fired, dropping the man to his knees before he fell forward.

"Are we clear back here?" Drake asked Morales.

"All clear," Morales said.

"Bring the boxes from the warehouse inside. We'll leave them for the Mounties to find." Drake said.

Drake pushed his PTT button and asked Holland about the second floor.

"Second floor's clear. You should come see Zheng's hobby room."

"On my way,' Drake said. "Marco, search down here and see if there's anything that will help us find Xueping. Liz, check with Kevin and see if we have anyone headed our way. We can't be here when the police arrive."

Drake ran down the hallway and up the stairs to the second floor.

Dan Holland was leaning against the wall in a large bedroom, next to an open closet door. In the center of the room was a raised round bed with a red silk bedspread. On the ceiling above the bed was a round mirror as large as the bed.

The blood from a dead bodyguard's head was seeping into a growing black stain on the red carpet to the left of the bedroom's door.

Zheng was lying on his back beside the bed. The black yukata, or summer kimono, he wore was open, displaying a full body tattoo in red and black, along with a black G-string and blood from a row of holes across his chest.

Drake shook his head, looking around the room. "Sex his hobby?"

"In a way," Holland said, hooking a thumb toward the open door of the closet.

"Closet?" Drake asked.

"Might be more than that," Holland said, pointing to the top shelf of a built-in bookcase next to the closest door. On each end of the shelf were two black air purifiers.

Drake walked to the bookshelf. Each air purifier had a small round camera lens hidden in the brand lettering across the front of the purifier.

Following Holland inside the closet, he saw it was a small video recording studio with a flat screen monitor on the wall above a small desk with drawers on each side.

Holland pulled one drawer back and picked out a Blue-Ray disc. It had a date and two sets of initials written in black on it. "Looks like Zheng enjoyed watching himself on that bed."

"Or people he wanted to blackmail," Drake said.

"What do you want to do with these?" Holland pulled open the drawer on the other side of the desk. "There has to be a hundred discs here."

"Leave them. The Mounties will be here, eventually. They'll want to know who Zheng was blackmailing."

Liz rushed into the bedroom and called out, "Drake? Time to leave. Kevin says a neighbor's out front, calling someone on his cell phone."

"Tell Kevin to pull around where Morales parked," Drake said. "We'll leave out the back through the woods. Take anything we found that will help us find Xueping and any link to China."

Holland followed Drake out of the closet and went into a small study that opened off the master bedroom. He came back holding a silver MacBook Pro in his hand. "If we're lucky, there'll be something more than dirty pictures stored on it."

Chapter Sixty-Eight

THE PSS GULFSTREAM G-650 landed in Seattle before midnight. Mike Casey was waiting at headquarters in the underground parking garage to meet his Sound Security and Information Solutions team.

"There's some food and coffee in the conference room," he said. "Help yourselves, if you're hungry. Then go home and get some sleep. I'll let the executive team tell me about your mission in my office."

Casey led the way up the stairs with Liz, Drake, Lancer and Mark Holland following his lead. When they reached Casey's office, they found a rolling tray loaded with breakfast croissants, orange juice and coffee waiting for them. A bottle of Weller Special Reserve Bourbon was sitting on his desk.

"It's not Pappy Van Winkle," Casey said, "But with what these special projects for the president are costing us, it'll have to do."

"We'll get paid," Drake promised, pouring himself a glass. "I just have to find out what he wants me to call what we've been doing. Anyone else want a glass?"

"Investigating China's new opium war against the U.S. would

cover it," Liz said, holding up a hand when Drake offered to pour her a glass of bourbon.

"I would," Mark Holland said, nodding to the bottle of bourbon. "When he's convinced China's intentionally killing Americans, he'll be mad as hell. He'll need to respond in a way that won't start World War III. That won't be easy to do.."

"We may need to help him with that," Drake said. "I have a few ideas."

"Did you find anything more in Vancouver linking China to all of this?" Casey asked.

"Mark found Zheng's laptop in his study," Drake said. "Kevin's looking at it now. There might be something more on it."

"That leaves Xueping and the Chinese general," Casey said. "We've shut down their Dark Net site and taken Zheng out of the game. What do we do about them?"

Drake knew Liz was waiting for his answer. They would let the president or China deal with General Wang, but he would deal with Xueping.

"General Wang is probably out of reach and we don't know where Xueping is," he said.

"I can reach out to friends and see if they know anything," Holland offered.

"Liz, the Coast Guard is part of Homeland Security," Casey said. "Do we know if they found anything when they searched Xueping's yacht that might help find him?"

"I can call and find out," Liz said, looking back at Drake. "But why can't we let the president and the FBI take this over? You uncovered the plot, identified the players, and prevented most of their fentanyl-laced pills from getting into the country. Isn't that all the president asked you to do?"

Casey exchanged a look with Drake before saying anything. The Special Forces Creed he'd told Liz about included praying for the strength to spit upon an enemy if captured. Drake had been captured and they'd been able to rescue him, but he knew his friend too well to think he would stop chasing Xueping.

"I haven't spoken to the president about what he wanted from us, Liz, but it's going to leave a bad taste in my mouth if we don't go after Xueping," Casey said. "He tried to kill Adam twice. That's unacceptable."

"Why? Because it's one fight you didn't win?" she asked.

"No Liz, it's because this fight is over when the other guy is dead," Drake said softly. "Xueping knew I was coming for him and he knows I won't stop until I find him. The only way he survives is by making sure I don't. I can't wait for him to come after me and kills both of us. That's what would have happened last time when he sent men to our condo, if he'd been successful."

Liz reached down and scratched Lancer behind his ears and stood up. "I'm going to find Lancer some water. Come get me in my office when you're ready to leave, Adam."

Drake watched her leave with a frown on his face. "She's never acted like this before."

"You weren't her husband before," Casey said.

"It's something else."

"Megan's the same way. Remember how she treated you when I was poisoned and in the hospital in San Francisco? She threated to leave me if I kept letting you put me in harm's way."

"You never told me that."

"I didn't need to. I wasn't willing to change back then. Now I am."

"What changed?"

"When the two cartel guys came to our home, and we made the girls stay in the safe room so they wouldn't see the bodies of the men we'd just killed."

"Was it because Megan was afraid of the girls losing their father?"

"I'd like to think she was worried about losing me too, but that was probably the biggest reason."

"It has to be something else with Liz."

"Then find out what it is. She's worried about something. Have you called Kate Perkins or the president?"

Drake set his glass down and stood up. "No, I'll wait until

they're in their offices. That Weller bourbon's not bad, by the way."

"Go get some sleep. I have a feeling you're going to need it when you tell the president what you're planning."

Drake found Liz sitting in her dark office, turned around in her chair looking out the window at the Seattle skyline. Lancer's head was in her lap and she was humming a tune Drake didn't recognize.

"Let's go home, Liz," he said.

Chapter Sixty-Nine

SAM XUEPING STOOD watch at the panoramic window in his off-the-grid waterfront home in the Discovery Islands of British Columbia, Canada. Eventually, someone would find him on his private island and come to kill him.

If it was General Wang, his fate was sealed. When Wang heard that Frank Zheng had been murdered along with six of his bodyguards, he would move quickly to wipe out any trace of his involvement in the plot against America.

It would take the general time to find him, but with the resources of the Chinese army and the MSS at his disposal, it would happen. A record of the purchase of the private island three years ago existed. It was as hidden as much as possible, but the transaction could be found by someone with the patience to follow the money trail leading to the sale and purchase of the island.

General Wang would not come to talk. He would send a sniper or a team of assassins to silence him without giving him a chance to explain why the plan was unraveling. Wang wouldn't accept that it was his order to kidnap the American attorney that gave the man a reason to investigate the death of his friend, the Australian agent.

The only chance he had to keep General Wang at bay was the threat of him being exposed as the person the government used to flood America with cheap and deadly fentanyl. China would execute him on the spot, if there was any sign of a scandal involving the Chinese government, and Wang knew it.

That's why it was imperative that Wang understand and believe the recordings of their conversations about the plot would automatically be released on the internet in the event of his untimely demise.

That was the reason he had arranged a call with General Wang that evening.

He had a better chance of surviving if it was the American attorney who came after him. The only way to get to his island was by boat or seaplane. Since acquiring the property, he had installed perimeter surveillance radar that provided wide-area detection and tracking that pinpointed the GPS coordinates of any potential intruder. The automated alarms would warn anyone approaching the island to stay away.

He had a new Bell 206 helicopter in an outbuilding that looked like a shop or large storage facility. He knew how to fly and could be in the air in minutes.

He moored an XO EXPLR boat with twin 250 horsepower Mercury outboard engines at the dock below the house that could maintain a speed of fifty knots over the waters surrounding the island and get him to safety.

And as a last resort, he had a hidden underground bunker at the end of a tunnel from the wine cellar where he stored a supply of heroin. If some government froze his bank accounts, he had access to something as good as gold that he could use in an emergency.

Each month, a seaplane dropped a waterproof package of heroin at night close to the island. With a GPS asset tracker tag attached to the package to help him find it, he used a sea kayak to recover the package and return unseen to the bunker through a hatch concealed in a retaining wall that ran along the waterfront below the home.

Besides the bullet-proof windows in the home and the motion detectors all around it, his personal chef and bodyguard was a former Chinese Special Forces Falcon commando.

Before he called the general, he decided to get an update from his Vanguard 438, or Operations Officer, on the General's activities.

While he waited for a reply to his encrypted text message, he walked to the kitchen to get a cup of tea. Feng, his chef, was busy preparing a hot, spicy soup with vegetables and little sausages for his midday meal.

"Check all the perimeter radar installations before the end of the day," he told Feng. "We may have unwanted visitors soon. I don't want to be surprised when they show up."

"Yes, boss."

Xueping's cell phone pinged with the arrival of an encrypted text from his Vanguard.

> W has men watching your office and home.

> He's staying in Macao at his favorite hotel with new bodyguards. Instructions?

> Who are the new bodyguards?

> Not PLA or MSS. They look like private mercenaries, not Chinese. No one we know.

> Find out who they are and where he found them.

> If they're contract, I want to know how loyal they are to him.

> Can we take one to find out?

> No. I don't want W to know he's being watched just yet.
>
> Understood. 438 out.

General Wang was nervous if he hired private security. When he'd met personally with the general, the only person with him had been his aide-de-camp. If his security wasn't from the army, it meant Wang was looking over his shoulder and expecting the worst.

Xueping left the kitchen with a cup of tea and a smile on his face, as he walked out onto the deck and sat in the deck chair where he enjoyed a Cuban cigar each night.

If the general didn't trust the Chinese army, he wondered how Wang would react if he knew about his high-ranking friend in the CCP? The Chinese Communist Party was the only one that could have given the green light to strike at America.

He didn't have a secure way to reach his high-ranking friend, but General Wang didn't know that.

He was looking forward to calling the general later that night and savoring the perverse pleasure he was going to get from giving him more of a reason to keep looking over his skinny little shoulders.

Chapter Seventy

DRAKE SLIPPED OUT of bed at sunrise and went for a run with Lancer. When they returned to the condo, Liz was in the kitchen with one of their wedding gifts, a red Cuisinart omelet pan on the stovetop. All the ingredients for an omelet set beside it on the counter.

"I thought you two might be hungry," she said.

Lancer's bowl of Blue Wilderness Salmon recipe food and water were on the floor and a pitcher of orange juice was on the breakfast table.

Drake saw she'd nibbled on a piece of dry toast on a saucer, next to a glass of water on the counter.

"You thought right, but aren't you going to have an omelet with me?"

"I didn't sleep well. Toast is enough. How was your run?"

Drake moved over to give her a hug.

Liz smiled and pushed him away. "Hug me after your shower. Want your omelet now?"

"Yes, please. Are you sure you're all right?"

Liz had her back to him, whisking eggs for his omelet, when she nodded her head and said, "I'm fine."

She didn't sound very convincing, but he didn't push it. She would tell him if something was wrong.

Drake sat down at the breakfast table and poured a glass of orange juice. "Did you call your friend at DHS while I was out?"

"She was in a meeting. I left a message for her to call me."

The omelet with spinach, mushrooms, and cheese she served him was perfect. His Blue Mountain coffee was rich and mild, and the orange juice was cold and tangy. But when Drake kissed Liz to thank her for his breakfast, he left to take a shower, feeling something wasn't quite right.

When he finished showering, shaving and dressing casually for a day at PSS headquarters, he found Liz was sitting at the breakfast table with her phone to her ear.

"Thanks Sandy," Liz said. "If you're out my way, come see me. I owe you lunch or dinner."

Drake poured a second cup of coffee and sat down across the table from Liz.

"The Coast Guard didn't find anything on his yacht," she told him. "They went through everything, including the yacht's navigation system and onboard computers. There was nothing that would help us find Xueping."

"It was a long shot, anyway," Drake admitted. "He has the money and resources to be anywhere in the world. We might never find him."

"Will you keep looking?"

He knew what she wanted him to say. "Liz, if something turns up, we'll look at our options. I'm not obsessed with the man, but he needs to pay for what he's done. That can happen in several ways."

"And by several people."

"Yes, it can. Do you want me to wait so we can ride together to headquarters?"

"Go ahead, I'll be along a little later."

Drake studied her face for an explanation until she said, "Go! I'm just a little slow this morning."

"There's no rush. I can call Kate and the president from here. Take all the time you need to get ready."

Liz kissed him on the check and left, leaving him with a frown on his face as he watched her walk away.

FBI Deputy Director Kate Perkins answered his call on the second ring.

"I just received an email from my contact with the RCMP about Frank Zheng being killed in his mansion," she said. "They think one of his enemies took him out."

"Sounds like it," Drake said.

"They also found boxes of counterfeit pills laced with fentanyl," Perkins said. "They're sending us samples to compare them with the ones we've seized recently."

"Seized where? Like maybe in Coeur d' Alene, Minot, Cleveland and Niagara Falls?" Drake asked.

"We think we got all of them. Thanks for the intel."

"Are you going to tell Canada that China was involved?"

"That's up to the president. If we told them now, they might have a closer look at what happened in Zheng's mansion."

"I was hoping you would say that. Do you have anything on where Xueping might be?"

"He has an arrest warrant outstanding for human trafficking because of the seizure of his superyacht," Perkins said.

"INTERPOL has a Red Notice out on him as well."

"Does law enforcement worldwide pay any attention to Red Notices?" Drake asked. "Aren't there sixty thousand INTERPOL Red Notices?"

"Sixty-nine thousand, two hundred and seventy, actually. We might get lucky, you never know."

"That's not good enough, Kate. The president needs to have this wrapped up before he takes any action against China. Could the NSA help us find him?"

"Probably, but the president would have to tell them to look for him. He would have to tell them why the FBI needs their help, because you know they will ask him."

"And as soon as he tells them, everyone in the intelligence

community and the entire government would know what China tried to do," Drake said. "The media would inflame the situation and we'd be at war. Let's forget the NSA."

"Do you have any ideas?"

"I might. We came back from up north with a laptop. Kevin's working on it. It might have something that will help us find Xueping."

"If there is, what will you do?"

"That's depends on where we find him. It's the president's call."

Chapter Seventy-One

DRAKE DECIDED to wait until he checked with Kevin McRoberts before he called the president. If there was something on Zheng's laptop that would lead them to Xueping, he wanted to know what the president planned on doing with the information.

Liz was in the bathroom with the door closed when he told her he was ready to drive them to headquarters.

"You go on," she said. "I'll be right behind you."

"Are you sure?"

"Yes. Go."

"All right. Love you."

"I love you too," she answered softly.

Walking down the stairs to their ground floor garage, Drake wondered if she was hanging back so she could drive her own company-owned Porsche Cayenne to work.

When he arrived at headquarters, he took the stairs to the third floor, where Kevin's office was at the back of the IT floor.

With the creation of Sounds Security Information Solutions at PSS, a growing number of intelligence analysts were being hired and housed within the IT division on the third floor. It was crowded. PSS needed to add on to the building or move somewhere. And he wasn't looking forward to either of those possibilities.

The PSS Director of the IT Division was leaning forward at his desk, studying the middle screen of three monitors when Drake knocked on the open door of his office.

"Morning, Kevin. You're in early."

"I didn't leave last night, Mr. Drake. I knew you wanted anything I could find on the laptop that would help you find Mr. Zheng."

"Did you find anything?"

"Not a thing."

Drake slumped against the door frame. "That's not what I hoped you were going to tell me, Kevin."

"Don't worry, Mr. Drake. I found a file about Mr. Zheng's mansion and it gave me an idea. Mr. Xueping owns a bank in Hong Kong that specializes in real estate loans, which makes sense because he develops real estate and buys casinos. Mr. Zheng financed the purchase of the mansion in Vancouver with a mortgage loan from Mr. Xueping's bank.

"I accessed Mr. Xueping's bank IT system and searched the records for all properties he purchased, and I found one anomaly—a small private island near Vancouver, B.C., in the Discovery Islands. It doesn't fit the profile of the other real estate investments he's made. This could be an off-the-grid hideaway where he's hiding. Here, look."

Drake sat down in Kevin's chair and looked at the online listing for an island on the market three years ago. A Chinese family in Hong Kong wanted $50 million dollars for a 1.2 square mile island off the east coast of Vancouver Island, British Columbia, Canada.

The island came with a modern waterfront home and several outbuildings on the western shore of the island. The rest of the property was forested with a peak in the center of the island three thousand feet tall. There was a dock below the home with a small boat moored there.

"Is there anything that indicates Xueping is there now?" Drake asked.

"Not that I could find. We could buy satellite imagery from a commercial provider and find out. There's a satellite imagery company I read about that's headquartered on Vancouver Island."

Drake got out of the chair and clapped Kevin on both shoulders. "Great work, Kevin. Call that company and find out what they can get for us. I want everything, high-resolution images, terrain mapping, radar, the works. I'll let Mike know what we're doing."

He took the stairs two at a time to the fourth floor and found Mike Casey talking with someone sitting in front of his desk.

The door was open, and Casey waved him in.

"Adam, you remember Chaplain Walker," Casey said, pointing to the man in the chair.

Drake stepped into the office and extended his hand to the six-foot-four-inch, broad-shouldered smiling man they both served with in Iraq and Afghanistan.

"Chaplain, you're looking good. Good to see you again."

"You mean I'm looking good for a man my age?"

"Not at all," Drake said. "You look as fit as you did in Afghanistan. You still serving?"

"No, I left last month," Walker said. "I wasn't as woke as command wanted me to be. You can't have a cohesive fighting force when you're told to make sure the men embrace everyone's differences based on their race, gender, ethnicity, and sex."

Drake and Casey laughed together.

Thomas Walker was a soldier's soldier. He spent four years at the University of Colorado majoring in philosophy and pre-law, and then reversed course and joined the army instead of his father's law firm. After twelve years of combat experience around the world as a Special Forces warrior, he went back to school for a Master of Divinity degree and returned to the army as a chaplain. Walker was a legend in the Special Forces community as a chaplain who understood the needs of the men he served with.

"What brings you to Seattle, chaplain?" Drake asked.

"I keep track of my men and they know they can call if they need help with something. One of them lives here in Seattle. He's having a hard time dealing with the death of his teenage son. His son bought counterfeit Adderall pills laced with fentanyl to help him study for a test, overdosed and died. His father wants to kill the dealer. He reached out to me and I'm trying to talk him out of it."

Casey looked at Drake before asking, "Is there anything we can do to help?"

Chaplain Walker stood and reached across the desk to shake hands. "Let me take you to dinner tonight and you guys can fill me in on what you do here."

"You name the time and place," Casey said. "I'll be there."

"Drake?" Walker asked.

"I need to take a rain check, chaplain. I need to stay home tonight. Maybe a night before you leave?"

"Sounds good. I'll let you know before I hit the road."

When Chaplain Walker left, Drake asked, "Why do you think he really stopped by?"

"I'll find out tonight. Why did you stop by?"

"I told Kevin to buy satellite imagery of an island Xueping might be on."

Chapter Seventy-Two

DRAKE WALKED down the hallway to his corner office on the fourth floor. The door of Liz's office was closed. When he knocked and opened it, she wasn't there.

He glanced at his watch and saw it was only a half an hour later than when he left her showering in the condo. He thought about calling to see if she was okay but decided against it. In any new marriage, he knew there were bound to be boundaries he didn't know about and didn't want to cross. Checking to see why she wasn't at work might be one of them.

Drake hung his blazer on the back of the door, rolled up his sleeves and sat down to make a short list of information he wanted to share with the president.

The president answered the call on the third ring. "I'm in the Oval Office Study with half a mouthful of a wonderful liverwurst and rye sandwich. Sorry."

"Would you like me to call back so you can enjoy your liverwurst?"

"I can eat while you tell me about your trip."

"We found Z. He isn't the head of a cartel any longer. His

main dealers in the U.S. have been arrested and the DarkNet drugstore is closed for business, permanently."

"Excellent! What about the other guy?"

"We think he might be on a private island."

"Do you know where the island is?"

"Up north, not far from where Z was living."

"Can you get him?'

"Do you want us to?"

"I want to send a loud measure to all the people responsible for killing a hundred thousand Americans a year," the president said. "If you can get him, do it."

"Does that mean you want him to stand trial in the U.S.?"

"Yes, if you're able to bring him in."

"How do you plan to punish his sponsors?"

"I have a few ideas. Let's finish this end of things first."

"Yes sir. I'll let you know when it is," Drake said.

"God speed, Adam.

Thank you, Mr. President."

Drake sat back to sort out his conversation with the most powerful man in the world. The president had authorized a kill or capture mission, with the emphasis on capture, using a private U.S. intelligence contractor, to bring back a Chinese national from a neighboring country without telling that country about it. What could go wrong?

Before he wasted time considering those possibilities, he needed to find out if Xueping was on the island. He left his coat on the door and took the stairs down to see if Kevin had been able to get the satellite imagery they needed.

"Just got them," Kevin said when Drake found him standing at the printer in his office. "I found a satellite imaging company in Vancouver, B.C., that works for the Revenue Services of British Columbia. They provide satellite imagery to the government so it can monitor newly developed properties that didn't get the permits they needed to avoid paying taxes. Go ahead to the conference room and I'll bring these along when they finish printing."

Drake borrowed a cup from the IT breakroom and took a cup of coffee with him to wait for Kevin.

"I bought everything they had on this island," Kevin said, as he spread copies of the satellite imagery along the length of the conference room table. "I'm not sure these are going to help much. The island is completely forested, except for this clearing around the house."

Drake leaned down to study the satellite imagery copied on a row of black and white photos on the table. The island's irregular shape reminded him of Ireland. As Kevin said, it was forested from one end to the other except for a long, rocky area bordering a cliff along the water on the northeast corner.

He picked up the photo with a better view of the waterfront house. Fifty yards up a slight slope was a modern mountain home at the edge of an acre of lawn and shrubbery. Two other outbuildings sat on the edge of a paved area at the end of a narrow road coming out of the forest.

"When were these satellite images taken?" Drake asked.

"The company said two weeks ago."

"Xueping was in Mexico until a week ago. We need something taken today or yesterday. The satellites they get the imagery from orbit every twelve hours. They can reprogram the surveillance coordinates of the satellites, so they should be able to get us something recent."

"If they have access to radar imagery, would you want it? I forgot to ask them for it?" Kevin asked.

"Yes, I want it. Infrared satellite imagery would be the best, if they can get it," Drake said. "We won't be able to identify who a person is, but at least we'll know someone's there."

"I can access the records of the Revenue Service and find out who's paying the taxes on the island," Kevin offered.

"Go ahead but be careful. I don't want anyone to know we're interested in the place, in case we go there to get Xueping," Drake said.

"They'll never know I was there," Kevin promised.

Chapter Seventy-Three

DRAKE TOOK the stairs to his office and saw that Liz wasn't in her office next door. Now he was worried.

"Liz are you okay?" he called and asked.

"I'm feeling a little under the weather this morning, to tell the truth. I think I'd better stay home today with my queasy stomach."

"Do you need to see a doctor?" Drake asked, as he sat down and opened the laptop on his desk to Google remedies for a queasy stomach.

"No, it's not that bad. I'll be fine."

"All right. Can I bring you anything that will help?"

"I can't think of anything, Adam. Get some work done. I'll see you tonight."

In the time he'd known her, she'd never been sick or missed a day of work. It wasn't like her and he didn't like it. If she wasn't feeling well enough to work, he was going to insist that she see a doctor. If she had a doctor, that is. She'd never mentioned one. Maybe Megan, Mike's wife, could recommend a doctor she liked. He'd try to remember to ask Mike when he saw him.

Drake opened a page on WebMD and started looking for

remedies for a queasy and upset stomach when Mark Holland, the new director of SSIS, knocked on his open door.

"Where are we on the hunt for Sam Xueping?" Holland asked.

"We have a lead but nothing actionable," Drake said and told him about Kevin's idea that Xueping might be on a private island in British Columbia. "We have satellite imagery of the island, but it's two weeks old. Kevin is trying to get something more recent."

"How do we get to this private island, if we find Xueping is there?"

"I haven't gotten that far. The island is remote. It probably doesn't have a ferry that goes there."

"So, access is by boat, seaplane or helicopter," Holland said. "Do you want me to get the coordinates for the island and see what's available?"

"If he's there, the president wants him captured and tried in an American court. We'll need to move quickly, so yes. Have Kevin show you the satellite imagery and see what transportation options we'll have."

"Do you want me to put a team together?"

"We'll use the same team we took to Vancouver," Drake said. "We won't know if we can take everyone until we know what transportation we'll use."

"I'll find out," Holland said, and left.

Things were coming together. It was time to meet with Mike.

Drake found him in the fourth-floor breakroom, spreading cream cheese on a bagel.

"Is Liz in?" Casey asked when he saw Drake.

"She stayed home this morning, queasy stomach."

Casey looked up with a frown on his face but didn't say anything.

"Are you headed back to your office? We need to talk, if you have time."

"I'm meeting with a new client in five minutes. How about after that?"

"Fine," Drake said. "Call me when you've finished."

On the way back to his office, his phone pinged with a message from Kevin.

> New satellite imagery just came in.

Drake messaged back that he was on his way.

Kevin was waiting for him in the IT conference room and handed him a copy of one satellite image.

"This is from yesterday," Kevin said.

Infrared satellite imagery showed the red hued figure of one man on the deck of the waterfront home and another man standing next to a vehicle parked next to an outbuilding.

"Do any of the others help ID Xueping?" Drake asked.

"No, none of these," Kevin nodded toward a stack of satellite imagery copies on the conference room table. "But the taxes for the place were paid from an account at the bank Xueping owns, in the name of Lewis Liu. Liu is the fourth most common Chinese surname, which doesn't tell us anything. But this Lewis Liu has a Canadian driver's license. Here's a copy."

Drake looked at the man's face on the driver's license by the name of Lewis Liu. It was the face of the man he saw in the casino in Brisbane, Australia - Samuel Xueping.

"That's him, Kevin. You found our man," Drake said. "Has Mark Holland been down?"

"He just left. After looking at the satellite imagery, he thinks chartering a boat will give you the best chance to surprise Xueping when you get there."

"Update the infrared satellite imagery as often as you can, in case he leaves the island. And see if there are ferries that pass close by the island. We might get lucky and find one we can hide behind."

"I'm on it."

Drake left to find Mark Holland. On his way up the staircase, Mike Casey sent him a message.

> Meeting concluded, come anytime.

On the fourth floor, he veered left down the hall to Casey's office.

"We found him, Mike. He's on an island off the east coast of Vancouver Island," Drake said as he entered the room.

"What did the president say when you called?"

"He wants us to bring him here to stand trial."

"How do we accomplish that?"

"I want to take the Vancouver team and go after him. Mark Holland thinks we need to get there by boat. He's trying to find a yacht we can charter."

"When do we leave?" Casey asked with a smile.

"As soon as possible, but I thought you wanted to keep Megan happy and manage things from here."

"I want to keep my wife happy, but this time it's different. If you're looking for a bare-boat charter, which I assume you are, so you don't have to explain to a captain and his crew what you're doing, you need someone to captain the yacht. I have experience, and Megan will understand when I tell her I'll stay onboard when you guys go do the dangerous stuff."

"Do you think she'll buy it?" Drake asked.

"Maybe not, but I need to get out from behind this desk. Besides, I can't let you have all the fun."

Chapter Seventy-Four

DRAKE LEFT PSS headquarters and drove to the condo to tell Liz he was leaving to go after Xueping. He found her asleep on the couch, with Lancer standing guard next to her when he entered the room.

He kneeled and waited for Lancer to come over. "Heh, Lancer. "How's she doing?" he whispered.

"She's fine," Liz said, sitting up and stretching. She was wearing her black FBI Academy sweatshirt, gray Nike running pants and running shoes. "What brings you home so early?"

"Did you go for a run?"

"I wanted to but didn't."

"Still queasy?"

"A little and tired," Liz said. "I slept all afternoon. You still haven't told me why you're here. You don't need to check up on me, Adam."

"Of course, I do, but that's not the reason I'm here. We found Xueping and we're going after him. The president wants us to bring him back to stand trial in the U.S., not Canada"

"When are you leaving?"

"Later today or tonight," Drake said, and sat beside her on the couch. "Xueping bought an island three years ago, and he's there now, we think. We need to get up there before he leaves."

"Where's up there?"

"His island's northeast of Vancouver Island. Holland is looking for a yacht to charter to get us there. Mike is going as our captain."

Liz got up suddenly and went into the master bedroom. He heard her close the door of their ensuite bathroom.

While she was gone, he went to the small office next to the master suite and picked up his go bag on the floor next to the desk. When he returned, Liz was standing in the kitchen, leaning back against the counter with her arms folded across her chest. She looked pale and might have been crying.

Drake walked over with a puzzled look on his face and stood in front of her. "Liz, what's really going on?"

She moved forward and snuggled against his chest. "I'm pregnant and I don't want you to go," she said softly.

He lifted her chin and kissed her. "That makes me very happy, Liz! Are you happy about being a mother?"

"I am, but also I'm scared. I do not want to be a single parent! Can't you let Holland and the team go after Xueping?"

"I have to do this, Liz. You aren't going to be a single parent. There are only two men on the island. I'll have eight men with me. I'll be okay."

Liz pushed him away, sniffling, and wiped her nose with the sleeve of her sweatshirt. "You can't promise that."

"No, I can't. But you've been with me when bullets were flying. You know I don't take unnecessary risks."

"When you get back, promise me we'll talk about this," Liz said.

"I promise."

"Then get going. Bring that Chinese S.O.B. back so I won't have to worry about him anymore."

DRAKE RETURNED to PSS headquarters a little before four o'clock. He found the men who were going after Xuiping planning the mission in the executive conference room.

Mark Holland had the latest satellite imagery projected on the wall and was tracing a line from Vancouver Island to Xueping's island.

"It's a hundred and two nautical miles from Vancouver, B.C., to Xueping's island," Holland said. "The seventy-foot pilothouse yacht I found is available, as a bareboat charter, and has a top speed of eighteen knots, or twenty miles an hour. Cruising speed is seventeen miles an hour. Using seventeen miles an hour, we can be there in six hours."

"How do we get from the yacht to the island?" Dan Norris asked.

"It has a thirteen-foot Zodiac tender with a fifty horsepower Mercury outboard."

"Do we know if we'll have a welcoming party?" Marco Morales asked.

"The infrared satellite imagery identifies two people," Drake said. "We'll take the Black Hornet nano drone and recon the island before we go ashore to make sure there aren't more."

"It looks like there's only one good landing place, right below that waterfront home at the dock," Norris said, pointing to the satellite imagery on the wall. "If he's prepared to defend himself, we're completely exposed going in. Can we swim a couple of men ashore somewhere else and let them hike to the house?"

"What about getting a second Zodiac for the yacht and landing two parties in different places?" Morales asked. "It looks like there's a road crossing the island that circles around the peak in the middle. We could land one Zodiac on the far side, hike across and surprise him from two sides."

"Mark, can we get a second Zodiac on the yacht?" Drake asked.

"There might be enough room on top for two Zodiacs. I'll check."

"Rules of engagement?" one of the tactical team members asked.

"We're going there to bring Xueping back alive to stand trial in the U.S." Drake said. "We do everything we can to make that happen, but we'll defend ourselves as necessary."

"Any other questions?" Holland asked.

There weren't any.

"Be ready to leave for the airport in one hour," Drake said. "We'll leave Vancouver on the yacht and reach the island by midnight."

Chapter Seventy-Five

THE OCEAN ALEXANDER 70 pilothouse yacht chartered by Puget Sound Security left its Granville Island moorage in Vancouver, B.C. at 7:30 PM PDT.

The yacht's passengers included the PSS CEO, it's Special Activities Director and in-house counsel, the Director of its new intelligence contractor subdivision, the head of the PSS HRT team and four operators.

Seven of the eight men had Tier One Special Forces operator experience, and the eighth man, Mark Holland, was the former head of the NYPD Counterintelligence Bureau.

Holland had chartered the yacht for the PSS's first annual corporate team building exercise, explaining to the charter service manager he needed a second Zodiac for a problem-solving exercise. He did not elaborate on the details of the exercise.

Mike Casey steered the yacht out into Burrard Inlet and headed north up the Strait of Georgia toward the Discovery Islands. Drake sat next to him in the pilothouse.

"Six hours is a long stint," Drake said. "Let's split it into two-hour shifts."

"Have you ever driven anything this big?"

"No, but I figure if there's anything to it, you'll show me how to do it."

"Do we have a plan when we get there?" Casey asked.

"A rough one. With two Zodiacs, we'll circle the island and drop one team off on the far side, as Marco suggested. Keep circling around slowly and when they tell us they're in place, launch the other Zodiac and race to the dock below the home. It will be sometime between one and two in the morning. We'll have the element of surprise on our side."

"When will Morales have a chance to recon the island with the drone?" Casey asked.

"From the yacht before we launch the first Zodiac, and again when we get close to the home on the other side."

"I'll check the yacht's navigation charts to determine how close we can get to the island," Casey said. "In the meantime, would you have someone bring me a cup of coffee?"

"Aye, aye captain."

Drake left the pilothouse and walked back to the galley to get Casey's coffee. On the way there, his phone buzzed. Kevin was calling from headquarters.

"Mr. Drake, I checked the latest infrared satellite imagery and there are more men on the island than we thought."

"How many more?"

"Four, bringing the count to six. They arrived three hours ago on the second to last earth orbit."

"Thanks Kevin. Let me know if there are more arrivals."

Drake poured two cups of coffee and returned to the pilot house, handing Casey one cup and sitting down in the chair next to him.

"Xueping's expecting us," Drake said. "Kevin says the latest infrared images show four new arrivals three hours ago."

"More security," Casey said. "That changes things."

Drake sipped his coffee and looked ahead in the evening twilight at the running lights on other vessels, while he thought about Xueping's beefed up security. If they were expected, the element of surprise was gone."

"We can't rely on the satellite imagery to show us where he's positioned his men. The images will be at least ninety minutes old," Drake said. "Marco will have to locate them using the Black Hornet's thermal and infrared sensors."

"Xueping's had time to install perimeter security radar and alarms. If he's expecting company, just knowing where his men are won't be enough. We're going to have a fight on our hands."

"I can't see a way to avoid one, but it needs to be a short one. I don't want the Mounties showing up before we have time to collect Xueping and get out of there. The president said he'd take the heat on this, but I don't want to spend years tied up in Congressional hearings and Canadian investigations about our involvement in the capture of Xueping."

"If he has perimeter radar, we'll need a diversion," Casey said. "What if we use the yacht as a distraction? Use the Black Hornet to locate the guards, drop off the Zodiacs, and come in behind the guards when they're distracted by a yacht racing straight toward the house."

"Leaving you on the yacht by yourself?" ask Drake.

"Sure, why not?"

"Because if they shoot at you on the yacht, you might want to shoot back. You can't do that and drive the yacht."

"Are you offering to stay on the yacht with me? Like old times and be my spotter?"

"Did you bring your sniper rifle?"

"As a matter of fact, I did."

"If I stay back, that means Holland would have to go ashore to give us six men in the Zodiacs. He's not an operator, Mike," Drake said.

"Even if he stays on the yacht, that's still five men with the experience going up against four Chinese triads. I like that match up."

"I don't. Let me think about it."

"Run it by the others. See what they think, before it's your turn at the wheel."

Chapter Seventy-Six

RUNNING up the Inside Passage six hours later, passing Cortes Island to the west, Mike Casey saw on the yacht's Lowrance chart plotter they were approaching the waypoint he set ten miles south of Xueping's island.

He slowed the yacht to five knots and stood to stretch. "AIS shows there are no other boats near the island. At this hour, I didn't expect any."

"What's AIS?" Drake asked.

"Automatic identification system," Casey explained. "It uses GPS, VHF radio and an AIS transponder to broadcast the location, speed and heading of a vessel and receive the same information from other boats in the area. Tell the teams we are thirty minutes from our first launch point."

Drake walked back into the main salon where the men going ashore had assembled.

Mark Holland was going over the insertion plan for the last time with the men when Drake interrupted him.

"We're ten miles south of the island and thirty minutes away from launching the first Zodiac," he said. "I'll have an update on the satellite imagery in ten minutes. Marco, I'll tell you when we're in range for your first recon with the Black Hornet."

"Roger that," Morales said.

"Anything we haven't covered?" Holland asked.

"When we have Xueping, is the dock at the home still the rallying point, if this goes south?" one of the HRT operators asked.

"I'll let you know if anything changes," Holland said. "The Zodiacs provide us plenty of options for exfil if we need to move the yacht away from the home."

Drake returned to the pilothouse as the yacht returned to cruising speed and called PSS headquarters for an update on the latest satellite imagery download.

"No change, Mr. Drake," Kevin McRoberts reported. "Still six heat sources, two in the home and four clustered together outside the home."

"Call me if that changes," Drake said. "We might get a break and find the four outside still hanging around the home."

"Roger that, Mr. Drake," Kevin said.

Drake rested his hand on Casey's shoulder and said, "Do you want me to take over so you can go below and get your rifle?"

Casey turned to look at Drake and saw he was dressed like the other operators. "You're going."

"I have to, Mike. I want Xueping to see my face when he realizes it's over. Holland's a good man, but he'll do a better job coordinating things from here with you than doing something he hasn't done before."

"Okay, understood. Get my rifle and range bag. He can use my binoculars and be my spotter," Casey said. "Even if no one's shooting at me, I can cover your six from here if you get in trouble."

Drake squeezed Casey's shoulder and went below to get his sniper rifle and range bag. He respected his friend's decision to honor Megan's request to leave the hard stuff to others. But he also knew Mike missed the action, just like he would if he made the same decision Mike had made.

The memory of her telling him she was pregnant, and that she didn't want to be a single parent, flashed through his mind. It startled him. He knew it was a distracting worry that got soldiers killed. One he couldn't dwell on.

Focus on the mission, Drake. There's time to think about all that later.

He shook his head to get rid of the thought and continued down the stairs to the stateroom he and Casey shared. He was beginning to understand what his friend had to think about as a father.

Drake brought Casey's .338 Precision Sniper Rifle and range bag up to the pilothouse and laid the rifle on the bench seat behind the two captain's chairs.

"Fifteen minutes from the first launch point," Casey said. "The charts show the waterways between these islands are incredibly deep, probably carved by the glaciers nearby. I can get the yacht within ten or fifteen feet from the shore, with the yacht's draft of five feet. We might not need to launch the Zodiacs. I'll bring the yacht in parallel to the shore and we can put one Zodiac in the water, swing it around and use it as a ramp across to the shore."

"That'll make exfil faster, if we don't have to send guys back to bring the Zodiacs around the island to the yacht," Drake said. "I'll tell them to get ready to put a Zodiac in the water."

He passed the information along to Holland in the salon and saw Morales in the stern, getting ready to send the Black Hornet on its first recon flight.

"Fifteen minutes from our first launch point, Marco, Drake said. "Kevin says the latest satellite images show two heat sources in the home and four outside standing around. Recon across the island and see if they're still there at the home. We might get lucky, cross the island and catch them napping."

"Roger that," Morales said. "Will we still land in two places, or do you want me to go with the first group?"

"We'll stick with the plan. Go with the first group and recon ahead of me. Get as close to the house as you can. If the guards are still at the home, use the drone to keep an eye on them. If they move out from there, let us know which way they're headed."

Chapter Seventy-Seven

CASEY PULLED the yacht within fifteen feet from the shore on the southwest corner of Xueping's island. With the Zodiac 400 swung around perpendicular to the shoreline, its thirteen-foot length allowed the men to easily step ashore.

Marco Morales led the way, as Charlie One. A former Army Ranger trained for Long Range Reconnaissance Patrol (LRRP) missions, he quickly found an old cattle or deer trail that curved away from the shore toward the other side of the island.

The trail entered a dark, mature Douglas fir forest a short distance from the shore. With the small amount of light from a waning Gibbous moon reaching the floor of the forest, Drake was thankful they all had Gen 4 flip-down night vision goggles on their helmets.

Drake, Bravo One, heard a click on his two-way radio as Alpha One, Mark Holland, reported, "Charlie has landed. Bravo team, what is your ETA?"

"Estimate fifteen minutes max for main body," Bravo Two, Marco Morales, replied from his position ahead of Drake on the trail.

"Roger that," Alpha One said.

Drake jogged ahead with one HRT operator behind him to close the distance between them and Morales. When Morales sent the drone up, he wanted to be there to cover him.

The trail remained flat for the most part as it circled around the base of the peak in the center of the island. Then it sloped down toward where Drake knew the house and dock were.

Drake pushed the PTT button on the Motorola P25 radio on his belt. "Bravo Two, what is your position?"

"Bravo One, the forest opens into a clearing. The house is on the other side, down by the water. I'm back in the trees fifty yards off the trail to the north. Suggest you go south the same distance. No sign of the guards. Sending the drone up now."

"Roger that, Bravo Two."

Drake saw the clearing ahead and stopped jogging. He stepped off the trail and motioned to move left by extending his left arm and swinging it from his chest to the forest. The forest had thinned out as it neared the clearing, but it provided enough cover to keep them from being seen unless someone was looking directly into the forest and saw movement.

He moved silently through the trees until he could see the house. Motioning for the HRT operator to move farther away, he dropped down and crawled forward until he had a clear line of sight of the clearing and house.

"Bravo Two, in position," he radioed.

"Roger that, Bravo One."

"Charlie One, what's your position?" Alpha One asked.

"Alpha One, we found a road leading to the house. ETA two minutes. Charlie One out."

"Roger that, Charlie One," Alpha One said. "We have the home in sight. Will turn toward the dock in two minutes."

Drake searched the area around the house for guards. An outbuilding that looked like a shop or garage was thirty or forty yards up a slight incline behind the house. Above the overhead doors was a loft or second floor with two wide and narrow openings in between them, reminding him of arrowslits in an old castle.

Across a large graveled area from the shop or garage was a greenhouse, a row of raised garden beds and a small tool shed.

The modern Pacific Lodge style waterfront house faced the water and the dock to Drake's left. The windows along the back of the building were all dark, leaving the area around it and the outbuildings in almost total darkness.

The sound of the yacht's two 825 horsepower diesel engines racing at full throttle toward the waterfront house brought the area surrounding it alive. A voice shouted orders and flood lights came on around the house and outbuildings.

The auto dim feature on Drake's fourth-generation night vision goggles kept him from being blinded by the floodlights. When he flipped them up onto his helmet, he saw muzzle flashes in the arrowslit above the shop overhead doors and heard AK-47s firing from across the clearing.

He hit the PTT button and shouted above the noise, "Bravo Two, tango locations?"

"Bravo One, two tangos up in the shop, two north of the house by the dock, and two by the greenhouse."

"Bravo Two, this is Charlie One. Taking fire from the top of the shop. Will flank to the north behind the greenhouse."

"Roger that, Charlie One. I'm receiving fire from the shop as well. I'll cover you flanking the greenhouse?"

Drake saw he had the best path across the clearing to the house. "Bravo Three, cover me. I'm moving in," he said.

When Bravo Three started firing, Drake jumped up and sprinted across the clearing to the back of the house. Bullets from the loft of the shop to his right hit the ground behind him as he ran.

Chapter Seventy-Eight

DUCKING his head around the southeast corner of the house, Drake saw the shooter in the loft had a one hundred fifty-degree range of fire toward the house and the water beyond.

The shooter at the other end of the shop would have the same range of fire back into the forest where Bravo Two was flying the drone. The two guards north of the house by the dock had clear shots at anyone moving in from the yacht, and that didn't include someone firing from within the home.

Something or someone had to change the equation, if they were going to capture Xeuping and get off the island.

"Charlie One, can you take care of the tangos by the greenhouse and down by the dock?" Drake asked.

"Roger that, Bravo One. Do you need help with the shop?"

"Negative, Charlie One. Bravo Two and Three will keep the shooters in the shop. I'm going after him in the house," Drake said.

"Copy that, Bravo One."

"Roger that," Bravo One and Bravo Three each said.

Drake moved along the southern end of the house toward the water. At the southwest corner, he looked around and saw there was a long, covered deck along the waterfront side of the house. No one was on the deck.

He grabbed the wrought-iron railing with his left hand and jumped over it onto the deck. With his HK 416 A-5 in the low ready position, he moved forward slowly, searching for any sign of Xueping or the man with him in the house.

Shielded from the floodlights on the other side of the house, it was dark enough on the deck to use his night vision goggles again. He stopped at the edge of a floor-to-ceiling window and peeked inside.

On the far side of a large great room, a man was standing next to a stone fireplace, holding an AK-47 with its barrel pointed toward a door at the other end of the deck.

The only way into the house from the deck was through the door the man was guarding. When he didn't see Xueping inside he walked slowly back to the end of the deck and slid over the railing and down onto the soft mulch of a flower bed.

As soon as he landed, the gunfire stopped. The only sounds in the night were waves coming ashore on the island's rocky shoreline.

Drake turned to move away from the front of the house and noticed movement in his peripheral vision. Fifty yards away, at the far edge of the clearing, a short man walked out from behind a small shed with a sea kayak lifted above his head. He was moving to the top of the slope, down to the water.

Xueping was leaving his men behind and trying to get away!

Drake ran across the clearing and found a trail with a rope handrail cutting diagonally across the steep slope. Xueping was thirty yards ahead when he started down after him.

When Xueping stopped to set the kayak down, Drake was fifteen yards away.

Sighting through the EOTech holographic sight on his assault rifle, Drake fired a single suppressed round past Xueping's right ear.

"That's as far as you're going tonight, Xueping. Raise your hands and slowly turn around."

Xueping stood still. "Are you Drake?" he asked, without turning around.

"Yes."

"Are you here to kill me?"

"Not if you cooperate."

"What does that mean?"

"My government will respond to your country's aggression. What you tell us about your attack on America will help the president decide what to do."

Xueping turned around slowly and faced Drake.

"Raise your hands," Drake repeated.

"Or what, you'll shoot me?"

Xueping reached down and started pulling the kayak toward the water. "It would be foolish of you to jump in after me, Drake. Glaciers feed this water and it's very cold."

"I won't be foolish, then," Drake said and fired a round into Xueping's left knee.

"Aagh!" Xueping yelled and fell across the front of the kayak.

Drake hit his PTT button and called Holland. "Alpha One, I have our man. He needs a medic. I'm fifty yards south of the house on the shoreline. Suggest we rally here and exfil as soon as possible."

"Roger that, Bravo One. We're coming to you."

"Bravo One, I'm 18 Delta and heading your way," Bravo Three said.

"Copy that, Bravo Three," Drake said. "Forgot you were a combat medic. Glad I chose you for my team."

"Actually sir, Alpha One made sure I was on your team. He wanted 18Ds with the older guys."

Drake smiled and shook his head. He knew he wasn't fully recovered from the injuries he suffered in Australia, but he also knew he could keep up with any of the younger men.

What he was beginning to think about was whether he still wanted to. He was going to be a father, and Liz wanted him to stop chasing after the bad guys. Sooner or later, he knew he'd have to decide whether to keep doing stuff like this or let the young guys handle it.

He just wasn't ready to start down that road yet. He still had to get this Chinese SOB off the island and back to the U.S. to stand trial.

Drake looked down at his adversary, moaning on the rocky ground beside the kayak.

You brought this on yourself, Xueping. If you'd left me alone on my honeymoon, you wouldn't be walking with a limp the rest of your life.

Chapter Seventy-Nine

WHILE BRAVO THREE worked on Xueping, Drake ran up the slope and took position behind the small shed four feet tall. It had a flat roof and was long enough to hang a sea kayak on its side. Near the end of the shed was a small two-feet-by-two-feet square door hinged at the top.

He moved along the side of the shed and reached down to see if the door opened. Lifting the bottom of the door up to see inside, he saw the top of a ladder that climbed up on the wall of a dark shaft.

Xueping must have made his way to the shed from the house through a tunnel, leaving a man inside to cover his escape. He wondered if the men guarding him knew he was leaving them to fend for themselves.

"Alpha One, the guards don't know they're guarding an empty house," Drake said. "Suggest you move offshore and send one tender in quietly for us. We might get out of here without another shot being fired."

"If they discover you have him, can you defend your position?"

"We will, but if you hear us shooting, send reinforcements in the tender."

"Roger that, Bravo One."

Drake heard the yacht pulling away from the island and, in the distance, the sound of outboard motors on the Zodiacs racing to it.

After a quiet ten minutes, three flashes of light from Bravo Three's tactical flashlight signaled the tender had arrived. By the time Drake ran down the slope, Xueping was on the floor of the Zodiac with duct tape across his mouth and Morales was waving for him to hurry.

The yacht was two hundred yards offshore, drifting away in the channel with its running lights off. As soon as Xueping was onboard, Casey started the yacht's diesel engines and pulled farther away from the island.

"Take him below," Drake told Bravo Three. "I'll be down to talk with him in a minute."

On his way to the pilothouse, Mark Holland handed him a beer. "If you hadn't seen him before he paddled away in his kayak, this would have been a wasted trip."

"We were lucky, Mark. He almost made it."

"Where are we taking him?"

"I don't know. I'll call Kate Perkins and find out."

He found Mike Casey adjusting something on the navigation system's screen in the pilothouse when he got there.

"I'm retracing our route along the waypoints we used to get here," Casey said, "Until you tell me where we're going," Casey said.

"My guess is Bellingham, Washington. It's the closest FBI satellite office. Hand me your sat phone. I'll call Kate and find out."

"Kate, it's me," he said when she answered. "We have him. Where do you want us to take him?"

"Bellingham. How far away are you?"

"Give me a moment, I'll find out," he said and turned to Casey. "Mike, how long until we get to Bellingham?"

Casey entered Bellingham as their destination in the nav system and said, "It's a hundred and sixty-four nautical miles from our position, say eleven hours."

"Kate, Mike says eleven hours."

"I'll meet you there. Any problems?"

"No, but there are five of his triad buddies we left on the island," Drake said. "They'll be looking for a way to leave when they realize we have him."

"Let Canada deal with them," she said. "We were never there, remember?"

"Never where?" Drake asked.

"I'll see you in Bellingham," Perkins said and ended the call.

Casey held out his hand for the sat phone. "I'll give the yacht's company a call later this morning and tell them we're exercising our option for another week on the lease. We have a few bullet holes to patch up."

"Maybe we can get the FBI to do that for us."

"Worth a try. How's Xueping doing?"

"He's okay," Drake said. "I'm going below to tell him what his future holds."

He left the pilothouse and took the stairs down to the four staterooms below.

Xueping was lying on the bed in the stern stateroom, staring at the ceiling. An HRT operator guarding him stepped aside at the door to let Drake enter the room.

"How are you feeling?" Drake asked and leaned against the side of the door frame.

"How do you think? You shattered my knee cap."

"Stop whining. I could have aimed higher."

Xueping glared at Drake. "Where are you taking me?"

"I haven't decided. It will either be to a dark site somewhere in the world, where you'll never see the light of day again, or to jail to stand trial as a terrorist."

"I'm not a terrorist," Xueping insisted.

"Yes, you are. You're not wearing a uniform and you attacked

America with your plan to kill as many people as possible. That makes you a terrorist."

Xueping grimaced in pain when he sat up. "It wasn't my plan."

"Yes, it was," Drake said. "We have a recording of you discussing it with General Wang."

Xueping paled and stared at Drake. "I didn't have a choice. You don't say no to someone like General Wang."

"You always have a choice. You just made a bad one."

"When you said you wouldn't kill me if I cooperated, what did you mean?"

"I know everything about your plan, Xueping," Drake said. "I know how you use your casinos to get fentanyl precursors to Ying's labs in Mexico. I know about the Dark Net platform you were going to use as a marketplace for counterfeit prescription drugs that Zheng would distribute for you to America. What I don't know is the best way to make China pay for what it's done and never tries anything like this again."

"If I cooperate, what will happen to me?"

"That's up to the president."

"China saw an opportunity," Xueping said quietly, "To take revenge against the West in its version of a new opiate war. The CCP can't forget the wars it fought with the West. Britain flooded the country with opium to win two wars. The similarities between then and now were too obvious to ignore. China knows it will fight a war with America someday. Why not let men of fighting age kill themselves with drugs they can't stop taking, and make it easier for China to win for once?"

Chapter Eighty

FBI DEPUTY DIRECTOR Kate Perkins was waiting in Bellingham at the Coast Guard dock when Casey used the yacht's side thrusters to ease it alongside. With her were four FBI agents wearing FBI raid jackets.

The FBI Deputy Director came on the yacht to meet Drake, leaving her escorts standing on the dock.

"He'll need to see a doctor," Drake said. "His knee needs attention. Other than that, he's fine."

"Did he tell you anything?"

"He admitted China wanted to make it easier to win a future war by killing as many young Americans as possible in what they're calling a New Opium War."

"The president's going to have a tough time responding to that, if it's true," Perkins said. "That's an act of war."

"That's exactly what it is."

"Have you talked with the president?"

"Not yet."

"Tell him we're detaining him for questioning under the Patriot Act, as a possible enemy combatant. We'll take him to

Washington. Ask him if he wants me to report directly to him. I knew what you were doing, but this wasn't an FBI operation."

"Of course," Drake said. "Ready to take custody of Xueping?"

"Yes," Perkins said, and waved for the FBI agents to join her.

Xueping was led out of the main salon to the aft deck, where FBI Deputy Director introduced herself. After advising him he was being detained for questioning under the Patriot Act, they marched him off the yacht between two FBI agents.

They left the chartered yacht with the U.S. Coast Guard to be repaired, and the men from Sound Security and Information Solutions were driven to the Bellingham International Airport in two black FBI vans. The PSS G650 Gulfstream was there to fly them back to Seattle.

When they were in the air, Drake called the president.

"We have him, sir," Drake reported. "Deputy Director Perkins took him into custody in Bellingham, and she's bringing him to Washington. She wants to know if you want her to report directly to you."

"That's best for now," President Ballard said. "Is everything okay?"

"No casualties, sir, on either side. Our neighbors might not know we were even there."

"I'll deal with it if they find out. Has he told you anything?"

"He confirmed China was behind this," Drake said. "They saw an opportunity to weaken us by killing fighting-age men. They see it as revenge against the West for what Britain did to them in the nineteenth century."

"How in the world did they think they could get away with this?"

"By blaming it on the triads and cartels, saying they had nothing to do with it."

"Adam, I have to be very careful with this. Can you come to Washington and lay this out for my team?"

"Mr. president, I'm in the air returning to Seattle. I can be there tomorrow."

"Come directly to the White House when you get here."

"Yes, sir. I'll be there tomorrow."

Drake laid his head back and closed his eyes. The last twenty fours had been a hastily planned mission that ended well with the capture of Xueping. It was Sound Security and Information Solutions' first task for the president, as an intelligence contractor, and it would put the company in the spotlight when word got out about the role it played in the capture of Xueping.

When it did, he would have to decide what he wanted his future to be with the new division of Puget Sound Security. He left his law practice when Mike asked him to serve as the company's house counsel and become a part owner. Then they developed the Special Project Division so he and Mike could lend a hand to protect the country when they saw a threat to the country the government couldn't or didn't want to take care of.

And now they'd formed a private intelligence contractor division of PSS to help the president when he had a special project he wanted to manage, without involving the bureaucracy that kept forgetting he was the president and commander-in-chief.

He cherished the opportunity to serve his country, but he wasn't going to continue doing it if screwed up his marriage or was a financial drain on PSS.

Drake felt a hand on his shoulder and looked up to see Casey standing in the aisle.

"The frown on your face just now tells me you're worrying about something," Casey said.

"The president wants me in Washington to brief his team about Xueping and China."

"Why are you worrying about that?"

"I promised Liz we'd talk when I got back about staying out of harm's way in the future, Drake said. "I don't want her to worry, but I don't think I can make the same commitment to her you made to Megan. She'll want to talk about it before I leave."

Casey dropped into the seat across the aisle and looked at Drake, with his chin held in his right hand. "We both know you want to keep doing what you've been doing since you prevented Secretary Rallings' assassination. Liz knows that too. Give it some time. You'll work this out."

"I hope so, Mike. I hope so."

Chapter Eighty-One

DRAKE WALKED OUTSIDE from Terminal One's baggage claim at Reagan National Airport and saw a man standing beside a white Ford Explorer at the curb waving at him.

"Mr. Drake, please come with me," he called out over the sounds of departing passengers talking and taxi cabs arriving and pulling away.

The young man's upright posture and neatly trimmed short hair hinted military, even though he was wearing khaki pants, white shirt and a blue windbreaker.

"I'm from the White House Transportation Agency," he said, holding out his hand to take the brown YETI duffel bag hanging from Drake's shoulder. "Staff Sergeant Nelsen, sir."

"Staff Sergeant," Drake said, unslinging the duffel bag and shaking Nelsen's hand. "Thanks for the ride."

"My pleasure, sir," he said over his shoulder while stowing Drake's duffel bag in the rear of the Ford Explorer. "I heard you were Special Forces."

"That was a while ago, sergeant."

Drake walked past the rear passenger side door, when the staff sergeant opened it for him, and got in up front.

"Hope you don't mind, staff sergeant," Drake said. "The view's better up here."

The five-mile drive to the White House took twenty minutes in light traffic, during which Staff Sergeant Nelson's description of his duties kept Drake from overthinking his meeting with the president's team.

If the president's team consisted of Cabinet members like the FBI Director, the Director of the CIA or the Secretary of Homeland Security, powerful insiders who might resent the president authorizing a new intelligence contractor to act without their involvement, the meeting could become counterproductive from the get-go.

A Secret Service agent was there to escort Drake through security to the West Wing of the White House and the president's small Oval Office Study, where three men sat at a round cherry wood table.

President Ballard got up to greet him and said, "Adam, you know Congressman Bridge. I don't believe you've met Pat Jefferson, my National Security Advisor."

"Adam, good to see you again," Congressman Matthew Bridge said as they shook hands.

The congressman's son was killed by a Chinese agent the year before windsurfing on the Columbia River. Drake had uncovered a Chinese intelligence operation was responsible when he agreed to help the president's friend and former campaign manager and discovered his son didn't have a heart attack but was poisoned. China had been trying to steal AI software for a new space weapon from the company where the son worked.

"The president's told me a lot about you, Mr. Drake," Pat Jefferson said, shaking hands.

"Call me Adam," Drake said. "You were 3rd Battalion, 75th Ranger Regiment, as I remember, and you're a leader on national security issues in congress. Nice to meet you, Pat."

"Would you like coffee before we start?" President Ballard asked Drake.

"No sir, I've had my quota this morning."

"I told Matthew and Pat what you told me about China and this New Opium War against the U.S. and the West," the president said. "Before I take this to the full National Security Team, I need to know what we can prove and what we're speculating about."

Drake sat across from the president and quickly compiled a list of facts in his head before he began.

"We can prove China is using Xueping's triad to provide a Chinese drug cartel in Mexico with fentanyl analogs and precursor chemicals. He ships them from Hong Kong to his casino in La Paz, Mexico, concealed in boxes of casino gambling chips. Ramon Ying, the head of a large Mexican pharmaceutical company, then uses a lab in company warehouses to produce fake prescription pills laced with fentanyl.

"Those pills are brought to America by Frank Zheng's Chinese triad via a DarkNet online site operated by Sam Xueping.

"Xueping was working with a Chinese General by the name of Wang. We have a recorded conversation between Wang and Xueping that confirms this.

"Xueping told me China wanted to weaken us by killing off as many young American men as possible, so they could win a future war. They called it a new opium war, using illegal synthetic fentanyl, like what Britain and European powers did to China during the two Opium wars in the mid-nineteenth century.

"I have personal first-hand knowledge of everything I just told you," Drake said.

The president nodded and asked, "What do you think we should do about it?"

"Before you do anything, Mr. President, have the FBI interrogate Xueping about the CCP's role in this. Then there are three things I think you could do. First, expose General Wang and China's role in this by imposing stiff tariffs on Chinese companies manufacturing fentanyl, and tell the world why you're doing it.

"Second, use the U.S. Cyber Command to shut down the

online networks being used to get fentanyl to Mexico and market fake pills around the world.

"Mexico plays a role in this, as well. They don't control customs and they are too corrupt to deal with the cartels. I know the leader of a guerilla group of Mexicans with U.S. military experience, who want to take their country back from the cartels. I think we should support their effort and help them do it.

"I'm not a diplomat," Drake said. "I'm sure there are a lot of things you could do diplomatically. That's just a short list of things I could think of that you could do now."

President Ballard looked around the table at Congressman Bridge and National Security Advisor Jefferson and asked, "Gentlemen, your thoughts?"

"Adam, do these Mexican men with military experience have dual-citizenship?" Congressman Bridge asked.

"The men I met do. I can't speak for all of them."

"What kind of support do they need?" Pat Jefferson asked.

"Money, materiel and any intelligence we can give them about the cartels," Drake said.

"Pat, how long will it take for the Cyber Command to put together a plan to take out these online networks?" President Ballard asked.

"Two or three days."

"Matthew, what's my political exposure if I do the things Adam's suggesting?"

"If we prove China planned and executed this act of war, every patriotic American will support you and cheer."

"Matthew, Pat, let's meet back here in two hours," the president said. "We have work to do."

Congressman Bridge and the president's advisor got up, came around the table to shake Drake's hand and left the Oval Office Study.

"Adam, will you stay and have dinner with me tonight?" President Ballard asked. "There are a couple of things that require your talents I'd like to discuss."

"Of course, Mr. President. Anything you want to discuss, especially if it comes with dinner with you at the White House."

Chapter Eighty-Two

DRAKE OPENED the door for Liz at Paddy Cloyne's Irish Pub and signaled to the hostess they needed a table for two. On their way back to the condo after an afternoon of house hunting in all the right neighborhoods of Bellevue, Washington, Liz wanted to stop and try Paddy Cloyne's "best I've ever eaten" fried pickles.

He'd thought jokes about pregnant women craving pickles and ice cream were folklore. But Liz's doctor had explained yesterday at their first prenatal visit he should expect late night calls to run to the store for weird things, like pickles.

After hearing his child's heart beating for the first time yesterday, Drake didn't care how many late-night runs he had to make in the next seven and half months to keep Liz happy.

It was happy hour, and the pub was full of men drinking mugs of beer and watching baseball on wide screen TVs. Their female companions leaned across tables to be heard above the noise, drinking cocktails or glasses of wine.

They were seated next to a window that looked out to the street and before Liz sat down and was handed a menu, she'd ordered fried pickles and a glass of water. Drake smiled as he admired the glow on his beautiful wife's face and ordered a mug of Guinness.

"Did you like the last house we saw in Somerset?" Liz asked.

"It was all right."

"What didn't you like about it?"

"Nothing in particular. It just didn't grab me. Did you like it?"

"I liked the kitchen, but it didn't have the study you're looking for. Will we ever find a place we both like?"

"We'll keep looking until we do," Drake promised her.

When her fried pickles and his Guinness arrived, Drake looked to see if the Mariners were playing, as a "Breaking News" banner rolled across the bottom of every wide screen TV and the pub quieted down to watch.

President Ballard was in the Brady Press Briefing Room in the West Wing of the White House, waiting for reporters who were hurrying in to find their seats.

"China's Ambassador just left the Oval Office," the president began. "China's accusing the U.S. of an unprovoked cyberattack on some of China's private pharmaceutical and chemical companies. I thought I should set the record straight before this becomes a big deal and it's the only thing you'll be reporting on tonight. The United States did not launch a cyberattack on private Chinese companies. Let me repeat that. The United States did not launch a cyberattack on private Chinese companies."

"U.S. intelligence does have evidence of a plot involving Chinese triads and Mexican cartels working together to flood the U.S. with cheap synthetic opioids, mostly fentanyl."

"China does produce the analogs and precursors needed to make fentanyl, that make their way to Mexican cartels that use them to make illicit fake prescriptions. Other countries do as well. But we have no direct evidence that China or the CCP supported or directed criminal drug trafficking activity that's killed over a hundred thousand young Americans, when they overdosed last year."

"Rest assured, if we had evidence that China or the CCP did do such a foolish thing, it would be considered an act of war, and I wouldn't be standing here calmly telling you about it today. I would be preparing our armed forces for war. China understands that," the president said.

"I can announce today that we are taking active measures to stop the triads and Mexican cartels from bringing these deadly drugs into the U.S. We have a fentanyl crisis in America, and we will hold anyone directly involved in this drug trafficking personally accountable. We will also hold any individual or group of individuals accountable who support or cooperate with the triads and cartels, and we will take swift and direct action against them as well. That's all I have. Thank you," President Ballard said and left the Press Briefing Room.

The silent pub erupted in reaction to what they heard the president say.

"Did he say we're going to war with China?"

"I'm all for it, if we hit those Chinese companies."

"I've always said it was a mistake to get too cozy with China."

"We've been down this crisis road before. Nothing will change."

"What does he know that he's not telling us?"

Drake reached over and took Liz's hand. "He played that well," he said. "We don't have direct evidence China used the triads and cartels as proxies, and we would never hit a "private Chinese company" because every company in China is controlled or bankrolled by the CCP."

"Will China get the message?" Liz asked.

"They'll be hell to pay if they don't."

THE END

Next in the Adam Drake series

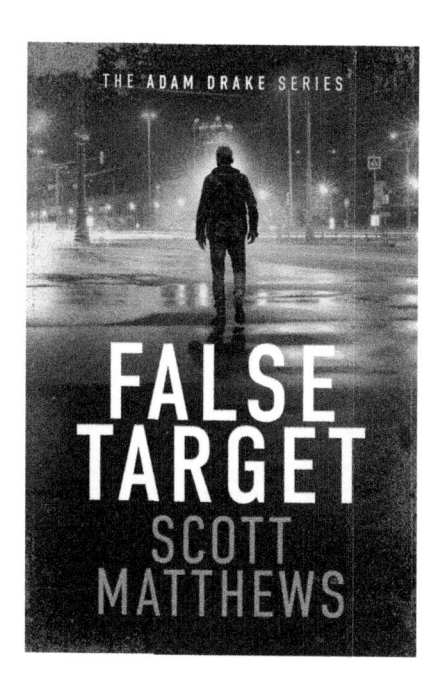

The stakes couldn't be higher for Adam Drake.

A girl trafficked and sold to the highest bidder, a teenager dead from toxic drugs and a Chinese deception on a global scale.

When Adam Drake agrees to help his former army Chaplain track down the killer of his friend's son, he finds himself in a dark world of cover-up, deceit and international spies.

With Taiwan's freedom hanging in the balance, the girl's life is not the only thing relying on Drake's next step.

Printed in Great Britain
by Amazon